FIRE IN THE SKY

ALEX SIGMORE

Dark Woods Press

FIRE IN THE SKY: EMILY SLATE MYSTERY THRILLER BOOK 17

Copyright © 2025 by Alex Sigmore

All rights reserved.

This is a work of fiction. Names, characters, places and incidents are products of the author's imagination and are used fictitiously and are not to be construed as real. Any resemblance to actual events, locales, organizations or persons, living or dead, is entirely coincidental.

No part of this book may be reproduced in any form or by any electronic or mechanical means, including information storage and retrieval systems, without written permission from the author, except for the use of brief quotations in a book review.

1st Edition

Print ISBN 978-1-957536-84-2

Description

A chilling message from the capital drags Emily Slate out of safety and back into the storm, to confront her greatest threat yet.

After receiving a devastating call, Emily and Zara are forced to return to D.C. to confront the conspiracy that has splintered the FBI and put their lives at risk.

But the city of magnificent intentions hides more than just political secrets. Two agents, sidelined like Emily, are found dead under suspicious circumstances, signaling the sinister forces at work are escalating their plan.

With the FBI under direct attack, the rules no longer apply. Stripped of her badge's protection, Emily finds herself outside the law for the first time, racing against a shadowy adversary with more than just her career on the line.

Navigating a labyrinth of lies without her standard arsenal, Emily must rely on her wits and Zara's unshakeable loyalty. They are all that stand between the FBI and its complete destruction. As the body count rises and the web of deceit tightens, Emily faces a chilling question: How do you catch a traitor in an organization built on trust?

Chapter One

IT CAN'T BE TRUE.

The woman who has been my mentor ever since I joined the FBI is dead.

At least, that's what the text says. A text that by all rights we shouldn't even have.

Zara looks up, her eyes searching mine. She's looking for confirmation—to see if I believe it or if I think this is some kind of hoax. And having been on the receiving end of some very *disturbing* letters in the past that have only led to pain, I'm not sure I'm willing to leave anything to chance at the moment.

"It has to be a code of some sort," she says, fumbling with the phone. "Right?"

I stare at the phone, trying to think. Here we are, undercover in a field office in New Mexico, two thousand miles from Washington D.C. and only one person is supposed to know we're here—our boss. To everyone else, in this office and everywhere else, I'm not Emily Slate and she's not Zara Foley. For the past five weeks we've been masquerading as junior agents who are just coming up in the ranks, hiding our true identities due to a breach at the FBI. A breach that has placed me and five other agents in the crosshairs.

Strike that, *nine* other agents now—according to my boyfriend and fellow FBI agent Liam Coll, who *also* isn't allowed to know where we are.

We've been sequestered in the middle of the desert, trying to keep our heads down while the FBI investigates and tries to get to the bottom of this breach. But I don't do so well sitting on my hands. And were it not for an urgent local case that had just come up, I would already be on my way back to D.C. to straighten this whole mess out.

But the point of us being here is so we're walled off from our department, like a perverse version of witness protection, except we still get to keep working. That was one of my stipulations. Otherwise, this was never going to happen. I'm not about to spend months on end in a cabin somewhere waiting for someone else to decide my future.

And yet, our most recent case almost exposed our true identities. Were it not for a few good agents in our field office, I'm sure our cover would have been blown by now. But the point is no one is supposed to know we're here and they're not supposed to be able to contact us. Especially not Zara's current squeeze and FBI informant-slash-collaborator, Theo Arquenest.

And yet, somehow, he's managed to find us and get a message to Zara. A message telling us that the woman who brought me into the Violent Crimes division and who was my boss for three years of my career is dead. No other details, no explanation. Just a cryptic note.

"We need to verify," I tell Zara. "That has to be the first priority." A gust of wind catches some dust from beyond the parking lot, blowing it in our direction, though I don't even bother to shield my eyes. I've gotten used to it.

"How do we do that?" she asks. "We're in a communications blackout."

"I'll contact Caruthers," I say. "We have the emergency number."

Zara turns the phone off. "Wait," she says. "We have no way to verify if this is even *from* Theo. It could be someone masquerading as him. What if whoever is targeting you is trying to draw you out?"

"Okay," I say. "So what do you suggest? We can't just do nothing."

She glances back at the bar behind us. The one where we're supposed to be celebrating a job well done. Where all our colleagues are probably starting to wonder where we've gone. "I... don't know."

"Yeah, that's what I thought," I say. "Which means we need to go back."

"Em, we can't just *leave*," she replied. "What about Strong? What about Agent Dent? Don't you think it's gonna look a *little* suspicious if we both try to take time off at the exact same time?"

"So?" I ask, turning and heading for our car. Only a few minutes ago I was entertaining the idea of staying out here longer—of building some semblance of a life instead of living out of a suitcase until this situation is resolved. But this text has changed everything. We can't afford to sit around and wait for someone to contact us. Not with something like this.

"So we'll blow our covers," she says, trotting behind me. "Everything we've worked for. And we might be giving whoever breached the FBI exactly what they want." She places a gentle hand on my shoulder, stopping me in place. "C'mon, we need to think about this."

She's right—sometimes I'm too rash. Maybe it's one of those trauma responses Dr. Frost talked about all the time. Maybe Theo *didn't* send the message after all—and someone *is* trying to draw me out.

But... what if Janice really is dead? And if that's the case, then don't I at least need to go back to find out what happened? Don't I owe her at least that much? After everything we've been through... after everything she did for me...

My mind is buzzing and I can't keep the thoughts from coming faster and faster, trying to mentally plan how to make this a reality. Setting up flights—or more likely bus fare, considering we won't be able to use the company dime. But that means it will take longer—maybe too long to be of any help.

I know Caruthers would say to stay where we are—which is precisely why I don't want to call him. I don't need to give him a heads up that we're coming back. And if this does all end up to be a hoax, then we come back, no harm no foul. I'm sure with our recent success that I can convince SSA Strong to give Zara and me a few well-deserved days off. In fact, I think it's perfect timing.

"Would you just wait a second?" Zara calls after me but I'm already halfway to the car. I can hear the commotion and congratulations being passed around inside the bar. I know if I tried, I could see all our colleagues inside, celebrating.

I'll put in our request to Strong tonight.

"*Emily!*" I spin around, finding Zara has fallen behind, standing in the middle of the dusty parking lot staring at me.

I'm running too hot—being too rash. I know it. But if I slow down it means I have to actually think about that text message. I have to consider the implications of what it could mean. And that means facing the reality that she might really be gone.

"I have to try," I say, holding my hands out to my sides.

She glares at me, staring me down like I'm an eight-hundred-pound bear. It's an intimidating stare, I admit. Finally she breaks eye contact and curses. "Your stubbornness is going to get us both killed."

I shrug. "I can't help it. Plus, how much fun do you think I'll be if you make me stay here? We can't just give up on her, Z. She doesn't deserve that."

"No, she doesn't," Zara concedes. "But if we're going to do this, we're going to be smart about it. We're not just barreling back into town, guns blazing. We need a plan."

"Thank you."

"What about Liam?" she asks. "Are you telling him we're coming back?"

"I can't contact him for another three days," I say. "And I hope we're back home by then." I can't call Liam directly because I am a hundred percent sure his phone is being monitored. But we have a system that's been working for us: we have a series of pre-paid phones we've been using to get in touch, though the calls are limited to five minutes at a time and we can't use any names. It might not be perfect, but it's allowed me to get by these past few weeks. But because our next call isn't scheduled for a few days, he doesn't even have the phone on yet. I can't call until the prescribed time frame.

I know she's probably thinking he's the first person we should confirm these details with. But I can't wait three days to find out. I'll let him know we're on the way when it comes time, but I'm not waiting around in the meantime.

"Okay," she says. "We both know what Caruthers would say—"

"Yeah, not an option."

"Okay then, guess we're going back," she replies and walks past me to the car.

"I'm thinking we need to stick to ground transportation," I say. "Just in case you're right. Buses, trains."

She nods. "Agreed. It's not direct, but it's safer. We also need to use this as an opportunity."

I screw up my features. "For what?"

"If someone *is* watching for you, I want to know who they are," she says. "Which means we need to be on the lookout for anyone who might be looking for *us*. Anyone who might be following us."

"Good idea, we can run interference protocol," I say.

"With just the two of us?"

I open the driver side door, giving her a wink. "Well, as much as we can manage."

"As soon as we get back I'll start working on an exit strategy," she says. "But you gotta give me a few hours. If we're going to do this, we're not half-assing it. I don't want to get caught with our pants down because we were in a hurry or sloppy."

She's right. I have to give her at least that much. If someone really is trying to bait us, they'll be on the lookout. They'll be waiting for us to pop up and show our hand. We both need to account and be prepared for that.

"What do you want to tell Strong?" she asks as we're headed back to the apartments.

"That we need a breather," I say. "Remember, this was our 'first' big case. We're supposed to be frazzled and maybe even a little traumatized. I mean, we both almost died." I give her a little smirk.

"Yeah, I guess we have been operating beyond our means for a little while," she replies, her voice full of sarcasm. "Just need a little break."

She goes quiet as I drive and I know she's thinking about Theo. About how he could have gained access to her phone considering they haven't talked in a solid month. He wasn't supposed to know where we were… so how did he find us? She's already been on edge about him—I imagine this is the tipping point.

"Do you want to—"

"Nope," she cuts me off. "I don't."

"Fair enough," I reply. "Let's just get back and we can get to work." As the road stretches out before me, I realize this might be the last time I ever see this place that I called home for a brief time. And I can't help but feel a slight ache in my heart that I might be leaving it all behind.

But there are bigger considerations to worry about. I can't get bogged down in sentimentality.
I grip the wheel tighter, my focus sharpening.
One way or another, I'm going to get answers.

Chapter Two

I CATCH sight of the Washington Monument before anything else. It isn't the tallest building in D.C., but it's often the brightest, especially late at night. The lights reflecting off the white, polished marble have a mirroring effect, turning the obelisk into a kind of beacon.

A lighthouse, calling me home.

It's been two and a half days since we left Albuquerque. Thanks to Zara's resourcefulness and given the fact I haven't slept in an actual bed since we left, I made it back in record time. First it was a train from Albuquerque to Denver, then a bus from Denver to Kansas City where I picked up another train that took me down to Atlanta, and then finally one last long-ass bus ride up the Blue Ridge mountains until I finally reached D.C. It's been a gauntlet, but a necessary one.

I watch as the lights from the city pass by before the bus pulls into the terminal station. It's a little after two in the morning and I'm struggling to keep my eyes open. But I don't dare sleep.

After a quick stop near Charlottesville around eleven, there are only sixteen people left on the bus, and I know their seat numbers and have created a general profile of each of them. Despite being beside the toilet, sitting in the back gives me the best possible angle on everyone and allows me to keep a low profile. I'm wearing a dark blue oversized hoodie that's pulled tight around my face, my hair hidden from view. My only bags are a small backpack and a larger bag underneath the bus. We decided traveling light was the best option. I've been watching like a hawk for the past two days, scrutinizing and profiling every stranger who gets within a hundred feet of me. Never have I been this on edge.

Because we know virtually nothing about the people targeting us, we decided it was best if we both took different routes and met up here. It was risky, but if they're looking for both of us, single travelers would have an easier time getting around. And so far, it's been a smooth trip. According to the schedule, Zara should already be here and making her way to the safehouse.

The pneumatics of the bus finally release and the door opens at the front, the rest of the passengers stand to shuffle out.

Except one of them doesn't move. 11B. He's also in a hoodie; we picked him up in Charlotte and he hasn't moved from his seat since. He's tall, with a dark beard and hair that's graying at the temples. The only movement I caught from him was a slight head turn about four hours ago where I think he clocked me. It could have been nothing more than him getting more comfortable for the ride, but then again, it could have been a warning.

I don't move, staying hunched over, pretending I'm asleep. The bus driver looks in his rearview. "Everyone off. Last stop for tonight," he says.

The guy doesn't stir. I tense, expecting anything. He could have been sent to monitor me, or take me down at the first possible chance. Now that there's only three people left and the station is relatively deserted at this time of night, it would be the perfect opportunity.

The bus driver makes a grunting sound as he gets up and heads back. My sweaty fists clench as he approaches the man. "Hey, buddy," he says, giving 11B's shoulder a shake. "Last stop. Time to get off."

The man groans slightly and then begins to stir. Finally he looks up, blinking at the bus driver. "Where are we?"

"D.C.," the bus driver says.

"Oh." The man looks around the bus, his eyes passing over me without pause. "Right. Sorry." He hauls himself up and out of the seat before making his way to the front. The driver watches him for a brief second before turning and heading my way, presumably planning to rinse and repeat.

But before he can reach me I fake a yawn and check my phone, even though I know exactly what time it is. "Sorry," I mutter. "Long day." I grab my backpack as relief washes over his face that he doesn't have a drunken passenger to deal with.

"No problem, ma'am," he says. "You have a good night."

"You too," I say, heading down the aisle. Instinctively, I check my surroundings once I'm outside, but there's no sign of the other passenger. No telling where he went. A few stragglers are on their phones and one is getting into an Uber, but otherwise the place is deserted.

I turn and begin the long walk to my next rendezvous point.

A lone female walking in the dead of night is not a good look, which is the reason for the oversized hoodie. Not that I expect to be out here too long, but Zara had hoped it might deter any attention by making me look bigger than I am, even if just a little.

Fifteen minutes later I'm headed down Jefferson street, the light wind buffeting against my form. My backpack is on my back and my other bag is in my free hand. I pull out my phone and order a ride-share, making sure there's no one around who could be following.

Another ten minutes passes before the car shows up—

thank God for overnight drivers—and I slip in the back, giving him the address. As he drives I fight to keep my eyes open, the warmth of the car combined with the fact I've gotten no rest these past few days a dangerous combination.

When the rideshare pulls up to the house I snap back awake, realizing I must have fallen asleep as I don't remember the trip here. I curse myself before thanking him and heading to the building that sits like a brownstone between two other buildings. I have to climb three steps before reaching the main door, where I find the buzzer for apartment 8E. I press it quickly.

"Password," Zara says, unusually chipper.

"Let me in or I'll kill you," I reply.

"Password accepted," she says and the door vibrates for a short second as I pull the door open. As I head through the passageway I think I catch a flash of movement at the far end of the block. I pause, watching the dark spaces for a second before deciding it was my imagination. Still, I'm on edge.

I make sure the door is closed behind me before heading up the stairs to the second floor. The building is old, complete with ornate wood detailing and a tile floor on the main level. On the second floor I head down to the unit at the end of the hall. As I approach I note the security camera that has recently been installed above the door, fresh sawdust on the floor under where it was drilled into the wood.

The door clicks as I approach and I'm able to open it with ease before closing it again. "Hello?"

"In here," Zara calls. The small hallway opens into a kitchen and living area with a small dining table on the other side of the kitchen. Zara sits at the table, her laptop in the middle and what looks like a half dozen devices connected to it in some way or another.

I sling my backpack on the nearby sofa and roll my other bag beside it. "You've been busy. I saw the camera."

She taps the screen of her computer, noting three other

camera views that I *didn't* see, all of them looking at various access points to the building. "Had to secure the place first," she replies. "Any trouble?"

I flop down on the single couch in the living room. A cloud of dust erupts from the cushion and I have to wave it away as I cough. "No, but I feel like my nervous system has been through hell. My hands are practically shaking."

"You need sleep," she says. "And you probably haven't eaten much since Albuquerque, have you?"

"Did *you* run into any trouble?" I ask, ignoring the question.

"I thought I had a tail when I got to Illinois, but I can't be sure," Zara replies. "I had to make a small schedule change which ended up getting me here about fifteen hours ago."

"Who was it?" I ask.

"No clue, might have been nothing. Just some suspicious-looking guys on my route. I figured better safe than sorry."

I think back to the guy on my bus who could have been nothing more than a sleepy passenger. "Yeah, I get that."

Zara nods down the hallway. "I took the bedroom on the left; hope you don't mind. We're going to need supplies. Groceries if we're going to be here a few days. The less we go out, the better."

I sit back up. "We didn't come all the way back here just to sit around."

"Great," she says, turning to me. "Then you can do the shopping. I need to connect with a few of my contacts here. See if I can't get us some equipment."

"Equipment?" I ask.

"We need untraceable phones, for one," she replies. "And the stuff I have here is barely sufficient. It needs an upgrade, as soon as possible."

"You sound like you expect the army to come down on us." I sit forward, wiping the dust off the nearby coffee table. When I first started with the FBI I used this building as a safehouse for some of my undercover jobs. Because of the nature of the work, I couldn't risk anyone following me back to my actual house. Funny how I'm back here again. But the best part about this is the FBI has no record of this address, as it would have been a security issue. Which means no one should know we're here.

She closes the laptop, though two of the devices she's hooked up are still blinking. "I don't know what to expect. That's why I want to be prepared." She comes over and gives me a hug. "Glad you made it. I'm exhausted."

"Yeah," I say, hugging her back. "Me too. Get some rest. I'll keep watch."

She shakes her head as she pulls away. "Nope. Got it all locked down. You can sleep too." She heads into the kitchen and pours herself a glass of water.

"You mean if I open the door—"

"Alarm goes off," she replies.

"Oh," I say, hesitating. "I guess that makes sense."

She takes a long sip of water. "Right. So if you were thinking about sneaking out to see that boyfriend of yours you can just tuck that little idea right back down in its box."

I glare at her while she only gives me a smirk back. "Now why would I do that?"

Zara gives me an exasperated look. "Because I know you. You haven't seen Liam in what, five, six weeks? And now that you're within a few miles of him you might feel the urge for a midnight special. But you do that, and you put us in danger. Whoever is looking for you no doubt has eyes on your house."

"Ugh. I can't live like this forever, Z. I'm not going to look over my shoulder for the rest of my life. I'd rather just get this over with than draw it out any longer."

"Which is an excellent way to get killed," she reminds me. "Let me gather some information. I can find a safe way you can meet up with Liam. But until then we can't risk it."

I shake my head. "Then what are we supposed to do? Just sit on our asses and collect data?"

Zara sets the glass down. "We can't go in guns blazing. As cathartic as you think that might be. For now, we gather information. We don't even know if the text was real. I want to set up some surveillance, try to verify first."

I sit back, sinking into the couch again. "Fine. But you're not keeping me like this forever."

"Yeah, yeah," she says. "I'm going to get at least four hours. We can talk about this in the morning."

"It's *already* morning," I call after her but she doesn't respond. I shouldn't be angry with Zara, she's just doing what she must to protect us. I just hate feeling so constrained. We made it all this way just to stop now? Though, I'm not sure what I expected as soon as we arrived. She's right. We can't just show up at the FBI's front door and demand to know what's going on.

It takes me a few minutes, but I finally fish out the remote for the TV. It was hidden between the cushions on the couch. And honestly, this couch is the most comfortable thing I've been on in two days. I can probably just go to sleep here. As I switch on the TV I can already feel my eyelids growing heavy. I'll just throw something on in the background so it isn't so quiet.

But when I switch the feed over to the news channel, all thoughts of sleep disappear.

"Z!" I call.

She comes running into the living room, toothbrush in her mouth. "Wha?"

I point to the TV.

And there, on the screen is a picture of Janice—her official FBI picture, actually. And below her image is the copy: *Decorated FBI Agent Found Dead.*

Chapter Three

I TASTE metal in my mouth when the news report ends, my fingers gripping the remote so tightly my knuckles have gone white. There's no longer any question. The text was real. Apparently the story has been running all day and we're just now catching it.

"How did we miss this?" I whisper.

"Emily." Zara's voice comes from somewhere distant. "Emily, breathe."

The room swims back into focus—faded floral wallpaper, the smell of industrial cleaner barely masking years of cigarettes, a crack in the ceiling that reminds me of a lightning bolt. Everything seems too sharp suddenly, too real.

"I need to see Liam," I say, already reaching for my jacket.

Zara steps between me and the door. "Nuh-uh. That's the worst possible move right now."

"I don't care."

"Then start caring." Her voice hardens. "It's three in the morning. You show up there in the middle of the night, you might as well send up a flare announcing you're back."

She's right. I *know* she's right. But the need to see Liam, to hold something familiar when everything else is slipping away, pulses through me like a second heartbeat.

"Then we'll find another way," I say, dropping back onto the edge of the couch. The cushion sags beneath me, springs protesting. I check my watch. "He'll stop and grab a quick bite before work tomorrow."

She narrows her eyes. "I thought he fixed you breakfast every morning."

"When it's the two of us, yeah. But when he's by himself he doesn't bother. I know his routine. We can intercept him on his way to work."

Zara crosses her arms. "And if someone's watching him too?"

"That's what you'll be there for." The plan forms as I speak it. Am I being irrational? Yes, but at least I know it. And this isn't just a personal desire—though I will admit seeing him again will be nice. We need to know what's been going on inside the Bureau for the past five weeks. We're not going to do this blind. "We can redirect him, find somewhere private to talk."

She studies me for a long moment, that silent judgement barely seeping through. It's asking a lot, I know. But she knows we could really use the intel. Finally, she sighs.

"You are a pain in my ass, you know that?"

THE COFFEE SHOP SITS ON THE CORNER OF 7TH AND E, morning commuters streaming in and out with paper cups clutched like lifelines. Bikers ride past in the bike lanes, some in suits and others in full racing gear. Zara is across the street, baseball cap pulled low, sunglasses in place despite the overcast sky. I wait half a block down, inside the entrance of a bookstore that hasn't quite opened yet. The teenage employee setting up gives me suspicious glances but says nothing when I buy a magazine from the rack near the door.

At 7:42, right on schedule, Liam pulls up in his gray sedan, parking alongside the building in one of the twenty-minute-or-less spots. Even from this distance, I can see the exhaustion in the slope of his shoulders, the way his steps lack their usual purpose. It's almost shocking—he's worn down, looking more worse for wear than I'd expected. What the hell has been going on here?

I text Zara:

> In position. Ready.

She responds immediately:

> You're clear. Go.

I fold the magazine, tuck it under my arm, and step out onto the sidewalk. Timing is everything. I move against the flow of pedestrians, calculating each step until our paths will intersect just before he reaches the coffee shop. My heart races at seeing him again, of actually being this close to each other.

Ten feet away, I let the magazine drop. Pages scatter across the sidewalk, and as Liam automatically stoops to help—always the gentleman—I'm there beside him.

"Don't look up," I murmur, crouching to gather papers. "Keep your eyes down."

His body goes rigid. "Emily?" The word comes out barely audible.

"Follow me. Act normal." I stand, clutching the reassembled magazine, and start walking toward the alley between the coffee shop and the neighboring building. Without looking back, I know he's following.

The alley smells of coffee grounds and yesterday's rain. I

lead him behind a dumpster, out of sight from the street, and finally turn to face him.

The impact of seeing him hits harder than I expected. His eyes are rimmed with red, stubble darkening his usually clean-shaven jaw. Before I can speak, his arms are around me, pulling me against his chest so tightly I can feel the strength of his heartbeat through his coat.

"What are you doing here?" he whispers into my hair, but his arms tighten, contradicting his words.

I allow myself three seconds in his embrace—one, two, three—before pulling back, scanning the alley entrance. "You know why."

"But…the news just broke yesterday—you didn't fly—"

"No," I whisper. "Theo contacted Zara three days ago. Liam, what happened?"

"Wait, *Theo*?" he asks. "How did he—"

I shake my head. "I have no idea. We got the text, but then couldn't respond. I couldn't call you because—well, because we're off schedule. And I sure as hell wasn't about to call Caruthers."

Liam's gaze drops. "I was going to relay it to you next time we talked."

I run my hand across his stubble. I've never seen him like this before. "Are you okay?"

He gives me a terse smile. "It's been a tough few weeks. Things at work have been… tense." He pulls me close again and I can feel the desperation in his grip. For the first time his mouth finds mine and it's almost like he's gasping for connection—as if he's been drowning without it.

Finally, he pulls away and I find myself breathless. "I missed you."

"Not nearly as much as I've missed you."

"How are the dogs?"

"Depressed," he says, smiling. "Every day I come home without you and their little heads just go down." The words ache in my chest. "But we're doing okay. We're holding it together."

I give him the same look Zara gives me when she knows I'm lying.

He leans closer. "The department has been fractured. Everyone is separated from everyone else. I haven't seen Elliott and Nadia in weeks. And all internal communications are coded—mandatory messages only. The department has been reduced to a virtual standstill. And now... with Janice..."

"Liam, what *happened?*"

"I don't know," he says. "I haven't seen the autopsy and I doubt they'll let me. All I know is it wasn't in the line of duty."

I screw up my features. "What are you saying? That it was a natural death?"

He shrugs. "I just know they're not planning on putting her name on the wall." I wince. When an agent dies in the line of duty they're name is emblazoned on the Wall of Honor as a "service martyr." The fact that she isn't receiving that honor means her death must have been something else— accidental, perhaps. But then again, a high-ranking FBI Agent accidentally killed? There's no way there won't be an investigation.

"Who's running point?"

"That's way outside my pay grade," he says. "I barely know what I'm doing day to day."

My mind races, trying to connect dots that may or may not be there. "When's the last time you saw her?"

"A few days ago," he says. "I told you about it on the phone. She and Caruthers were talking... this *Underground* business. I've been looking, but I still don't know what it means."

"Could she have meant underground as in a real, physical place?"

He checks his watch. "No idea. Em, I'm going to be late. And if something's off, they might start looking into it.

They've got IA all over the place, especially after what happened with Janice."

I hold him by the shoulders. "When's the funeral?"

"You can't—" he begins.

"When?"

He sighs. "Wednesday. Arlington. *Don't* go. Whoever is looking for you might—"

"No one will see me," I say. "But I need to get a lay of the land. We can't just sit back and wait for someone else to figure this out. I spent five weeks doing that and look where it got us."

A smile touches the edge of his lips. "You were in New Mexico, weren't you? That kidnapping case."

I glare at him with feigned frustration. "I'm getting a little tired of people knowing what I'm up to."

He smiles. "I just know your handiwork. But someone else might have noticed as well. You shouldn't be here, but I'm glad you're not there anymore. I think it might have been too tempting to resist."

A siren wails nearby, causing me to tense and glance down the alleyway. But it passes harmlessly, fading into the city.

"Em…"

"I know." But I don't move, memorizing his face like it might be the last time I see it. "Be careful. Watch your surroundings. I'll be in touch again soon."

"I know how to handle myself," he reminds me gently.

"I seriously doubt that, Mr. Coll." My words may be playful, but they barely mask the real worry beneath them.

He touches my cheek, his fingers warm against my skin. "I'll tell the dogs you'll be home soon."

"Count on it," I say.

He nods, then hesitates. "Emily, whatever's happening… Janice was in the middle of it. This isn't just a coincidence."

"I know." It's why we're here. Running away has never

been in my nature. If something's hunting us in the dark, I'd rather face it head-on than wonder when it will find me.

Liam sees it in my eyes—the stubbornness, the bull-headed determination that both frustrates and draws him to me. He doesn't argue further, just pulls me in for one last kiss that tastes of goodbye.

Then he's gone, stepping back into the flow of morning commuters, shoulders squared as if carrying a new weight.

Zara appears at the mouth of the alley, scanning for threats. "Everything okay?"

"No," I answer honestly. "But we got what we came for."

"And the funeral?"

"We'll need to plan carefully. I can't be recognized."

She doesn't waste breath arguing. "You're killing me, Smalls."

We separate, taking different routes back to the warehouse. As I walk, I can't help but scan faces as they pass, looking for anyone or anything that might be out of place. Instead of feeling like home, the city feels different now… foreign. Almost like a hostile force. Someone out there has me in their sights, and I still have no idea why.

The answers are here, somewhere. And someone knows what happened to my boss. Despite what everyone keeps telling me, I'm going to uncover them.

No matter what it costs.

Chapter Four

"BAD, BAD IDEA," Zara whispers for what seems like the hundredth time as I affix the blonde wig over my hair. Arlington Cemetery isn't just your average run-of-the-mill graveyard. It's a national monument that requires a security check before entering, which leaves me with two choices. I can either try to sneak in—and probably get shot in the process, *or* I can use a fake ID. We toyed with the idea of me going in as Special Agent Claire Dunn, considering I still have my ID and clearance from New Mexico. But if Liam is right, and we made more of a splash out there than we meant to, then I don't want to trip any alarms. Giving up even my fake badge could alert someone that I'm not where I'm supposed to be—raising questions and possibly an investigation.

Thankfully, Zara managed to get in contact with some of her old suppliers here in the city and procured us a couple of new fake IDs. This way I can be just a normal citizen who just happens to be visiting the cemetery and not throw up any red flags. My plan is to go in with one of the morning tour groups and just stay behind to catch the funeral at eleven.

But regardless of the ID, people in this town know my face. I can't just show up to an event full of my former coworkers and expect no one to recognize me. Which is why I'll be keeping my distance, but also will be in disguise. Cue the wig, the black overcoat and the hat, along with an oversized pair of glasses, hopefully obscuring most of my face. I won't be out of place because lots of people wear large glasses at funerals—regardless of the weather—because they don't want to show their tear-streaked eyes.

We're alike in that regard, at least.

"Well?" I ask, turning to Zara after I've made sure the wig is on tight.

"Nope, don't like it," she replies. "I told you, you should have gone with red."

I huff. "It doesn't matter; it's just for a few hours. Plus, red stands out more."

She gets up in my face, pulling strands of the wig off my newly-glossed lips—another suggestion of hers to make me not look quite like myself. "Yeah, but this doesn't work with your skin color. You're too pale to pull it off."

"I thought I was getting a tan from the desert," I say, pulling on my long overcoat.

"Oh, you did. You were even *paler* before. Practically transparent."

I swear she just likes winding me up. "Seriously, is it enough? Can I pull it off?"

She scrutinizes me for a minute. "I guess. I still say you should sit with me and we can both watch from the telephoto lens."

I shake my head. "Can't. I need to get an eye on the people *at* the funeral and your lens will have limited maneuverability. Whoever is behind this will be there, I'm sure of it." I still can't quite believe Janice is gone. It feels like she'll just show up out of nowhere and complain that I've broken cover for no reason. In fact, I keep hoping that will happen, though I know it's unlikely. Still, I'm not leaving anything to chance until I get a look at that autopsy. For all I know, this whole thing could have been orchestrated by Janice—but for what purpose I couldn't say. I just know I need to be there in person, no matter what.

"You ready?" Zara asks, pulling on her own ball cap that obscures her platinum blonde hair.

I tighten the belt of the overcoat. "Let's get going."

AN HOUR LATER I'M MIXED INTO A CROWD OF LOCAL TOURISTS, my fake ID in hand as we're fed through the security system. There's a metal detector, which means I didn't bring my sidearm with me; it's back in the car with Zara. I have to take off my hat and glasses, but they allow me to leave my coat on as I pass through the detector. Thankfully, the equipment I have on me is so miniscule it doesn't set off the machine. A Marine hands me my hat and glasses, flashing me a quick smile that I don't return. I reset my disguise and join the group of tourists who've gathered around our guide, already pointing out some of the features of the cemetery here at the entrance. I feel like this whole thing will be nothing more than a laundry list of "important" people buried here, but I'm not here for them.

Using subtle movements, I set the earpiece in my ear, making sure it's switched on. If the detector had been super sensitive, I didn't want the Marines to pull it out of my ear as that would have looked too suspicious. Thankfully it wasn't an issue. But as I get it set I'm scanning what parts of the cemetery I can see from here. No sign of the funeral detail for Janice's service later.

"Are you picking me up?" I whisper once the earpiece is in.

"Loud and clear," Zara says. "No trouble at security?"

"Wouldn't be talking to you if there was," I say. "Do we have an idea of where they'll be burying her?"

"There are over twenty services scheduled today, six of them at eleven and they don't publicize a list. You'll have to start searching."

Great. That means wandering aimlessly around until I happen to hit the right one. And this is not a small place. The cemetery covers six hundred and thirty-nine acres, which means I'm going to need to hoof it if I want to find the right service. Alternatively there is a bus that provides access around the grounds, but that would be just another way to draw attention that I'm looking for a specific service. My hope is to blend in as seamlessly as possible.

"Moving now," I say and silently make my exit from the group while no one is really paying attention. The Marines don't seem to care and the tour guide is so wrapped up in what he's saying he doesn't notice. Heading over the hill, I glance at a small gathering of people dressed all in black, but the group is too small to be the one I'm looking for. Only a few family members and a priest. There are also five service members, all armed with rifles for the military salute.

That's one thing I don't think I'll ever get used to about places like this. That a human life all comes down to a few people around a gravesite and then that's it. Everything we work for, everything we strive for, buy, sell, love, hate, and experience is reduced to little more than a hole in the ground. Not even that in my case. I'll be a pile of dust if I have my way. And then it's all gone. It's hard to imagine, especially given how complicated my life is right now. But one day—none of it will matter.

I don't like thinking about it. Dwelling on death has never been conducive for me and now is *definitely* not the time. I need to find Janice's site so I can get eyes on the attendees—figure out who is there that doesn't belong. Will someone else be there doing the same thing, maybe even looking for me? Probably. But like I told Liam and Zara, I owe Janice this much at least. She's the reason I'm in this job—she saved me when she didn't have to—kept me from a life of deskwork when I should have been benched. She was always there, almost like a parent or a guardian.

I'm not sure what I'll do now that she's gone.

I crest another hill, the sweat starting to run down my back from moving so quickly, despite the chill in the air. From here I spot two more services beginning to gather, one significantly larger than the other as cars pull up alongside the burial location. I can see from here those are FBI-issue vehicles, the kind we use on a regular basis to keep from using our personal cars.

"I have eyes on it. South side of the cemetery, close to the Coast Guard memorial," I mutter.

"Moving into position," Zara replies and I catch the rustle of equipment on the other end. I make my way down the hill in the direction of the gathering. There are at least a hundred people or more, all of them milling about as some get out of nearby cars and others come from all directions to pay their last respects. To anyone else, I look like just another patron, gathering for the service. I catch sight of Caruthers already at the grave site where the hole has been temporarily covered with a green cloth tarp. The casket sits on two heavy nylon belts that will be used to lower it into the ground once the service is over. Caruthers stands beside the casket, kind of staring at it almost as if he's looking *through* it. His face is heavy with resignation and worry, and he looks a good five years older than he did the last time I saw him a little over a month ago.

Liam wasn't lying. This thing is taking its toll on everyone in the office. Not even the upper brass is safe.

More people begin to gather and a man I've never seen before takes the first chair beside the dais where the priest will speak. He has dark silver hair that's combed back and out of his face, but still seems long and luxurious. And he wears a dark pair of sunglasses not too dissimilar from my own. He isn't speaking with anyone else, instead he sits in the first seat normally reserved for family and waits.

I know little to nothing about Janice's personal life. She was a workaholic, a lot like me, so I don't think she had kids. But she also never talked about it, so as far as I know, she could have had a completely different life back at home that we knew nothing about. In fact, that would have been the smart play.

Smarter than dating someone in the same department anyway.

The priest begins motioning and everyone gathers around the site. I notice four agents standing off to the sides, each of them with their eyes on everyone and everything. Not only are they backup security in case it's needed, but they're searching—just like I am. Which tells me someone else suspects there's something a little funny about a fifty-nine year old woman dropping dead for no apparent reason.

"Thank you all for coming," the priest says as everyone who wants a seat takes one. I'm situated about five rows back, behind a pair of tall people. So far I've seen Caruthers, Michaels, Dyer, Rutherford—the list goes on. People I've known and worked with for years, they're all here. Even my therapist, Dr. Frost. It's strange not to see Janice among them. I even catch sight of Elliott who is standing off to the side—though Nadia isn't with him. Usually those two are inseparable. I wonder if they've been compartmentalized as well. Liam said he hadn't seen either in weeks. Is everyone working their own division now? How can the department function like that?

And then I see him: Liam. He looks like he's running late as he jogs to the site from the opposite direction I came from. He doesn't scan the crowd, just blends in seamlessly.

"Whew, close one," Zara says in my ear. "I thought he wasn't going to make it."

I don't reply because I'm close enough that someone

might hear me. And I don't want anyone thinking I'm talking to myself, or worse, spying. I want to say something to him, to go and comfort him, because he looks like he needs it. He looks even more strung out than he did yesterday—like he's not getting enough sleep. My heart wrenches knowing I can't just go home with him after this is done. I just want to sleep in my own bed, beside him, with the dogs at our feet. Funny how much I took that for granted until it was gone.

"Today we are here to celebrate the life of Janice Veronica Simmons," the priest says. "A dear friend, a fierce and loyal agent and a determined, yet caring person."

"Veronica?" Zara asks in my ear. "Did you know her middle name?"

I subtly shake my head. Janice was not the kind of person to share personal details about her life. And I doubt I'll learn anything from this service I didn't already know. People are always the most complimentary right after a death.

But as the priest continues to speak, I find I can't take my eyes off the casket itself. It's so hard to imagine she's in there—just... dead. It almost doesn't feel real.

A series of gunshots cause me to jump, shaking me from my thoughts. I instinctively go for my weapon, until I realize it's the military salute. Seven men, all with rifles pointing into the air. They fire again, and then pull back for one final time. Once they're done, they step back.

Funny, I hadn't realized Janice had been in the military. Not that it surprises me either. In fact, it actually makes a lot of sense. She was good at her job and didn't suffer fools easily. She was sharp, quick on her feet, and ruthless. All of which could have started with a military career.

And before I know it, the service is over, everyone shuffling away. I was so preoccupied with the service, I barely even looked at who else was attending. Anyone who stood out like they didn't belong. Anyone who might want to stick around to watch the fruits of their labor.

But as I scan the crowd, most people are getting up to leave as two men begin ratcheting Janice's casket into the ground. My gaze lands on Liam for a split second and we lock eyes, even though he's just looking at a pair of thick sunglasses. It's like he can see right through them. He doesn't give anything away, just turns and heads back the way he came, mixing into the crowd.

It's not until it's almost too late that I feel the presence beside me.

"Hi, Emily."

I nearly jump back, almost losing my balance before the woman beside me. She's about six inches shorter than I am, dressed in her work clothes but also wearing a wide-brimmed hat with a mesh veil.

"Nadia…" I say, catching my breath. "Where… how did you know it was me?"

She beams at me. "I thought I saw you walking up. You have a distinctive gait. But I wasn't sure it was you until I saw you reach for your weapon when the guns went off."

I'm completely dumbfounded. I have a *gait*? Like a horse?

"She's right, you do walk weird," Zara says in my ear.

"You were supposed to warn me if anyone was coming," I hiss.

She chuckles on the other end. "This was more fun."

"Is that Agent Foley?" Nadia asks, still smiling. Enough people have dissipated that I don't feel the need to hush my words anymore. We're not near anything that could be considered a listening device and I highly doubt someone planted Nadia here—she's part of my team after all. Still, I don't like the implications—no one was supposed to know it was me.

"Yes," I say. "We needed to do some recon on the funeral."

"Because you suspect foul play," Nadia says. No questions about where we've been, or everything that's happened. Agent

Kane is right back to business. It's like we haven't even been gone, which, I have to admit, is nice.

"It's good to see you again, Nadia," I say. "How are you so quiet?"

She shrugs. "Part of my nature, I suppose. Are you here undercover?"

"Not officially," I say. "Zara and I… we found out what happened. We had to come back."

She nods. "I understand. Things have been very weird since you left. Today was the first time I've seen Liam in weeks. Elliott and I have been sequestered—"

"Seems like there's a lot of that going around," I mutter. "Do you know what happened? Liam said it was some kind of accident."

She shakes her head. "I tried making inquiries, but they shut me down. Then two days ago, I was put on administrative leave. They said it didn't have anything to do with my requests but… I mean, come on."

"*Who* shut you down? Who's in charge?" I ask, my frustration leaking through. "Was it Caruthers?"

"Caruthers delivered the news, but I don't think it was his doing. He seemed hamstrung, like he wanted to say more, but couldn't. I asked if I could still come to the funeral and he said yes, but after this I'm on leave until further notice."

This is worse than I thought. Liam boxed in, Nadia on leave… it means Elliott is the only one of us left who might be able to get some real information. "Did you talk to her lately? To Janice?"

"Never got the chance," Nadia says. "She was making a lot of inquiries, though. She wasn't content just to sit around."

"I know the feeling," I say, glancing around. I catch one of the FBI agents who had been watching the funeral—Donnely, I think—lingering. I can't tell if he's clocking me or not, but I don't want to take the chance. "Look, I gotta run. I shouldn't even be here. We need to find a way to compare notes. Can Elliott get away for a few hours without anyone noticing?"

"Sure," she replies. "They're not monitoring us as far as I can tell. At least, I haven't seen anyone. And I've been keeping a close eye."

"Zara will find a way to reach out," I whisper. Then I take her hand quickly, giving it a quick shake. "It was great seeing you again. Take care."

A confused look crosses her face. "You too." I turn and head off just as Donnely begins walking our way. With my hat and sunglasses I doubt he recognizes me, but I don't want to take the chance. I hurry back to the same gate I came from, my stride quick and purposeful.

"Zara will find a way?" she chirps in my ear. "What am I, a magician?"

"That's exactly what you are," I whisper. "Plus, you heard her. If we want answers, we're gonna need one."

Chapter Five

I SLIP INTO THE SAFEHOUSE, disabling the security system as soon as I'm inside the door and I remove the heavy overcoat and sunglasses, along with the hat. It feels like peeling off a layer of skin. Despite the chill outside, I'm soaked to the bone with sweat and need a quick shower. As I'm pulling the wig off, the little lock on the door beeps once before the door opens, revealing Zara. She closes the door with a soft click and reactivates the security system.

"Clean getaway?" I ask.

"Cleaner than yours. Donnely saw you."

"He saw a blonde woman in a large hat and overcoat," I say. "He didn't see *me*."

Zara sets her camera with the telephoto lens on the counter. "If they come knocking, we know who to blame. What the hell is going on at the Bureau?"

It's a good question. Zara knows as much as I do, but it does seem that things have gotten much worse since we left. "I wish I knew."

She heads over to the curtains by the two windows that face out towards the street and pulls them tight, shrouding the room in darkness as I hit the light. "Any ideas about how to get everyone here cleanly?"

She heads back for the computer setup in the "dining room." "I like how we went from *maybe* we'll talk to Liam to getting *everyone* together," she says.

I shrug. "The opportunity presented itself. Nadia was right there. Plus, I think it's a good idea if we can all compare notes. Maybe with all of us, we can piece together whatever they obviously want to keep hidden."

"It's a risk. What if—" she stops herself.

"What if what?" I ask.

"Nothing," she replies. "Give me a few hours. I'll come up with something. It'll need to be somewhere off the beaten path. Where no one will be expecting us."

The thought of the five of us being together again sends something like hope surging through my chest. I haven't seen my old team since before Albuquerque—and really, since before I went down to St. Solomon on my undercover op when all this started. But I don't like the hesitation in Zara's voice. She's obviously not telling me something and I'm not sure she wants me to ask about it. Ever since she began looking into Theo's background she's been—different. Like she's being weighed down by an invisible shroud. And I don't like it. I don't like seeing my friend this way: reactionary, cautious, subdued and… angry. That's not her.

"Hey, Z…" I begin. "…I should have checked with you before telling Nadia you'd reach out. I wasn't thinking. I know that's not an easy—"

"No, it's fine," she says and I believe her. Something else is weighing on her, and I have a good idea what it is. I just hope it doesn't affect her concentration.

"Okay," I say. "I'm going to take a quick shower and wash some of this sweat off. Be right back."

She doesn't reply, instead keeps a laser focus on the computer in front of her. I consider trying harder, but if Zara wanted to talk, she wouldn't be shy about it. I just need to let her be and hope she comes around before this eats her alive.

～

THE FOX AND HOUND SITS NESTLED BETWEEN A BOOKSTORE and a vintage record shop, its wooden sign weathered by years of DC rain and snow. Inside, the lighting is dim, warm amber casting shadows across worn leather booths and dark wood paneling. A proper English pub, transplanted to the heart of a little town called Ashleigh, about thirty minutes outside the city.

We arrive separately. Zara first, claiming a corner booth with sight lines to both exits. Me second, baseball cap pulled low, moving quickly through the small dinner crowd. Thankfully the place isn't packed. To the best of my knowledge, none of us have ever been here before and it's so far removed from typical DC types of places that I don't expect to see anyone we know. At least, I hope we don't.

Nadia and Elliott arrive together. Through the window, I watch them approach—Nadia's confident stride alongside Elliott's more measured pace. Just the sight of them loosens something tight in my chest and brings a smile to my face.

Liam enters last, ten minutes later, as planned.

"You look terrible," Nadia says by way of greeting, sliding into the booth beside me. But her eyes are warm as she pulls me into a fierce hug.

"Missed you too," I say into her hair, breathing in the familiar scent of her shampoo.

Elliott remains standing, eyes methodically sweeping the room. "This location is less than ideal. Too many variables. Did you see the security cameras? If someone figures out what we're doing—"

"It's perfect," Zara counters. "Noisy enough that we won't

be overheard, busy enough that five people meeting won't draw attention."

Liam slides in next to Zara. The booth is tight with all five of us, elbows bumping, knees touching. It's a far cry from how we are used to meeting, all of us in the office or at our own desks. Or during the short period when I was SSA, in the small bullpen on the other side of our department. I catch Liam's eye and he smiles like we're in on our own little secret. Seeing him again has re-energized me in a way I can't explain. It's like I've been dying of thirst in an ocean.

A server approaches. We order drinks—nothing strong, just enough to look like friends meeting after work. When she leaves, the facade of casualness drops.

"This is nice," Nadia says, looking around at our faces. "Though I could have done without the circumstances."

Elliott's expression remains neutral, but he places his hand over Nadia's on the table—a gesture so uncharacteristic I almost do a double take. Their relationship has evolved while I've been away. I glance at Zara, who I know is dying to comment, but she holds it in.

"Thank you all for coming," I say. "I know it's a risk."

"A calculated one," Elliott answers. His eyes, ever observant, never stop scanning the room.

"Honestly, we're just glad you're alive," Liam says. "News has been scarce since you two left. But we should be as quick as possible." His knee presses against mine under the table and I feel a surge of electricity through my core. It's taking a considerable amount of willpower not to just yank him into the pub's back room right now. But I can't ignore why we're all here. And even though she was never part of this group, I still feel Janice's absence.

"First, let's go over what we know. Janice died six days ago, but not in the line of duty," I say. "What else?"

"The details of her death are being classified," Zara offers.

"By who?" I ask.

"Not Caruthers," Nadia says. "He claims not to know anything more than we do."

"The department heads have also been strangely quiet," Liam adds. "I mean, I know I haven't been in this office as long as the rest of you, but I thought it was common practice for a department to be informed of the details when a Deputy Director dies—especially one who used to run your department."

"That's at the discretion of the department head," Elliott says. "There's no hard and fast rule."

I nod, taking a sip of water to ease my dry throat. "Is there an investigation?"

"Most likely," Elliott replies. "But any record or details surrounding it have been either classified or hidden."

"Which means someone doesn't want anyone looking into her death," Zara says.

"How did you even hear about it?" Nadia asks. "I thought you two were in communications blackout."

"Theo," Zara replies, though something darkens her face as she says it.

"Oh," Nadia replies, looking like she wants to ask a follow-up question but decides against it.

"None of this is right," I say. "Unless Janice happened to have some kind of terminal disease none of us knew about."

"She did like to keep things close to the chest," Liam offers.

"Has there been any communication from any of the other agents who were targeted?" I ask.

"We don't have that kind of information," Elliott replies, his tone cold. "In fact, none of us should even be speaking. It's against the new protocol."

Nadia's hand tightens around Elliott's. Something passes between them, a silent communication I can't quite read.

"But… that would be counterproductive," Elliott concedes after a moment, his expression softening almost imperceptibly.

The shift is subtle but significant. I've known Elliott for a while now, watched him maintain rigid adherence to protocol through situations that would break most people. This willingness to bend—that's new. It has to be Nadia. Their relationship has deepened into something that even Elliott's iron-clad principles can't override.

"No one has heard a word from them," Liam says, leaning a little closer. "But Janice was the one who told us that was by design. For their protection. Just like you. They were each sequestered." I can sense the worry practically wafting off him. He may be glad to see me, but my presence here is a risk. The whole point of us being in New Mexico to begin with was to insulate us from whatever was happening. But as I look around at my friends and colleagues I realize that protecting us may have hurt everyone else. We haven't been here to help them navigate all these changes—or push back against them.

"I think we need to track down the other agents," I say.

"How would that help?" Nadia asks.

"I don't know, but they were isolated under Janice's order. Do they even know she's dead? If Theo hadn't contacted us —" I shoot a quick glance at Zara. "—would *we*?"

"I would have found a way to tell you," Liam says. "Eventually."

"That's my point. With the Bureau so fractured, information comes slowly and in pieces. And I think someone wants it that way. What if Janice was getting close to something—the heart of all this? What if she was working the case and someone thought she was getting *too* close?"

"You mean you think it was a hit," Nadia replies.

"I'm not ruling it out. Can you?"

She and Elliott share a quick look. I can tell they're skeptical but also they can't refute it.

"But how are we supposed to prove that if we can't even look at the autopsy?" Liam asks, lowering his voice at the word *autopsy*. There may not be a lot of people around, but people are passing by our table periodically.

"I want to look at her apartment. If that's where she died—"

"It wasn't," Nadia interrupts. "It happened at work."

I turn to her. "*What?*"

She nods. "Yeah. I heard one of the other agents talking about it. Myers found her in her office. Called it in. But that's all I know."

I turn to Liam. "Then why wasn't she given a place on the wall? She was clearly working." Even dying in her office should be considered *in the line of duty*.

He gives me a bewildered look. "I have no idea."

This was why we all needed to get together. Because we don't know what we know until we can share openly. "Any chance you can get into her office?" I ask Elliott.

"I'm sure it's been sealed by now."

"I could do it," Nadia says. "I could bypass the security. If my access hadn't been revoked."

I narrow my gaze. "That's probably why you were put on leave. They realized you had the skills to gather evidence about it. *Fuck.*" My hands are in fists and I want to slam them on the table, but I don't.

Liam wraps his hand around mine. "Em, it's okay."

But I don't think it is. There's a coverup going on here, and I need to find out why. "I still want to take a look at her apartment. She knew the department was in trouble. She may not have kept everything in her office."

"Are you sure that's a good idea?" Zara asks. "You're not supposed to be here. If you get caught—"

"I know," I say. "But if I'm not going to investigate I might as well be back in New Mexico."

"Oh," Nadia replies. "*That's* where you've been. I thought that kidnapping case might have been you. Even though that other agent—what's her name—took credit."

"Yeah, Agent Dent," I say. "She's a good egg. Solid agent. She covered for us."

I see Liam visibly exhale. Grinning, I shove his leg. "What, didn't think we could handle ourselves out there?"

"I just don't like the idea of you being so far away," he says. I grin, then notice Zara staring at the table. This *love talk* probably isn't doing anything to lift her spirits about Theo.

I clear my throat and change the subject. "Okay. I'm going to check out her apartment. Tonight. In and out, quick."

"I'm going with you," Liam replies.

"No, I need—"

"You need backup," he says. "And I'm not letting you go in there alone. We don't know what we're dealing with. In fact, none of us should be doing *anything* alone until we have a better picture of what we're up against. Agreed?"

"Yeah," I mutter, knowing he's right. "Agreed." Everyone else nods. "But until I get back, let's keep a low profile."

"We need a way to keep in touch," Zara says. "An untraceable one." She hands out a prepaid phone that's already been removed from the package to each person at the table. "We can use these maybe twice before they'll be useless. Each number is programmed using the first two digits of our service numbers."

"Thank you, all of you, for agreeing to do this," I say before we begin to part. "I know you're putting a lot on the line here."

"None of us thinks this is right," Nadia says. "But I think I speak for everyone when I say we're just glad you're both back."

I exchange a glance with Zara. "Us too. We'll be in touch again in a few days. Until then, keep your heads down and your ears open."

Nadia and Elliott head out together, just as they arrived. Zara is next, giving me a knowing smile as she leaves me and Liam for a brief moment.

"I wish we had more time," I say.

"We will," he says. "Once all of this is over." He runs his hand gently down my cheek, sending a shiver through my spine. "See you tonight?"

"One-fifteen A.M.," I say. "Don't be late."

"Wouldn't dream of it," he says and kisses me so quickly I think I've imagined it. Then he's gone.

I pay the tab with cash, and take a different exit than Zara. Using the routes she prescribed; it will take me an hour to get back to the safehouse.

But I don't mind. The ghost of Liam's kiss lingers on my lips the whole way back.

Chapter Six

I study the access panel outside Janice's building, the blue glow illuminating Liam's face in the darkness. He stands close, his shoulder pressed against mine. I grin because I know it's no accident.

"You sure this will work?" I ask, watching him scroll through his phone.

"No, but do you have a better idea?" He's using a remote cracking program and assured me I didn't want to know where it came from. Still, it's odd having him try to break into our old boss's apartment. I wonder if Janice somehow foresaw this moment—us standing here in the shadows, trying to piece together why she's gone. The thought sends a chill through me that has nothing to do with the night air.

I scan the roads around us. Janice's building sits in a heavily-wooded section of town where the trees are taller than the buildings. But that doesn't mean we're obscured from sight. Quite the opposite, actually. We're out in the open and someone could come by at any minute. Which was why I wanted to make sure that if we were going to do this, it would be during the dead of night.

Liam taps a sequence into his phone. The screen connects wirelessly with the building's security system, numbers scrolling rapidly across the display. It takes thirty seconds before the access panel blinks green.

"Bingo," he says. "But the timestamp will show entry at 2:17 PM today, not now."

"Smart." I give him a sideways glance. "When did you get so good at this?"

A ghost of a smile crosses his face. "I had time to learn some new tricks while you were away." He pauses. "What would you have done if I hadn't been here?"

I shrug. "Climbed in through a window?" In truth I didn't have a plan. But I've been trained to adapt. Maybe I could have followed another resident inside, or found a way up on the roof. There have to be at least three different ways into the apartment.

The lobby is deserted at this hour, security cameras panning empty space. We avoid them as much as possible and take the stairs instead of the elevator, moving quickly but unhurried—just residents returning home late, nothing suspicious.

Janice lived on the seventh floor, apartment 714. The hallway is silent except for the soft hum of the building's ventilation system. Liam pulls out a lock-pick set as we approach. He gets to work on the door's deadbolt as I stand guard.

"You're becoming a regular safe cracker," I whisper.

"Don't congratulate me yet. I've only done this a handful of times so far."

I have no idea what awaits us inside, other than no one should be home. As far as I know Janice lived alone and didn't have a family. Still, there's no telling what kind of precautions a Deputy Director of the FBI would take with her personal living space. We need to be prepared for anything.

The door opens without a sound. We step inside, closing it

behind us. I expect to see a panel near the door, or at least a blinking light somewhere indicating we've tripped a silent alarm and only have seconds to disarm it. But that doesn't seem to be the case.

"No alarm system?" I whisper.

"That is strange," Liam replies, glancing around. "I mean, I'd be willing to bet most of the people in this building have alarms. So why not her?"

I take a few minutes to inspect the hallway, turning on the lights, thinking we've missed it. But there's no sign of a system anywhere. And nothing is beeping to let us know it's about to alarm.

The apartment is... not what I expected. I realize with a pang that I never knew where Janice lived, never visited her outside the office in all our years working together. The woman who shaped my career, who trusted me with impossible missions, remains a mystery even now.

Her living room is bathed in shadows, moonlight filtering through sheer curtains. Clean lines, minimalist furniture, but with unexpected touches of warmth. A handwoven throw draped over the sofa. A collection of small pottery pieces arranged on a shelf. Books—real, physical books—lining one wall.

Liam moves toward the kitchen while I linger in the living space, my eyes slowly scanning across framed photographs on a side table.

The largest shows Janice on a beach, much younger than I ever knew her, maybe in her thirties. Her hair is longer, falling past her shoulders in loose waves. She's laughing, arm wrapped around a man I don't recognize. He's tall, athletic, with the kind of easy smile that invites trust. They look happy. In love, even.

"I didn't know she was married," I say, picking up the frame.

Liam appears at my shoulder. "You're kidding," he says, looking at the picture. "Really?"

"Maybe just a boyfriend?" I study the man's face, committing it to memory. Something about him seems vaguely familiar, like a face glimpsed once in passing.

"Could be." Liam's voice softens. "I wonder how many parts of her life she kept separate from work."

The question lands with unexpected weight. How long did I keep myself hidden from view? Even now, there are still things I don't let Liam—or anyone for that matter—see. Am I destined to become like her, to build a life completely insular from my work? Or maybe even give up the possibility of a "normal" life for the job?

I set the photo down, moving to another. This one shows Janice receiving an award, shaking hands with the Director—not our current boss, his predecessor. Her smile in this one is different. Professional. Contained. It's the Janice I knew.

"Check this out," Liam calls softly from the hallway.

I join him, finding him examining a series of framed photographs arranged in a neat line along the wall. They show Janice in various locations around the world—standing before the Eiffel Tower, on what looks like the Great Wall of China, beside a massive waterfall I recognize as Victoria Falls.

"What in the ever-loving hell? When did she have time to do all this?" I say.

"These span decades," Liam notes, pointing to the subtle changes in her appearance from frame to frame. "Some vacation photos, but others..."

He indicates a picture of Janice standing with three men in military uniforms. The background is nondescript, but something about their posture suggests covert operations.

"This wasn't a vacation," I agree. "This was work. The kind that doesn't make it into official files." That explains the military salute.

We continue our search, meticulous and thorough.

Bedroom, home office, kitchen, bathroom. Nothing obvious jumps out, no hidden safe or secret compartment. Just the mundane details of a life I never knew—favorite books, a collection of jazz records, a half-finished crossword puzzle on the nightstand.

I open her medicine cabinet to find what might be the most revealing evidence yet and my heart sinks.

"Liam," I call quietly.

He joins me in the bathroom doorway as I examine the array of prescription bottles. Lisinopril. Atorvastatin. Metoprolol.

"Heart medications," I say, reading the labels. "And recent refills, all of them."

Next to the prescriptions sits a collection of vaping devices, sleek and modern, arranged neatly on a shelf.

"She was treating a heart condition," Liam says, his voice hollow. "While vaping regularly."

I close the cabinet, my reflection fractured in the mirror as the door swings shut. "Maybe it was just a heart attack after all."

The words taste bitter, like surrendering. Like I've traveled all this way and put everyone at risk based on nothing but paranoia and grief.

Liam's hand finds mine in the darkness, his fingers warm against my skin. "But that doesn't explain why they're keeping her death so secret. Why they're not letting anyone close."

"No," I agree. "It doesn't."

We stand there for a moment, close enough that I can feel the rhythm of his breathing, smell the familiar scent of his aftershave. In the dimness, his eyes find mine, and something electric passes between us. All the things unsaid during months apart, all the worry and longing.

His hand moves to my face, thumb tracing the curve of my cheek. "I missed you, Emily."

"I missed you too." The words come out raw, honest in a way I rarely allow myself to be.

For one breathless moment, the world narrows to just this—his face inches from mine, his hand warm against my skin. Then reality crashes back. We're standing in our dead boss's apartment, conducting an unauthorized search that could end both our careers. Or worse.

I step back, clearing my throat. "We should keep looking."

Disappointment flickers across his face, but he nods. "Just testing your willpower." He swallows and I notice he has to adjust his pants ever so slightly. "Nicely done."

I grin as we return to the office, examining the desk drawers, the computer (password protected, beyond my skills), the filing cabinet. But there's nothing to indicate a secret case she's been working on, or why anyone would want her out of the way.

Finally, Liam checks his watch. "Em, I think we need to call it. There's nothing here."

I take one last look around, frustration burning in my chest. Nothing. We came all this way for nothing.

As we prepare to leave, my gaze catches on a small box tucked beneath the coffee table. I crouch down, pulling it out. Inside, I find more photographs, these older, their edges yellowed with age.

One in particular stops me cold. It shows Janice with the same man from the beach photo, but they're not alone. Standing with them is a face I recognize immediately—the man I glimpsed at her funeral, the one sitting in the first chair.

"Who's this?" I show Liam.

He studies it, shaking his head. "Don't know. Obviously someone she knew… a friend?"

I slip the photo into my pocket. "He was at the funeral. Did you see him? In the first chair. We should get Elliott to run facial recognition on him."

We leave the apartment exactly as we found it, erasing all

traces of our presence. Liam resets the door lock, and we take the stairs down to the service exit at the back of the building.

"We'll go separately," I say once we're outside. "Get this photo to Elliott."

Liam nods, hesitating as if there's something more he wants to say. But the moment passes. "Be careful," is all he offers before disappearing into the darkness.

I wait five minutes, then head in the opposite direction, keeping to the shadows. My mind races, trying to make sense of what we've found—and what we haven't. The medications suggest Janice's death could have been natural, but my instincts scream otherwise. The mysterious man in the photographs. The timing of it all.

Lost in thought, I don't notice the figure until we collide at a corner. The impact is jarring, shoulder against shoulder. I keep my head down instinctively, murmuring an automatic "Sorry" as I step to the side.

The man says nothing. No apology, no acknowledgment. Just continues walking, face obscured by the brim of a baseball cap, hands thrust deep in jacket pockets.

Something about the encounter raises the hair on the back of my neck. His silence. The deliberate way he kept his face hidden. Or maybe it's just my paranoia working overtime, seeing threats in every shadow.

I consider turning back, finding Liam, but he's long gone by now. And showing up back at home would only create more risk.

Instead, I change direction, taking a convoluted route back to the safehouse. Three extra blocks, doubling back twice, cutting through an all-night diner and exiting through the kitchen (with an apologetic smile to the startled cook). Basic counter-surveillance measures, but effective.

By the time I reach the safehouse I'm reasonably confident I wasn't followed. Still, I perform one final check before entering, scanning the street, the windows of neighboring buildings, the parked cars lining the curb.

Nothing unusual. No signs of surveillance. Just the ordinary quiet of a DC neighborhood after midnight.

Inside, I lock the door and lean against it, suddenly exhausted. The adrenaline that carried me through the night ebbs away, leaving bone-deep weariness in its wake. "Hello?" I call out, but there's no response. Zara isn't here. Strange, she didn't say she was going out. I feel a pull deep in my stomach until I see the little Post-it note by the computer.

E, had to run out. Back soon – Z.

I take a deep breath, calming myself. While it's not like her to go out late at night, it *is* in her handwriting, so the odds she was taken (or worse) are pretty low. She has been under a lot of stress lately—maybe she just needed some fresh air.

I pull out my phone and study the photograph from Janice's apartment again. Janice, younger and carefree. The man from the beach photos, his arm around her shoulders. And the third figure, the one I recognized from the funeral—smiling along with them. Three friends a generation ago. And yet, I don't know either one.

Who are you? I silently ask the stranger's face. *And what did you mean to Janice?*

More importantly—could he know why she died?

I tuck the phone away and check my watch. Almost three in the morning. I need to get some sleep, but I'll feel better once Zara is back.

I move to the window, carefully edging back the curtain to look out at the street below. The odd encounter with the silent man lingers in my mind, a discordant note I can't dismiss.

Is he out there now, watching? Or has all this just finally gotten to me? Am I so sleep-deprived that I'm seeing shadows around every corner?

The street is empty, not a thing in sight. But I can't shake the feeling that something has been set in motion—something that began long before Janice's death, before my exile from DC, before any of us realized we were pawns in someone else's game.

And now the pieces are moving faster, the endgame approaching. I just have to stay out of the spotlight long enough to see what it is.

Chapter Seven

THE PHONE SITS on the table between us, Janice's face smiling up from the screen like an electronic ghost. Zara leans in, studying the image with narrowed eyes.

"And you saw this dude at the funeral?" she asks, tapping the figure standing beside Janice.

"From a distance." I pace the length of our safehouse living room, muscle memory tracing the exact seven steps it takes to cross from wall to wall. "He wasn't trying to hide, right there up front and he was there the whole time. Now that I think about it, I don't think anyone other than the priest said a word to him. I'm not sure *anyone* knew who he was. I told Liam to get Elliott to find him."

Zara turns to her laptop. "Pfssh. Never send a child to do a woman's job."

I lean against the wall, watching her work. The safe house is quiet except for the tap of keys and the distant hum of traffic outside. Morning light filters through the blinds, casting striped shadows across the worn carpet. Zara didn't get back until around four-thirty, with some excuse about needing to take a long walk. We both know it was bullshit, but I have to let her come to me. Then again, I can only take so much of this until I confront her with it. Time will tell which one of us breaks first.

"You know, I've seen his face somewhere before," Zara mutters, staring at the screen. "Not in person, but..."

"A case file maybe?" I suggest.

She snaps her fingers over and over. "No. Somewhere else. It's right on the tip of my tongue."

Her fingers move rapidly across the keyboard, uploading the scanned image to a facial recognition database. Not the Bureau's official system—that would leave a digital footprint we can't afford—but an incognito image search, built from publicly available information.

"Sonofa—that's it, *that's* where I've seen him," she says after several minutes. "D.L. Mattingly. *Darren Mattingly.*"

"Wait, the attorney?" I ask. I've heard of the man, but never seen him. At least I don't think I have. When she turns the screen to me, I realize I *have* seen his picture somewhere before, probably on some billboard ten years ago. The photo shows the same man, older than in Janice's picture but unmistakable. Sharp eyes, distinguished gray at his temples, the confident posture of someone accustomed to commanding attention.

"Yep," Zara continues, scrolling through information. "High-profile defense lawyer here in DC. Specializes in federal cases."

"A defense lawyer?" I frown, trying to make sense of the connection. "Janice worked for the FBI. They would have been on opposite sides."

"Those must have been some fun court cases," Zara laughs. "Maybe they reconnected there? Opposing counsel becoming something more."

I think of the photo from Janice's apartment, the way she looked at him on that beach. There was history there, something deep and personal.

"We need to talk to him," I decide. "Find out what he knows about Janice's last few weeks."

Zara looks up at me, concern etched in the lines around her eyes. "That's risky, Em. He's a high-profile figure in DC legal circles. If we approach him directly—"

"I'm already a ghost," I remind her. "If I'm seen, it's a problem no matter who I'm talking to."

She sighs, recognizing the stubborn edge in my voice. "Fine. But I'm requesting a different cell when we're arrested. When do you want to confront him?"

"Tomorrow morning. You said he has an office downtown?"

"Twelfth and K," she confirms. "Mattingly, Ramirez, and Klein. Big corner office with a view of the Mall, according to their website."

"Too public," I muse. "We need to catch him somewhere more private."

Zara returns to her laptop, digging deeper. "According to his… shockingly curated social media, he's a creature of habit. Takes a midmorning walk every day around ten-thirty, weather permitting. Also apparently likes flowers. A lot."

I look over her shoulder; his feed is filled with images of different local flora, some of the photos good enough that I'd call them professional.

"Where does he like to walk?"

"Looks like Constitution Gardens. And from the number of photographs, I'd be willing to bet he's there for a good ten or fifteen minutes each day. Plenty of time to corner him. Alone."

I can't help a small smile. "It's perfect."

"It's as good a spot as any," Zara says. "But what's our approach? He doesn't know you."

I consider this, mentally cycling through options. "Direct confrontation. No pretense. He knew Janice well enough to attend her funeral without hiding. That tells me he's not afraid of people knowing they knew each other. He cared for her."

"But does that mean he knows something?" Zara adds softly.

I stand back up. "We'll find out tomorrow."

∼

CONSTITUTION GARDENS GLEAMS UNDER THE MORNING SUN, cherry blossoms beginning to bud along the pathways. I sit on a bench with a newspaper open in my lap, sunglasses concealing my eyes, my cap pulled low. Casual tourist attire, forgettable in a city full of visitors.

Zara's voice comes through the tiny earpiece hidden beneath my hair. "Okay, I see him. Coming in from the southeast path. Black overcoat, tacky gray scarf. Probably paid way too much for it."

"What are you, his tailor?" I whisper.

I don't look up immediately, letting him pass within my peripheral vision first. Darren Mattingly walks with purpose, each stride measured and deliberate. He carries a takeout coffee cup in one gloved hand, a sleek leather briefcase in the other.

He settles on a bench fifty yards from mine, facing the pond. From here, I can study him properly while pretending to read my paper. He looks older than he did two days ago, lines of fatigue etched around his mouth, shadows beneath his eyes. Grief, perhaps. Or something else entirely. He sips his coffee, oblivious to the fact he's being surveilled.

"I'm moving in," I say.

"Make it as fast as possible."

Yeah, yeah, I think. She's such a worrier lately. I fold the newspaper, tuck it under my arm, and stand. The path curves around the pond, bringing me closer to Mattingly's bench with each step. He doesn't look up, focused on something in the middle distance, lost in thought.

I stop directly in front of him. "Mr. Mattingly."

His head snaps up, startled from whatever reverie had claimed him. Wariness immediately replaces surprise, his posture stiffening.

"Do I know you?" His voice is deeper than I expected, with the careful enunciation of someone who makes their living with words.

"No." I remove my sunglasses, meeting his gaze directly. "But we have a mutual friend. Had, I should say."

Recognition flickers in his eyes—not of me, but of my purpose. He sets his coffee cup down with deliberate care and starts to rise. "Excuse me, I need to—"

"Janice Simmons," I say quietly.

The name stops him cold. He sinks back onto the bench, eyes darting to scan our surroundings.

"Who are you? Bureau?" His voice hardens. "I could have your badge for this kind of harassment."

"My name is Emily Slate." I don't hesitate. There's no point in obscuring my identity. It will only lead to more questions. I just have to hope I can trust Mr. Mattingly.

The effect is immediate. His expression transforms, hostility melting into something more complex—surprise, recognition, and a strange relief.

"*Oh*, Ms. Slate," he repeats, almost to himself. "Jan— Janice was very fond of you."

I sit beside him, maintaining enough distance to appear casual to any observers. "She was? What did she say?"

A ghost of a smile touches his lips. "Never details. Janice was too careful for that. But good things. Which, I don't have to tell you, was high praise coming from her."

The past tense lands between us like a physical weight. *Was*. Final.

"I'm hoping you can help me, Mr. Mattingly," I say. "I'm

technically not supposed to be here. But when I found out what happened… I had to come back. Do you know what Janice was working on? Before she died?"

He shakes his head. "We had rules. No work talk. It was the only way…" He trails off, then clears his throat. "The only way we could maintain what we had. FBI Deputy Director and defense attorney—not exactly a match made in professional heaven."

"How long?" I ask.

"On and off for years. Decades, really." He gazes out at the pond, the present seeming to fall away. "We met during the Rodriguez case in '98. She was a field agent then, I was a junior associate. We were… combustible together. But it was complicated."

"Because of your jobs?"

"That was part of it." He turns the coffee cup in his hands, a nervous gesture at odds with his otherwise composed demeanor. "Janice was married before, did you know that? Early in her career."

I shake my head. Nothing in Janice's official file mentioned a marriage.

"David Hastings. Military pilot. There was an accident…" Mattingly's voice tightens. "The three of us knew each other when we were young. She never got over it and frankly, neither did I. David was one of my best friends. For a long time we didn't talk. But once we started seeing each other again in court, it kind of… naturally developed. So we had what we had. Moments, stolen between cases and court appearances."

The revelation hits me like a brick wall. Janice—who lost her partner when she was young. Who knew and understood that grief. Who gave a promising young agent more chances than she deserved when something similar happened to her. But she never revealed why. I always thought it was just luck, that Janice was going easy on me.

The truth was she had felt that pain herself. She knew how deep it ran.

Why didn't she ever tell me?

I have to clear my throat to stop the tears from bubbling up. "Did Janice have heart trouble?" I ask, steering us back to the question that's been gnawing at me since finding those prescription bottles.

He nods. "She was diagnosed five years ago. But it was manageable with medication." His eyes find mine, sharp and knowing. "You think that's what killed her?"

"What did they tell you?"

"They said it was a heart attack," he says, appraising me. "But you don't believe it."

It's not a question. Something in his tone tells me he doesn't believe it either.

"Do you?" I counter.

He's silent for a long moment, watching a pair of ducks glide across the pond's surface. "No," he says finally. "But there's nothing I can do about it."

"Why not?" The question comes out more forcefully than I intended.

"Because I'm a defense attorney, Ms. Slate. I know exactly how the system works, where the barriers are, which doors stay locked no matter how hard you push." Bitterness edges his words. "And because I promised her."

"Promised her what?"

"To stay out of it. If anything happened to her." He meets my gaze directly. "We both knew the risks of a relationship in such a… volatile job. If anything ever happened to either of us, we walk away. No questions. No inquiries. No stirring up trouble."

A cold feeling settles in my stomach. "Did she know she was in danger? Was someone watching her?"

"We didn't talk about it," he says again, then glances down at the cup. "But I could tell something was weighing on her. She was on edge, worried. I could feel it in the room with us."

"What?"

"I wish I knew."

"Is there anything you can give me?" I ask. "Anything at all that might help me understand what was happening to her?"

He hesitates, conflict clear in his expression. "When I make a promise, I keep it."

"You may have," I acknowledge. "But I didn't. And I'm already in it, whether she wanted that or not."

He looks away, silent deliberation playing across his features. I wait, giving him space to wrestle with competing loyalties—to Janice's memory, to her explicit wishes, to whatever he might suspect about her death.

"I assume you've been to her apartment," he says finally.

I nod.

He drops his voice so low I have to lean in to hear him. "And her *other* apartment?"

My eyes go wide. "She had a safehouse?"

"Not exactly a safehouse. Not officially, anyway. But somewhere she would go when she felt... exposed at home. A condo in Arlington, registered under a shell corporation. We used to meet there sometimes, years ago now."

My pulse quickens. "She still used it?"

"About a month back, she mentioned she'd been staying there again. Didn't say why."

A month back. Right around the time agents began being targeted, including me. When Janice began warning people, putting safeguards in place.

"I need the address," I say.

He pulls out a sleek pen, writes on his napkin with practiced precision. His hand shields the writing from any potential observers.

"I'm giving you this," he says, folding the napkin and

passing it to me with the subtlety of a man accustomed to discreet exchanges, "because she believed in you. In all our time together, she never spoke higher of anyone she worked with. I know you won't let her down."

I tuck the napkin into my pocket. "Thank you."

He stands, buttoning his coat. "I have a hearing in thirty minutes. But if you find anything..." He hands me a business card with a number handwritten on the back. "That's my personal line. Not the office."

I pocket the card next to the napkin. "I'll be in touch."

He starts to walk away, then pauses, looking back. "She trusted you, Ms. Slate. More than most. That meant something."

Then he's gone, striding back toward the city's gleaming buildings, leaving me alone on the bench with a folded napkin burning in my pocket and the weight of Janice's trust heavy on my shoulders.

"Did you get all that?" I say to Zara through the mic.

"Every word," her voice confirms in my ear. "Are you... okay?"

I swallow hard. I just learned more about my boss in five minutes than I did in five years of working with her. It's a lot to process. "Meet me back at the safehouse in an hour. I need time to think."

As I walk away from the pond, I can't shake the image of Janice and Mattingly together—the FBI agent and the defense attorney, finding moments of connection despite the professional chasm between them. How many other parts of her life remained hidden from those who thought they knew her?

And more urgently—what secret had she discovered that was worth dying for?

Chapter Eight

"Do you believe him?" Liam asks.

I'm back in the safehouse, trying to relax on the couch with a cup of tea courtesy of Zara, but I'm finding it difficult. My heart hasn't stopped pounding since I left my meeting with Mattingly, his words echoing through my head the entire way back. I think after I returned looking like I'd seen a ghost, Zara finally took pity on me and gave Liam instructions on how to reach the safehouse—meeting him halfway to make sure they weren't followed back.

She understands—maybe better than I do—that conversation was earth-shattering for me, dredging up more buried memories and skeletons than I care to admit.

Liam arrived in record time, almost like he'd been waiting for the call. And sitting across from him now is strange. We spent so much time apart and now here we are, back in the same room together. And yet there still seems to be something between us. I don't know if it's because I can't fully relax or if it's something else, but I don't feel like we should be dealing with anything personal until we have a handle on this situation. But another part of me wants to scale this table and rip his shirt off.

I'm not sure how much willpower I have in that department.

"Earth to Em," Zara chides.

I take a deep breath, inhaling the smell of Earl Grey before I answer Liam. "I think he's trustworthy. At least about this he is."

"It doesn't surprise me," Zara calls from where she's monitoring the computer in the dining room. "Janice wasn't the most trusting of people. She could have ten safehouses for all we know."

"I didn't get the sense it was a safehouse," I say. "At least he didn't make it seem that way. He made it seem more like *another* home. Maybe like a vacation property."

"I don't recall her ever taking a vacation," Liam replies.

That's true. Janice was a true workaholic… like me. Maybe that's why she saw something in me, maybe I was just a younger version of her. That being said, it wasn't like she ever tried to call me on it or insist I take copious amounts of time off. Maybe she liked that there was someone else like her in the office.

Or maybe she just recognized the need for people like us. There are some agents, like Agent Sutton who go home to families and work nine to five. They clock out and their day is done. And then there are people like me—much rarer, but we exist—who never clock out, as hard as we try. We're *always* working. And maybe she wanted to foster that attitude. Not that she could have ever dissuaded me anyway. The only way I would have ever stopped is if they had fired me.

"Em," Liam says softly, bringing me back.

"Sorry," I say. "Lost in thought."

"It's a lot," he says. "But if Mattingly was telling the truth, we need to take a look at this second location. She could have left something crucial behind."

"Agreed," I say, setting the tea down.

"Orrrrr it could be a tra-aaaap," Zara sing-songs from the

table. "How can we trust Mattingly? We don't even know him."

"He seemed genuinely upset at her death," I say.

She tsks. "Sweet, innocent Emily. He's a lawyer. He lies for a living."

I purse my lips and stick out my tongue at her. She returns the gesture. "So you think he's in on it?"

"No, just that he may have his own secrets to hide. They obviously didn't want the knowledge of their relationship public. He may have just been feeding you false information so if you ever have to go public with any of it he can deny it."

"No," I say. "You didn't see his face." I turn to Liam. "You believe me, right?"

"I think we need to be cautious," he says. "We still don't know why you and the other agents were targeted. We can't afford to be reckless."

"Let me at least do some recon on this property," Zara says. "We can stake it out for a few days, keep watch, make sure no one else has eyes on it."

"A few *days*?" I flop back on the couch. "This is never going to end."

"She's right, Em," Liam says. "I know you don't want to hear it, but better safe than sorry."

I huff. "Okay, yeah. Let's… get surveillance set up."

"I'll take care of it tonight," Zara says. "Maybe I can rope Nadia into helping since she's not doing anything but sitting around her house."

I turn to Liam. "I just want to come home."

He takes my hand. "I know. Me too. It isn't fair. But this is the only way to get ahead of these people. We can't keep reacting. We need to find a way to turn this around." He's right. They both are. In my gut I know it. It's just when you've been sequestered in another part of the country away from the people you love with no answers it begins to grate on your nerves a little. I think if I hadn't had Zara there I might have *actually* gone insane. I'd been so close to rage quitting before that damn case came up... what would have happened if I'd just come back then? Could I have stopped all this? Saved Janice? Or was she already in too deep?

Liam checks his watch. "I need to get back. The dogs need to be fed and walked and it'll take me a good hour to get back home." Even though our house is less than thirty minutes away, given all the precautions we're all taking it makes everything that much more complicated. Liam's car isn't anywhere near here and he'll need to double back every few blocks to make sure he's not being followed. That's another thing. If we end up rushing into Janice's place without the proper precautions, it could wind up exposing all our hard work so far. Meaning we would have come back all for nothing. I can't forget that I'm not the only one who is affected here. *Everyone* is putting themselves on the line for me.

I get up and wrap my arms around Liam, never wanting to let go. He holds me just as hard, like I might disappear if he lets go. I have missed this so much. Just this simple act that I ended up taking for granted. Finally he leans down and his lips find mine. I don't want this moment to end. I don't want to break the connection, but I feel that longing and desire in him too. Finally, I pull away, even though it's the hardest thing I've ever had to do. "Be safe," I say, placing my hand on his chest while I catch my breath.

"I will," he replies. "You haven't seen the last of me. I know it sucks, but staying here really is the best thing for now."

I nod, not wanting to argue. I'll take as much time with him as I can get. Who knows how much we have. Maybe the fate that befell Janice is what awaits all of us at the end of this.

We say our goodbyes and he heads out, leaving behind nothing but the scent of his cologne. I hate how sentimental I'm being about all of this. That isn't like me. Usually, I can keep my head and leave my emotions out of things like this. I think it's this constant stress—it's like a pressure cooker that keeps building and building. And eventually, something is going to have to give.

"You okay?" Zara asks. She hasn't moved from her computer, but she's watching me with a trained eye.

"Yeah," I say, even though I don't believe the word as I say it. "...no. But it doesn't matter. It is what it is, right?" I turn to her. "What are you working on over there?"

"Just... tracking down the equipment we'll need for the surveillance," she replies. I'm not sure I believe her either and I'm not sure how long I should wait until I begin to press. It's that caginess of hers poking through again.

"How long do you think it will take to set up once you have everything?"

"An hour," she says. "At most. But the kicker is tracking it all down without making any waves. We're operating way off-grid here. Everything takes a thousand times longer."

"Tell me about it," I say. I take in a deep breath, looking around the apartment. With little else to do, I might as well make myself useful. "Feel like food?"

"I could never not eat, you know that," she replies, her focus still on the screen.

"Lo Mein?"

"Sounds perfect to me." I head to the refrigerator to flip through one of the paper menus stuck to the front with a magnet. Would placing an order through my phone or the computer be quicker? Yes, but things like that come with a whole host of additional data we don't need to be leaking right now. Which means it's down to a paper menu and a landline. Like a freaking neanderthal.

As I grab the nearby phone and dial, I can't settle the unease in my stomach. No matter what we do, they have always been one step ahead of us. And I'm not sure there's anything we can do to change that.

I hope I'm wrong.

Chapter Nine

IT'S BEEN NEARLY a full week since we've been back in D.C. and I feel like all we've managed to do is confirm what we already knew and little else. If this were one of my regular cases I would say it was the slowest one in history. What's worse is there isn't much I can do about it. Whereas normally I would go out and work every angle possible, I have to limit my time outside due to possible exposure. I've already had to call SSA Strong twice and extend our leave. I made something up about a sick relative, but that is only going to hold for so long. Eventually Strong is going to want us back at our desks for our next assignment.

"You shouldn't be doing this alone." Zara's voice in my ear is tight with disapproval.

I crouch beside Janice's second residence—a modest Arlington condo tucked into a quiet development where nobody asks questions. Three days of surveillance has confirmed it isn't being watched. At least, not by anyone we've been able to detect.

"We've been over this," I murmur, examining the electronic lock. "You're my eyes out there. I'm the safecracker."

"You're just trying to one-up Liam." The concern in her voice would be touching if it weren't so annoying right now.

"You're just mad because this is the second breaking and entering you've had to miss out on." I pull out the electronic bypass tool Liam provided, a sleek device that looks like a smartphone case. "Going radio silent for entry. I'll check in once I'm inside."

"Emily—"

I tap the earpiece, cutting her off. I love Zara to death. I would literally take a bullet for her. But she has been annoying the crap out of me lately and I know it has to do with what she won't talk about: the big, six-thousand-pound elephant in the room named Theo. Since coming back she hasn't said one word about him, not even that she wants answers. She hasn't tried to contact him— doesn't even know if he's in town. But I know my best friend. She's plotting something and it's only a matter of time before I figure out what it is.

The bypass tool connects to the door's security system, running through thousands of possible combinations in seconds. Janice would have had better security than this, which means she wanted it to appear normal from the outside. The real protections will be inside.

The lock clicks. I pocket the device and draw my weapon, holding it low against my thigh as I ease the door open.

The entrance hallway is dark, curtains drawn against the afternoon sun. I step inside and close the door behind me, standing motionless, letting my eyes adjust to the gloom. Listening. Nothing but the soft hum of a refrigerator, the distant sound of traffic outside.

I scan the floor, walls, ceiling. When I see it I can't help but grin.

A nearly invisible tripwire at ankle height, stretching across the hallway. Beyond it, a pressure plate disguised as a normal floorboard. Amateur mistakes to miss them. I step carefully over the wire, avoid the pressure plate, and continue deeper into the condo.

The living room appears ordinary at first glance—sofa, coffee table, TV. But the normalcy is a veneer, staged for casual observers. A delivery person dropping off a package from the front door wouldn't notice anything unusual. But I do.

The furniture is positioned for optimal defensive sight lines. The heavy ceramic vase on the side table—perfect for grabbing in a close-quarters fight. The slightly misaligned rug that likely conceals a floor safe.

I move through the space methodically, checking for additional security measures. Another tripwire connected to what looks like a silent alarm. I avoid it, making my way toward a closed door at the back of the living room. I feel like a spider, each step has to be carefully calculated and my knees keep ending up at my chest as I try to give the alarms as wide of berth as possible.

Once I reach the back of the hallway, I take a breath, exhaling slowly. Trying the handle, I'm not surprised to find it locked.

The lock is more sophisticated than the front door's, but not impenetrable. I pull out a set of picks and get to work, careful not to rush despite the prickling awareness that every second I spend here is another second where it can all go wrong.

Calm down, Emily. This isn't your first rodeo. You know how to do this and you know rushing will only make things worse.

The lock yields after forty seconds. I ease the door open, weapon raised, and find myself staring at exactly what I'd hoped for.

Janice's war room.

The space was once a bedroom, now transformed into an operation center. Three walls covered in corkboards, whiteboards, maps. Papers pinned in methodical arrangements, even a red string connecting seemingly disparate elements. She really went all out. A desk dominates the center, three laptops arranged in a semicircle, all closed.

I holster my weapon and retrieve the earpiece from my pocket. "You should see this—it's like her command center."

"About freaking time," Zara's voice returns immediately. "Find anything useful?"

"Just getting started." I scan the walls, taking it all in. "It's...a lot."

"Describe it."

"She has a whole setup here. More in depth than anything I ever saw in her office. And there are names," I say, moving closer to the nearest board. "Faces."

And there, in the center of the largest board—my own face stares back at me. My official Bureau photo, taken three years ago. Around it, string connects to other agents. Some I recognize, others I don't. Nine faces total, arranged in what appears to be chronological order.

"She was trying to connect us," I murmur, half to myself. "All the agents who were targeted."

I read off the names for Zara: "Thomas Mercer. Sarah Abernathy. Marcus Chen. Miguel Ortiz. Danna Williams. Vanessa Estes. Curtis Carrillo. Sfiyyah Scott." Names that mean nothing to me, yet Janice had connected them all together, connected them to me.

"Running them now," Zara responds, the click of her keyboard audible through the earpiece.

I move to another board, this one covered in what looks like financial records, bank statements, shell companies. Janice was following money trails, trying to connect the dots. Many of the documents have notes scrawled across them in her distinctive handwriting.

The third wall focuses on locations. Safe houses, foreign embassies, remote compounds. Photos taken with telephoto lenses, satellite imagery, property records. Some have red X's drawn through them. Dead ends. She was putting in some serious legwork to collect all this data. Not that it seems like it amounted to much.

"She was doing this all on her own," I say, scanning the documents. "Outside official channels."

"Em," Zara's voice interrupts my thoughts. "Those names. All specialized in covert operations or financial crimes. Four of them...Chen, Williams, Estes and Scott are deceased."

I stop cold. "They're... dead?"

"Yeah," she replies. "Others I'm still missing data."

The timeline matches our own exile. "What are the causes of death?"

"Chen in a car accident. Scott was killed in a home invasion. Williams from a heart attack—like Janice. I don't have a cause of death listed for Estes."

My gaze drifts to a smaller board partially hidden behind the door. This one contains personal photos. Janice with Mattingly in various locations over the years. Janice receiving commendations. Younger Janice in what must be academy graduation photos.

And there—Janice with her first husband. The pilot. David. They look so young, so happy. His arm around her waist, her smile unguarded in a way I never witnessed during our years working together.

I understand now why she kept so much of herself hidden. The compartmentalization wasn't just professional caution—it was emotional armor. After losing David, she'd built walls to protect herself from that kind of pain again. I recognize the strategy because it's the same one I employed after losing Matt.

"Em?" Zara prompts. "You still there?"

"Yeah." I shake off the reflection. "Just... this is a lot. And it's weird... seeing another side of Janice."

I turn my attention to the desk, carefully checking for additional security measures before approaching it. The laptops will require passwords we don't have. But in the drawer, I find a leather-bound notebook, its pages filled with Janice's cramped handwriting.

"Found her notebook," I tell Zara. "She was documenting everything old-school."

"Smart. Can't be hacked."

I flip through pages of observations, theories, dead ends. The handwriting is hurried and unpolished, like she was trying to write her thoughts as fast as she thought them. I'm not sure it amounts to much; it's mostly just theories and suppositions. Little else.

The most recent entry is dated three days before her death:

Another block. Access denied to P-level files. Someone has noticed my searches. T says watch my back. DL insists I drop it. Can't. Won't. Too many gone already. ES next if pattern holds. Need to warn her, but direct contact compromises us both.

ES. Emily Slate. Me.

My throat tightens. She was trying to protect me, even as she pursued answers that were getting her nowhere.

A sound from outside catches my attention—a car door closing. Voices. I freeze, hand instinctively moving to my weapon.

"Someone's here," I whisper to Zara. "Can you see anything from the surveillance feed?"

"Checking." A pause. "Just neighbors. Couple with groceries, heading to their own unit."

I exhale slowly, forcing my heart rate to steady. Paranoia is heightened in these situations, but sometimes paranoia keeps you alive.

As I turn back to the desk, something catches my eye. A flat package that's fallen against the desk in a haphazard way. As if dropped there in a hurry. I glance up, realizing the window to the room has been cracked at the top, though the window covering prevented me from seeing it as soon as I came in the room. It's open just wide enough to allow a thin envelope through. I try moving the window to close it, but it must be locked in place somehow. She kept the window open? For what?

I crouch down to examine it. A padded envelope, no markings, unsealed. But uncategorized, like everything else in the room.

"Found something," I tell Zara. "A package. Looks like someone might have dropped it through the window."

"Can you see what's inside?"

I hesitate, considering the possibilities. It could be evidence, something Janice was waiting for. It could also be a trap—explosives, toxins, any number of dangers.

"Going to check it," I decide. "But I'm being careful." *Please don't explode.*

I place the envelope on the desk and use a pen to gently open the unsealed flap. No wires visible. No suspicious powder. Inside, I find a USB drive and a single sheet of paper folded around it.

The note is typed, no signature:

J,

What you asked for. Took longer than expected. Security was tighter than anything I've seen. But it confirms your suspicions. He's involved, but may not be the mastermind. Someone higher is pulling strings.

Be careful. They're watching you.

-A

"Zara," I say, my voice tight with urgency. "I think it's information about her case."

"What kind?"

"The kind Janice never got to see." I carefully place the USB drive and note back in the envelope. "From someone named *A*. Mentions someone else, but doesn't say who."

"*A*?" Zara sounds surprised. "Big help there. That could literally be anyone."

"Would you sign your real name?" I take one last look

around the room, committing as much as possible to memory. "I'm going to document what I can and then get out."

I use my phone to photograph each board systematically, making sure to capture every name, every connection, every question mark. Janice spent months building this web of information; we can't let it go to waste. At the very least it means we can begin contacting the agents who've been targeted that haven't been killed yet.

As I work, I can't help but notice the parallels between us. Janice living a double life—Bureau Deputy Director by day, rogue investigator by night. Keeping secrets from everyone, even those closest to her. Working alone because trust was too precious, too dangerous to extend.

Isn't that exactly what I'm doing now? Operating outside official channels, keeping secrets even from some of those I love, pursuing answers that powerful people want buried?

Will I end up like her—alone in an apartment with walls covered in questions that outlive me?

"Hey," Zara's voice interrupts my thoughts. "You've been in there twenty minutes. Time to move."

She's right. I've pushed my luck far enough. I take one final photograph of Janice's last journal entry, then carefully replace the notebook exactly as I found it. The envelope with the USB drive goes into an inside pocket of my jacket.

I retrace my steps through the condo, careful to avoid the same trip wires and pressure plates. At the front door, I pause, listening for any movement outside before easing it open.

The afternoon sun is blinding after the dimness inside. I squint against it, scanning the parking lot, the neighboring buildings, any place a watcher might hide. Nothing seems out of place.

I lock the door behind me and walk away at a measured pace. Not too fast, nothing that would draw attention. Just another resident returning from an afternoon errand.

Two blocks away, I round a corner and lean against a wall,

suddenly exhausted. The adrenaline that carried me through the break-in ebbs, leaving me hollow.

"I'm clear," I tell Zara. "Meet you at the rendezvous point in thirty."

"Copy that. And Em?"

"Yeah?"

"Good work." Her voice softens. "Janice would be proud."

Would she, though? Or would she be frustrated that I've stepped into the same dangerous investigation that got her killed?

As I navigate back toward the safe house, taking a deliberately circuitous route to shake any potential tail, I can't help but wonder what secrets the USB drive contains. Who was the note referencing? And more importantly—who is A?

For the first time since returning to DC, I feel like we might have something solid, a thread to pull that could unravel whatever conspiracy got Janice killed. And maybe—just maybe—keep me from being the next name on that board with a red X through it.

But as I weave through afternoon crowds, anonymous in a sea of faces, another thought surfaces. What if this is exactly what they want? What if finding the USB drive wasn't luck or timing, but a calculated move in a game I don't yet understand?

I touch the envelope through my jacket, feeling its weight against my ribs. One way or another, I'm about to find out.

Chapter Ten

THE SAFE HOUSE hums with a palpable tension. Zara sits at the kitchen table, hunched over her laptop, fingers dancing across the keyboard in rapid bursts. The USB drive from Janice's second apartment is connected, its tiny light blinking as Zara works to break through its encryption.

I pace the small living room, seven steps across, turn, seven steps back. Waiting has never been my strong suit.

"Anything?" I ask for the third time in an hour.

Zara doesn't look up. "Still working on it. This isn't amateur encryption. Whoever A is, they know what they're doing. Janice probably had a cypher. We aren't so lucky."

I drop onto the couch, springs protesting beneath me. My mind keeps circling back to those photographs on Janice's wall. Nine agents including me. All targeted. Four already dead. The rest scattered to the winds or in hiding.

The heavy clacking of the keys draws my attention. She's practically stabbing each one as she hits it, the frustration on her face unmistakable. Zara is one of the smartest people I know and the fact that this is giving her so much trouble pains me to watch. But it isn't really about the USB or the fact we're stuck in this safe house or even that we're on the run from the FBI.

I can't take it anymore.

"Are we going to talk about it before you break your computer?"

"What?"

"You know what."

Her fingers pause for a fraction of a second, then resume typing. "Nothing to talk about."

"Zara." I move to the table, sitting opposite her. "You haven't mentioned him once since we got back to DC."

"Because we have more urgent things to deal with." Her tone is carefully neutral, eyes still fixed on the screen.

"You have literally saved my life more times than I care to admit," I remind her gently. "That means we talk about the hard stuff."

She finally looks up, her expression guarded. "What do you want me to say, Em? That I'm worried about him? That I'm angry he might be involved in all this? That I don't know if I can trust him anymore? And that all of this is so damn confusing I'd rather not think about it at all?"

"Any of that would be a start."

Zara sighs, pushing away from the laptop. "Fine. You want to know what I'm thinking? I'm thinking I've been played and I may be the reason all of this has happened. I may be the reason Janice is dead."

The bluntness of her statement catches me off guard. "What do you mean?"

She sighs. "I should have done a thorough check on Theo when I first met him after that whole ordeal with Simon. But *nooo*, the prospect of dating someone mysterious was too exciting."

"The FBI vetted him, Z," I say.

"But *I* didn't!" It comes out with such force I lean back. Zara is never this on-edge and she has been ever since New

Mexico. Ever since she admitted she thought something was wrong with all this…with Theo.

"I have run every background check I can think and it always comes up roses and cherries," she says. "It's too clean. Too manufactured. And it's all a lie."

I think back to all the cases we've run with Theo, all the cases he's helped us close. In each one he'd been a dependable partner. An asset— reliable, his intel solid. But there had always been something… elusive about him, something that never quite added up. I didn't want to see it for Zara's sake, because I wanted her to finally find someone who could match wits with her.

"How bad do you think it is?" I ask.

"I don't know." Frustration edges her voice. "That's the problem. I don't know, and I can't move forward until I do."

"So what's the plan?"

"I'm going to find him." Her eyes meet mine, determination replacing guardedness. "He's here in DC. And when I do, I'm going to get answers."

I reach across the table, covering her hand with mine. "Let me help."

She pulls away, not unkindly but firmly. "You have enough on your plate. Four dead agents, four more unaccounted for. Janice's death. This USB drive." She gestures to the laptop. "I need to do this on my own."

"Zara, it's too dangerous. If Theo is involved—"

"Then I need to know the truth. Nothing else can make this right."

I recognize the resolve in her voice, the same tone she uses when she's made up her mind and nothing short of divine intervention will change it. Still, I try one more time. "At least let me back you up. You don't have to—"

Something on her computer sends off an alarm signal. She switches over to the video feeds to see a person walking up to the front of the building. Instinctively I grab my weapon.

But when the person looks up at the camera and waves, I realize it's Nadia.

"How the hell...?" Zara asks.

"Liam," I say. "He must have told her. Even after I made it clear to him not to let anyone else know about this place."

"I tried to tell you," Zara says. "You let one person in, you might as well invite the whole neighborhood."

"Well, don't leave her stranded out there," I say.

Zara opens the front door with a quick buzz, and we watch Nadia make her way up the stairs and down the hall to our door, which Zara unlocks with a click.

Nadia slips inside, securing the three locks behind her before turning to face us. "Hey," she says.

"Hey," both of us say, looking at each other as Zara disables the alarm from her computer.

"Sorry for just showing up out of the blue, but I couldn't sit home by myself for a second longer knowing you two were out here working your asses off to try and get to the bottom of this thing. Plus, it's kind of lonely at my place by myself. Turns out I don't do well just sitting around."

"I know the feeling," I tell her. "Did Liam give you the location?"

She nods. "Well, I kind of had to pull it out of him. But I haven't told Elliott. And I won't if you don't want me to."

"Why not?" Zara says turning back to her work. "It's only our lives we're exposing."

"Ignore her," I say. "She's having a tough day. Thank you for coming." I stand and give Nadia a quick hug.

"I really didn't mean to interrupt anything." She shoots a worried glance from me to Zara. "I would have called, but I didn't want to risk it. And I was very careful getting here."

"It's fine," Zara finally says. "Sorry. Em's right. I don't mean to be a bitch. We're just under a lot of stress."

For the next forty minutes, we wait in relative silence while Zara works. I bring Nadia up to speed on what we found at

Janice's second apartment, showing her the photos I took of the evidence boards. She studies them carefully, taking her time with each one. I've learned Nadia is something of a walking encyclopedia. She can recall things most others can't at a moment's notice. It's probably why she's such a good agent.

"These names," she says, pointing to my phone screen. "I recognize Chen and Williams. They were part of the task force that took down the Brighton syndicate two years ago."

"Financial crimes unit," I recall. "They traced money laundering through offshore accounts."

Nadia nods. "Major case. Several high-profile arrests, including two senators and a defense contractor executive."

I file this information away, another piece to the puzzle. Were these agents targeted because of that case? What did they uncover that made them dangerous?

"Got it!" Zara suddenly exclaims, straightening in her chair. "God. Fucking finally."

We gather around her laptop, peering at the screen as she navigates through the newly accessible files.

"What are we looking at?" I ask, trying to make sense of the folders appearing on screen.

"Surveillance data," Zara says, opening files. "Lots of it. Photos, audio recordings, location tracking…"

She opens an image file. The photograph shows a man in his fifties, silver-haired, sharp-featured, exiting a black town car. Even from the grainy surveillance photo, I recognize him immediately.

"Son of a—" My breath catches. "Fletch."

Joaquin Fletch. Information broker and all-around asshole. I spent a month undercover working to crack his operation before everything at the FBI sidelined that investigation. Part of which required Zara dressing me up in a formal cocktail dress and ended with me dangling from a seventh story-balcony trying to avoid his bodyguards.

"There's more," Zara says, opening additional files. "Locations, meetings, phone records... it looks like he met with each of the agents on that list."

The data unfolds before us, a methodical documentation of Fletcher's movements over the past several months. And there—timestamps showing Fletcher meeting with each of the agents from Janice's board, one by one.

"That can't be a coincidence," Nadia says quietly.

I study the timeline, connecting dots. "Fletch meets with these agents. Weeks or days later, they're reassigned, they disappear, or they turn up dead."

"Correlation doesn't equal causation," Zara cautions. "This shows they met, but not why or what was discussed."

"Who compiled all this?" I ask, scanning the meticulously organized data. "This isn't Bureau work. The methodologies are different."

"Private intelligence maybe," Nadia suggests. "Or a foreign agency feeding information to Janice."

"The question is whether we can trust it," Zara says. "For all we know, this could be carefully constructed misinformation designed to point us in the wrong direction."

She's right. In our world, evidence can be manufactured, breadcrumbs laid to lead investigators astray. And someone good enough to crack Bureau security would be good enough to create convincing false trails.

"Even if it's legitimate," I say, "it doesn't give us much to go on. Fletch is in the wind. And I can't get close to him again —he knows my face and that I'm *not* Emily Agostini."

The weight of this realization settles over us. Our best lead might be a dead end before we've even started.

"Hey... uh, guys," Nadia says suddenly, attention shifting to the surveillance monitors set up in the corner of the room. "Isn't that the condo you're monitoring?"

We move to the screens, watching as a figure in dark clothing approaches the building I was in only hours ago. The camera angle isn't ideal—we can see the person's back but not their face. Average height, slim build, moving with the confident stride of someone who belongs there.

"Another drop?" Zara suggests.

We watch as the figure enters the building—using an access code, not forcing entry—and disappears from our exterior camera view.

"I've got them on the hallway cam," Nadia says, taking point on the monitor and switching feeds.

The interior camera shows the same figure moving purposefully down the hall toward Janice's door. They pause and knock, but when there is no response they leave again, still keeping their face angled away from the door. We follow them back outside as they walk past the outdoor windows of Janice's condo and pause at the window that's part of her war room. The figure slips something through the window before heading back off again.

"It's her contact. We need to follow them," I say, already reaching for my jacket.

"Oh no, you're not leaving me behind again," Zara says, right on my heels.

"I'll stay here," Nadia says. "Guide you."

Zara grabs her keys. We realized after about three days here that taking ride shares everywhere or waiting on public transportation wasn't ideal. Zara managed to have a rental vehicle delivered to an address down the street under an assumed name which we've been using on and off since. "We can intercept them before they're too far."

We move quickly, slipping out the back exit of our building and into Zara's nondescript rental sedan parked in the alley. By the time we pull onto the main street, Nadia's voice comes through our earpieces.

"Target exiting the building now. Heading east on Wilson."

"You should have let me drive," I mutter as Zara navigates

the streets with practiced precision, cutting through side roads to position us ahead of our target's likely path. I'd have had us there in half the time.

"And kill us both? No thank you," she shoots back.

"Got 'em," I report as we spot the figure walking briskly along the sidewalk, head down, hands in pockets. "Still can't see their face."

"Don't get too close," Nadia warns. "If this is who we think it is, they're clearly experienced. They'll spot a tail."

We hang back, maintaining visual contact without drawing attention. The figure leads us through residential streets, eventually turning into a coffee shop on a busy corner.

"What now?" Zara asks, parking across the street.

"We wait," I decide. "See if they come out, where they go next."

Ten minutes pass. The figure emerges, coffee cup in hand, and continues walking, now heading toward a more commercial district.

"They're approaching the Metro station," Nadia says, tracking their movement on a map. "If they go underground, we might lose them."

"I'm going on foot," I say, opening my door. "Circle around, be ready to pick me up if they emerge from another exit."

"Be careful, and keep your head down," Zara says, eyes meeting mine. She's right—in the tension I'm likely to get spotted on a traffic cam. I can't let the lead go, but at the same time I don't need to announce my presence.

I follow our target at a safe distance, weaving through evening commuters. They don't head down into the Metro station as expected, instead turning right and entering a nondescript apartment building half a block away.

"Change of plans," I murmur. "They've entered a residential building on M Street. Gray brick, six stories."

"I see it," Zara responds. "What's the play?"

I scan the building, noting the security camera above the entrance, the keypad access system. "We can't follow them in without risking detection. But we need to know which unit they're in."

"There's a bagel shop with outdoor seating across the street," Nadia suggests through the earpiece. "And it's a beautiful day."

"I could go for a bagel," I say, crossing the street and claiming a table with a clear view of the building entrance. Zara joins me minutes later, setting two bagels and a couple cups of tea on the table to complete our cover as casual patrons.

"What do we think?" she asks quietly, eyes on the building. "Is this our mysterious *A*?"

"Maybe," I say. "The timing fits. Delivering information to Janice's apartment even after her death suggests someone who doesn't know she's gone. Or someone maintaining cover. *Or someone looking to bait us.*"

"We need to identify them," Zara says. "Find out what they know, who they're working for."

Nadia's voice comes through our earpieces again. "While you sit back and relax, I'll be running facial recognition on building residents and cross-referencing with Bureau databases and public records."

"Let us know what you find."

"Will do," she replies. "I've got eyes on all exits through traffic cams. If they leave, we'll know."

"Guess we're here for the long haul," I say. "Still happy you came along?"

Zara gives me *the eye*. "I would have preferred cupcakes."

∾

THE EVENING DRAGS ON AND MY ADRENALINE PLUMMETS ALONG with the sun. I hate stakeouts. We switch tables twice to avoid looking suspicious and Zara has continued ordering. We pretend to be deep in conversation while in reality we're just watching the building's exits. By the time we're on our third tea and bagel of the evening I decide to venture back into the deep end. Maybe it's just the boredom of a stakeout. Or maybe it's because I feel responsible and can't help it.

"About Theo," I say quietly, having muted my earpiece. "I understand why you need to find him yourself. Just... keep me in the loop? Please? No solo heroics."

She's silent for a moment, then nods once. "No solo heroics," she agrees. "But I need to face him alone when the time comes."

"Deal." I give her a playful shove and she sort of chuckles. It's not much, but I'll take it.

"Hey guys," Nadia says over the comms. "I think I might have something."

"We're here," I confirm. Nadia probably saw that we muted for a second. I don't like keeping her out of the loop, but that's not my call. Zara will bring her in if she wants.

"So I've gone through all the rental records I could find. Unit 4B is rented to a James Merritt. No criminal record, no Bureau file, seemingly unremarkable background. Unlike everyone else in the building. Not even a parking ticket."

"Seems hard to believe," I say, catching Zara's eye.

"That's just it," Nadia continues. "The background is perfect. Too perfect. Like it was carefully constructed to withstand casual scrutiny but not deep investigation."

"A cover identity," Zara says, giving me a wiggle of her eyebrows.

"I'll keep digging," Nadia promises. "But for now, he's looking like our best option. That's more than we had this morning."

"No, you know what? That's good enough for me." With a name I'm not as keen to sit here all night and wait for our Mr.

Merritt to show himself. I promised myself we wouldn't stay on the defensive any longer. "We're going in."

"We are?" Zara asks.

"Odds are he's not coming back out anyway and I don't feel like camping out in the car, do you? He's our best lead. Let's get in there before he figures out he's being watched and disappears. If he hasn't already."

"Guess we're going in," she says, depositing our cups in the nearby trash. "At least I'll be able to show you how to properly pick a lock."

Chapter Eleven

"REMEMBER," I say as we approach the service entrance at the rear of the building, "we don't know what his connection to Janice was. He could be an ally or—"

"Or he could be the one who killed her," Zara finishes. The edge in her voice betrays the guilt she's been carrying. If Theo is somehow connected to all this, she blames herself for not seeing it sooner.

"Let's not jump to conclusions." I test the service door. Locked, as expected. "Third time's a charm?"

Zara pulls out a device similar to the one Liam used and attaches it to the keypad, though hers looks newer. "Third time for you. Now you get to see how a pro takes care of this."

I sigh. "I miss knocking on doors and getting straight answers." All this cloak and dagger crap is beginning to weigh on me. I'm not used to needing to cover every action we take or double and triple back every route. Life used to be so much simpler.

"The good ol' days?" Zara whispers.

"Yeah, just being… sentimental, I guess."

The door clicks open. "See, *that's* how you do it." Zara pockets the small device.

"Yeah, yeah." We move through the service corridors, taking the stairs instead of the elevator. Fourth floor, Unit 4B. The hallway is empty, quiet except for the distant sound of a television from another apartment.

Zara kneels before the door, examining the lock. "Standard deadbolt. No electronic security that I can see."

"Want me to do it?"

She gives me a look that would wither plants. "You wish."

As Zara works the lock, I keep watch on the hallway. Nadia's voice comes through the earpiece again: "Still clear outside. Just be on guard. There's no telling what's in there."

"We noticed," I mutter.

The lock returns with a hard click. It sounds like a spring broke inside, but the lock yields. Zara stands, one hand moving to her own concealed weapon. We exchange a nod—ready for anything. Our mysterious man might have already absconded out a nearby window.

I push the door open slowly, scanning the darkened apartment beyond. No movement, no sound. I step inside, Zara close behind me.

The attack comes without warning.

A shadow detaches from the wall to my right, moving with shocking speed. I barely have time to raise my arm to block the strike aimed at my throat. The impact sends pain shooting up to my shoulder.

"Contact!" I shout, more for Nadia's benefit than Zara's, who's already engaged with our attacker.

The apartment erupts into chaos. Furniture topples as we grapple in the darkness. My training kicks in—muscle memory taking over where conscious thought is too slow. Block, strike, evade. My opponent is skilled; his movements precise and economical. No wasted energy.

"Em!" Zara's voice, tight with urgency.

I catch a glimpse of her struggling with the attacker, just

before he sends her crashing into a side table. The lamp topples, shattering on the floor.

I launch myself forward, driving my shoulder into his midsection. He grunts but doesn't go down, instead grabbing my arm and using my momentum to throw me. I roll with the impact, coming back to my feet in time to see him advancing on Zara.

"Hey!" I grab the first thing within reach—a heavy book—and hurl it at his head.

He turns, ducking the projectile, giving Zara time to recover. In the dim light filtering through the windows, I finally get a clear look at our attacker. Tall, athletic build, close-cropped hair. James Merritt, I presume.

"Emily, status?" Nadia's voice in my ear, tense with concern.

No time to respond. Merritt closes the distance between us with two quick strides. I block his first strike, countering with one of my own that he deflects easily. We trade blows, testing each other's defenses.

He's good. Professional. The kind of fighter who's spent years honing his skills.

But so have I.

I feint to the left, then drop low, sweeping his legs. He jumps over the sweep, but Zara is there, driving the base of her palm up toward his chin. He twists away from the worst of it, but the blow still connects.

For a moment, the three of us separate, circling warily in the confined space of the living room.

"You're better than I expected," Merritt says, his voice calm despite the exertion. The first words he's spoken, carrying the faintest trace of an accent I can't quite place.

"Likewise," I respond, keeping my guard up.

He shifts his weight, preparing for another attack. I tense, ready to meet it. But instead of charging, he feints, then throws a decorative paperweight from the nearby shelf directly at my face.

I duck, the projectile missing me by inches. When I look up, Zara's vaulted over the couch and has him in a hold, arm around his throat. She has him pinned in a way that she could choke him out in less than five seconds.

"Enough," he says. "Finish this."

I hesitate, confused by his words. "What?"

"Do what you came to do," he insists, not struggling against Zara's grip. "At least give me that dignity. I expected this might happen eventually."

"*What* might happen?"

"The kill," he says simply. "That's why you're here, isn't it? To tie up loose ends?"

Understanding dawns. "We're not here to kill you."

He studies my face, searching for deception. Finding none, his expression shifts to confusion. "Then why the break-in?"

"We need information about Janice Simmons." I keep my distance, hands visible but ready to move if needed. "About the work you were doing for her."

Zara holds tight, her gaze shooting between us. "The drop you just made," she says.

"Ah, I see. J, correct?" He goes limp, no longer tight in Zara's grip. My weapon is at my side but I motion for Zara to release him. She hesitates a moment then steps completely away from him in one move, giving me a clean shot if necessary. Merritt stays where he is. "You must work with her. Either that or you're planning on killing her."

"She was our boss," I say. "And she's already dead."

The change in his demeanor is subtle but immediate. The tension in his shoulders eases, though he remains alert. He reaches slowly for a light switch, illuminating the room.

In the light, I can see him more clearly. Mid-forties, as his file suggested, with the weathered look of someone who's spent time in harsh environments. Sharp eyes that miss nothing. Despite the fight, his expression is composed, almost businesslike.

"Jimmy?" an elderly voice calls from the hallway. I note the door is still open from where Zara broke the lock. A woman pushing a walker with tennis balls on the feet slowly appears in the frame as I hide my weapon behind my back. "Is everything okay?"

Merritt grimaces then holds up a finger at us as he addresses the woman. "I'm fine, Mrs. Kominsky."

"I heard a crash," the woman says, trying to look over his shoulder as he blocks us from view. "Sounded big."

"Just an accident," he replies. "My *friends* and I were moving some of my furniture around and didn't look where we were going. I'll need a new lamp, I'm afraid."

She tries to peer over him again. "Are you sure? I can call the super."

"That won't be necessary Mrs. Kominsky," he says with a soothing voice. "Everything is fine, I promise."

She hesitates. "If you're sure. But you let me know if you need some help, okay?"

"I absolutely will," he says, assisting her to turn her walker and head back to her apartment. After saying his goodbyes he quietly closes the door, noting it won't latch properly now. "Guess I'll be paying for that."

"Sorry," Zara says. "I didn't realize—"

"It's fine," he says, waving her off. "I'm sorry to hear about your boss. I had hoped when I saw the announcement on the news it wasn't her, but I'm not surprised. I knew she worked with the US Government, just wasn't sure which branch. She was investigating her own department, then?" He rights an overturned chair and gestures for us to sit.

"What line of work are you in, Mr. *Merritt?*" Zara prompts.

"Information acquisition. Sometimes security. And..." he pauses, choosing his words, "...problem solving."

"You're a mercenary," I translate.

He inclines his head slightly, neither confirming nor denying. "J hired me a month and a half ago. Said she needed information on a man named Fletch. Specifically, his movements, contacts, communications."

"Joaquin Fletch," I clarify.

"The same." His eyes narrow slightly as he examines me more closely. "Oh. Yes. You're the one in the cocktail dress. The Constitution Hotel. I didn't recognize you out of context."

"What did Janice want you to find?" Zara asks, still on edge but following my lead in engaging with him.

"Patterns," Merritt answers. "Mr. Fletch met with each of the agents J identified. Always briefly, always in public locations, but with care taken to avoid surveillance. It took a lot of work to even find evidence of the meetings ever happening."

"My meeting with Fletch was a carefully orchestrated operation," I say. "Part of a bigger case to determine what kind of threat he posed to the FBI."

"From what I can tell, Mr. Fletch isn't the kind of person who is reckless. He's exceedingly careful with who he associates with and where he's seen. How did he pop up on your radar?"

I exchange a glance with Zara. "A contact brought the case to us."

"And this contact… he's reliable?"

"That's to be determined," I say. "What else did you find? After the agents met with him?"

"The agents would be reassigned, disappear, or die under circumstances that, while seemingly accidental, struck me as… convenient."

The room feels suddenly colder. "That information was on the USB drive you left for Janice."

He nods. "My final delivery. I always complete a contract."

"Was there anything else?" Zara asks. "Anything you didn't include in your report?"

Merritt hesitates, considering. "There was one final thing. The name *Solitaire*. Mr. Fletch referenced it occasionally, but never in the same context twice. I didn't include it in the original report because I couldn't determine if it was a person, an operation or something else entirely. But the more I thought about it, the more I decided she should know. She paid for it, after all. Hence the most recent drop earlier today. But again, for all I know, it could be nothing."

"What about something called the Underground?" I ask, recalling Liam telling me about the conversation he overhead between Janice and Caruthers while we were still in New Mexico.

His brow furrows. "I'm not familiar with that term in this context."

Now it's my turn to study his face. Either he's telling the truth or he's an exceptional liar. Given his profession, either is possible.

"When was the last time you met with Janice personally?" I ask.

"Never did," he replies. "All communication was through secure channels, dead drops. Standard procedure for this type of work."

"But someone like you must have done your homework before taking the job," Zara says. "Did she seem ill? Under stress?"

"She seemed… cautious," he answers after a moment. "Hypervigilant. But otherwise… physically healthy."

I exchange a glance with Zara. Another piece suggesting Janice's death wasn't natural. Not that we needed more convincing.

Merritt watches our silent communication, then rises from his chair. "I suppose if you're not here to kill me, I should probably leave town for awhile. Her unexpected death and your visit suggest things are accelerating."

"Wait." Zara steps forward. "You're familiar with the players in this game. Do you know Theo Arquenest?"

I glare at her, my expression screaming *What are you doing?* But she ignores me.

Merritt pauses, his expression carefully neutral. "I know of him. Not personally. His reputation is... complicated."

"What does that mean?" The tension in her voice is palpable.

"It means his allegiances shift with the wind," Merritt says. "If you're working with him, I'd advise caution."

"He was the contact who brought Fletch to us."

"In that case, I would be *extremely* cautious," he replies. "Now, I'm going to pack. Mrs. Kominsky may be old, but she's not stupid. She'll start the rumor mill about two women who showed up at my apartment unannounced. There will be questions. More than that, I suggest you don't remain in DC much longer either. Whoever eliminated your friend isn't likely to stop there."

As he disappears into the bedroom, I lower my voice. "Nadia, did any of that come through?"

"I got about half of it," she replies. "Are you two okay?"

"We're fine," I confirm quietly. "Run the name *Solitaire* through every database you can access."

"Right," she responds.

Zara moves closer to me, her voice low. "Do you trust him?"

"About as far as I can throw him," I reply. "But his information matches what we've pieced together so far."

"If what he said about Theo is true—"

I place a hand on her shoulder. "One step at a time. We follow the evidence, not assumptions."

She nods, but the doubt lingers in her eyes. Theo's specter

stands between us, a question neither of us has the answer to yet.

Merritt emerges from the bedroom with a single duffle bag. "I'd appreciate a five-minute head start before you leave. Professional courtesy."

"Where will you go?" I ask, not expecting a real answer.

He offers a thin smile. "Best you don't know. Best I don't know what you plan next either. I sincerely hope I never see either of you again. But, that being said, best of luck."

"You too," we both say in unison.

He pauses at the door. "J was good people. For someone in her position, anyway. Whatever got her killed—it's bigger than you think. Watch yourselves."

Then he's gone, the door closing softly behind him.

Zara and I stand in the aftermath of the encounter, surrounded by the scattered evidence of our brief, violent meeting. Another thread pulled, another layer revealed.

"Our fingerprints are literally everywhere," Zara says.

"Yep."

"No way we can wipe the whole apartment."

"Nope." I take a deep breath as our gazes meet. "Fuck it?"

She nods. "Fuck it."

As we leave through the service exit, the night air cool against my skin, I can't shake the feeling that we're being watched. Maybe that's just my paranoia, which has been ratcheted up to twelve ever since returning. But with each step deeper into this investigation, the shadows around us seem to grow larger and more dangerous.

Solitaire. The Underground. Fletch. Theo. Janice's death.

And nine agents in the middle of it all, being taken out one by one.

Maybe we should have stayed in New Mexico after all.

Chapter Twelve

BY THE TIME we arrive back at the safehouse, it's after midnight and I'm wiped. My sides hurt from Merritt's attacks, and I'm completely dehydrated, despite having a week's worth of coffee in me. And since we only have two beds, Nadia volunteers to head back to her place until tomorrow.

Zara and I move wordlessly through the apartment, making cups of warm tea before heading off to our respective bedrooms. Our havens from the outside world. I can't stop going over what we've uncovered. The fact that Fletch could be connected to all this is maddening. But at the same time, the fact that he could be behind all of this and at the same time be the solution to our exile is intoxicating. If we can just find some evidence that connects him to these deaths… then it won't matter if he was dealing in classified FBI documents or not. We'll be able to find everything we need to shut him down, and get our lives back to normal.

My eyes snap open as the morning sun filters through my window. My mug of mostly untouched tea sits on the nightstand beside me and I realize I'm still in my clothes. I must have fallen asleep before I could even get undressed. I peel the clothes off, feeling the dirt and grime of yesterday, and hop into a quick shower. Fifteen minutes later I've towel-dried my hair and head back to the apartment's kitchen only to find Liam already there, in the middle of cooking breakfast.

"Hey," I say, furrowing my brow. "Where did you come from?"

"Day off," he says. "I got up early and fed and walked the dogs, ran some errands, then made my way over here. I'm getting better at it—it only took me forty-five minutes this time."

I take a seat at the dining room table where Zara's equipment still sits, taking over most of the surface. Liam sets a cup of hot coffee in front of me and goes back to his prep work. "This kind of reminds me of when we first started dating," I say, grinning. "Though I would have preferred if you'd stayed the night."

"So do I," he says, shooting me a grin. "How did it go at the other apartment? Any leads?"

I lift the edge of my oversized shirt to show him the bruises on my ribs. "You could say that."

"Em," he says, dropping the knife and coming over to inspect the injuries. "What happened?"

"Nothing I couldn't handle," I say, pulling the shirt back down over the bruises. "Just an interrogation."

"Please tell me you had backup," he replies.

"She did."

We both turn to see Zara making her way down the hallway. Her hair sticks in five different directions as she yawns. "But she kicked his ass in the end."

"I wouldn't take it that far," I say as I give Liam the lowdown of everything that happened yesterday. With some prodding, he eventually goes back to his work in the kitchen as he listens to our discovery of the USB drive at Janice's place, and how we eventually tracked down Merritt.

"So he believes Fletch is involved in the deaths of these agents?" Liam asks.

"As far as we can tell—and that may be what Janice was working on as well before she died," I say. "But it makes sense, doesn't it? This all started with our investigation into Fletch. It logically follows that he's elbow-deep into it."

"Technically it started when *someone* gave us the Fletch contact," Zara murmurs as she takes a sip of her coffee. She's standing off to the side, occasionally glancing at the screen of her laptop.

"You think Theo is connected to all this?" Liam asks.

"I don't see how he can't be," she replies.

"The point is, we need more information. We need something concrete on Fletch. The FBI still has the data Zara downloaded from his computer—"

"—which is encrypted," she reminds me.

"Right, but I was thinking maybe you or Elliott could get us access, if we had that drive we might be able to—"

Liam shakes his head before I even finish. "I've already tried. Caruthers has told me it's off-limits, because it involves you. I imagine Elliott will get a similar answer, considering we all work, or *worked* together."

"What does that mean? Is another team working on it?" Zara asks.

"No idea," Liam says as he spoons a couple of over-easy eggs onto two plates. He places some sizzling bacon right beside them before adding a scoop of hash browns from a small pan he pulled from the oven. The man is a certified wizard. He sets one plate in front of me and another at the only other empty seat, indicating it's for Zara.

"Oh," she says, realizing the food is for her. "I get to try the famous *Coll cuisine*." Her eyes are wide with anticipation.

"Don't call it that," I say, my mouth already full of eggs. *God*, I have missed this. Liam's cooking is second to none. I swear he uses some kind of crack cocaine in this food because it is *that* damn good.

"Oh, I'm *not* calling it that from here on out," she says

after she's taken a few bites. I can tell the food is having the same effect on her as it is on me. After a solid month of eating nothing but takeout or canned whatever, having a home-cooked breakfast is literally manna from heaven.

"Em, I have some bad news for you," Zara says working on a piece of bacon. "He's my boyfriend now."

I chuckle as I clean the rest of my plate. I can't help but notice the grin on Liam's face as he watches me inhale it. But I don't care. I don't think I realized how badly I needed this.

He takes one of the other chairs near the laptop and takes a seat. "It's good to see you happy."

"How could I not be?" I ask, pushing the plate away. "Thank you. That was amazing."

"He does this for every meal?" Zara asks.

"More or less," I say.

"I'm gonna need you to split yourself in two," she says, pointing her fork at Liam. "Cause this is ridiculous."

"Thank you?" he says.

"I mean my God, I almost had an orgasm over here," she says, finishing her plate.

"O-*kay*," I say, "Enough from the peanut gallery." I turn back to Liam. "We need to find some way to connect Fletch to these other agents. He's met with all of us in various capacities. What we don't know is if those meetings were officially sanctioned or not. Obviously ours was—it was part of the larger operation. What I'm wondering is if these other meetings were something similar, or off-book."

"Without access to our regular resources, that's going to be hard to uncover," he says. "We can only ask so many questions before people get suspicious and you saw what happened to Nadia. I can pretty much guarantee if we ask the answer will be no."

I return my attention to Zara. "Is there any way to get into the FBI database from outside? Anything you can do?"

She shakes her head. "I wish there was. But breaking into

one of the most secure servers on the planet? Even with the right equipment—which would cost as much as a new Lamborghini—it's unlikely to happen. And even if it does, getting away clean is even more unlikely."

"In other words, impossible."

"For just you and me, yes."

"So that leaves Fletch."

Liam's brow forms a *V*. "What about him?"

"Since we have no way to track down the other agents and have no other leads, we're going to have to infiltrate his operation. Find what we need from his side."

"But… your cover…" Zara says.

She's right. My cover with Fletch isn't ironclad. Not since my true identity was leaked to Detective Peregrine. Still, we don't know *who* leaked it or who even knew. It's possible they leaked it to Fletch as well, but just as likely he's in the dark.

"I agree with Zara," Liam says. "Going after Fletch directly is too much of a risk. If he knows who you really are he'll kill you on sight."

Great, two against one. I seem to keep running into the same problem— wanting to go do something, and everyone around me telling me it's too dangerous. It doesn't matter that they're right. We never would have gotten anything from Merritt if we'd just waited around. In fact, he probably would have disappeared on us. The fact remains that we can't just sit back and hope things will go our way.

"There might be another way," Zara offers. "According to Merritt's data, Fletch uses the same security company for most of his meetings. Apex Protection Services." She grabs the laptop and pulls up information. "Much smaller operation, less sophisticated security, but still connected to Fletch's activities."

"You think we can get information from them?" I ask.

"Worth a shot," she replies. "Their digital security is decent but not impenetrable. I could find a way in, see what they have on Fletch's movements, maybe communications records."

"It's still risky," Liam cautions, "but less insane than walking straight into Fletch's operation again."

"Okay," Zara says. "Lemme start working on a way into this place."

"At least take a shower first," I tell her. "You don't need to do this *right now*."

She considers it for a moment, then nods and heads back down the hallway. "I'll be thinking of nothing but your food the whole time, *chef*," she calls, following it with an evil laugh.

Liam goes beet red and I can't help but chuckle. "If it's not you, it's her," he says.

"She just likes making people squirm," I say, helping him clean up the plates. "She kept me grounded out there. I was this close to losing it." I hold my thumb and forefinger half an inch apart. I lower my voice. "She was selling feet pictures online to make us some extra income."

He stops dead in his tracks. "That's a lie."

"Nope. And she was making good money at it too."

His eyes go wide. "Did she… I mean, did you ever—"

"Yes?" I ask. "Care to finish that sentence?"

"You know what? None of my business," he says and goes back to scrubbing the plates in the sink. I wait half a beat, then hug his waist.

"You're adorable, you know that? No, I never did it, but it wasn't for lack of trying on her part. Would you be upset if I did?"

"Nope," he says matter-of-factly. "You can do whatever you want."

A perfect answer. But I know deep down it probably would have bothered him. "It's okay, you know. I wouldn't be upset if you say it did."

He turns to me. "I don't ever want to tell you the choices

you make upset me," he says. "If that's what you genuinely wanted to do, I would have supported you."

I hug him harder, not wanting to let go. I wish we could stay like this forever.

"I'm worried about her," I confess. "All this business with Theo... it's like she's going to explode and I don't know what I can do to help."

"Just be there for her," he says. "The way you are for me."

I pull back. "I don't know. It's hitting her hard. She blames herself for bringing him into the fold—especially if he's involved with this Fletch business. She'll want to take responsibility for Janice's death, as well as the other agents. I'm afraid she's going to do something rash."

"How can I help?" he asks.

I'm afraid to admit I don't know. I don't want to start spying on her—she promised she wouldn't take action without letting me know. Still... I have a bad feeling deep in my gut about all this. I don't know how it's all going to play out. "If I knew, I'd tell you."

We hear the shower crank and while Zara starts belting out some '90s tune from down the hall, I worry about where all this is heading.

None of us are in a safe place and I'm not sure if we ever will be again.

Chapter Thirteen

I ADJUST my designer sunglasses as I step out of the cab in front of Apex Protection Services' glass-fronted headquarters. The March sun hits me square in the face, and even with the tinted lenses I have to squint. My stomach churns with that familiar mix of adrenaline and dread I always get before going undercover.

"You've got this," Zara's voice comes through the nearly invisible earpiece. She's parked in the car three blocks away, monitoring everything. "Just remember, confidence. No one is gonna stop someone looking like you do if you're dripping confidence."

"Easy for you to say. You're not the one doing it." The weight of the charcoal pantsuit feels strange after weeks in jeans and T-shirts. Emily Slate would not be caught dead wearing something this expensive, but Emily Agostini, executive with Thompson Intermodal with flexible ethics, owns ten just like it.

"Remember," Zara continues, because of course she can't help herself, "if anyone mentions St. Solomon, that's our abort signal. It means they know who you really are."

Jesus, we've gone over all the contingencies about fifty

times already, but Zara's anxiety is bleeding through. I can't really blame her. This is risky as hell, and we both know it. My cover as Emily Agostini might be compromised, but I'm hoping I'm not important enough in Fletch's world that he would have notified anyone about me.

The lobby is all polished marble and brushed steel, with a security desk that looks more appropriate for a high-end financial firm than a private protection company. I approach with the confident stride of someone who belongs here, someone who doesn't ask permission.

"Emily Agostini for Marcos Delgado," I tell the receptionist, sliding a business card across the counter. My fingers leave the tiniest smudge on the polished surface. "He's expecting me."

I've never met Delgado, but Merritt's information showed he's the Operations Director at Apex, the man who coordinates security for Fletch's most sensitive meetings.

"One moment, Ms. Agostini." The receptionist's fingers fly over her keyboard. She's wearing a ring that probably cost more than I make in a month. "Mr. Delgado isn't showing any appointments this morning."

I allow a flicker of annoyance to cross my face. "Joaquin assured me this wouldn't be a problem." I emphasize his first name, establishing familiarity. "I'm in town briefly and have critical information regarding his Milan acquisition." I glance at my watch. "I can wait five minutes."

The name-drop works like a charm. The receptionist makes a quick call, speaks in hushed tones, then hangs up with a practiced smile. "Mr. Delgado will see you now. Please take the elevator to the fourth floor."

As I cross the lobby, I scan for security cameras, noting their positions. Standard setup, nothing excessive. The marble floor clicks under my heels, and I feel sweat forming at the small of my back.

"I'm in the elevator," I murmur, pretending to check my phone. "Headed to the fourth floor."

"Nicely done back there. Just like that. All the way through."

The doors open into a reception area that's a more subdued version of the lobby. A tall man with salt-and-pepper hair and a tailored suit steps forward to greet me. His cologne hits me before he does—something expensive and woodsy that makes my nose itch.

"Ms. Agostini, Marcos Delgado." His handshake is firm, his smile doesn't reach his eyes. "This is unexpected. Joaquin didn't mention you'd be reaching out to us directly."

I mirror his smile—professional, cool. "Joaquin prefers compartmentalization, as I'm sure you know. The fewer people who understand the whole picture, the better." I glance around. "Is there somewhere we can speak privately?"

He studies me for a moment, then gestures toward a hallway. "Please. My office."

Delgado's office is spacious but practical. Floor-to-ceiling windows offer a view of the city, while framed military commendations line one wall. He motions me to a chair facing his desk. The leather is soft, probably real, not that cheap pleather crap you find in government offices.

"So," he begins, "Milan."

"The security arrangements were inadequate," I state flatly. "Joaquin was displeased."

"Our team followed his exact specifications." A hint of defensiveness colors his tone. Men like Delgado hate being called out on their failures.

I wave a dismissive hand. "I'm not here to assign blame. I'm here because Joaquin values your services and wants to ensure future operations run more smoothly."

"What exactly does he have in mind?"

"First, I need to understand the protocols you currently have in place." I cross my legs, settling in. My calf muscle twitches from tension—I've been on high alert for too long. "Walk me through how you typically handle his high-value transactions."

As Delgado begins explaining their security procedures, my mind catalogs every detail while simultaneously assessing the room. That's when I notice it—the almost imperceptible bulge in the smoke detector above his desk. I do a double-take. Is that…?

My pulse quickens, but I maintain my composed exterior. Shit. Shit. *Shit.* Years of training have taught me how to recognize FBI surveillance equipment, and that's exactly what I'm looking at. This office is under active investigation.

"Everything okay over there?" Zara whispers in my ear. "Your heart rate just spiked. I can practically hear it through the mic."

I adjust my bracelet, and continue my conversation with Delgado, asking follow-up questions about their security protocols while my mind races. Who's monitoring this office? Is it standard Bureau surveillance, or something connected to the agents' disappearances? Do they already suspect Fletch? And have I just walked into a hornet's nest here?

More importantly, have I just been caught on camera, exposing myself as an agent who's supposed to be out of DC? God, if I make it out of here alive, Liam is going to kill me.

"—and that's typically how we handle the rotation," Delgado is saying. I've missed half his explanation.

"Fascinating," I reply, buying time. "But tell me, how do you handle counter-surveillance? Surely someone in Joaquin's position attracts unwanted attention."

Delgado's expression shifts subtly. "We have comprehensive measures in place."

"Really?" I lean forward, lowering my voice. "Because your office is currently under surveillance."

His posture stiffens. "Excuse me?"

"The smoke detector above your desk," I indicate with a

slight nod. "Standard FBI surveillance package. Remote audio and video feed." I allow a small, knowing smile to form. "Joaquin would be very interested to learn you're being monitored."

Shock flickers across his face before he can mask it. "That's a serious allegation."

"It's not an allegation; it's a fact." I maintain steady eye contact. "The question is, what are you going to do about it?"

"Em," Zara says in my ear with more than a hint of concern. "What are you doing?"

I ignore her, focused entirely on Delgado, who's now staring at the smoke detector with barely concealed alarm. His left eye twitches slightly—a tell I've noticed in people when they realize they're caught in something bigger than they expected.

I have an opportunity here, however brief, to get everything I need in one fell swoop. But it's a risk.

"I could help you with this problem," I offer. "For a price, of course."

"What kind of price?" His voice has dropped to a near whisper.

"Information. About Joaquin's recent meetings with FBI agents."

His eyes snap back to mine, suddenly cold. "I don't know what you're talking about."

"Don't insult my intelligence, Mr. Delgado." I maintain my composure, though adrenaline is coursing through my veins so fast I can practically taste it—metallic and sharp at the back of my throat. "We both know Joaquin has been meeting with several agents over the past month. I need the details of those meetings."

"*Emily.*" Zara's voice is urgent in my ear. "If this really is Bureau surveillance, you need to get out of there, right now."

Delgado stands, moving to the window. "These are dangerous waters, Ms. Agostini."

"Then it's a good thing I know how to swim." I remain seated, projecting calm authority while my insides are doing somersaults. *This* is exactly why I hate undercover work. Nothing is straightforward, it's all a game and one wrong move can put you out of play permanently. "But we're both already in danger. That camera didn't install itself. Someone suspects you, which means they likely suspect Joaquin as well."

He turns back to face me. "And you're offering what, exactly?"

"I can tell you exactly who's monitoring you and why. I can help you disappear that equipment without raising alarms." I gesture around the room. "Or you can wait until they have enough evidence to move against you. Your choice."

I'm gambling everything on this bluff. If I'm right about the surveillance, Delgado's desperation might override his caution. If I'm wrong, I've just exposed myself as someone with knowledge of FBI operations. Either way, I'm playing with fire.

"Emily." Zara's voice cuts in again, higher-pitched than normal. "I'm getting some movement out here. I don't know what's going on. I say abort. Now."

My heart slams against my ribs so hard I'm surprised Delgado can't see it through my blouse, but I keep my expression neutral as he considers my offer. I've always been good at poker.

"I'll need to make a call," he says finally.

"Make it quick," I advise.

As he steps behind his desk to reach for his phone, I catch movement in the hallway outside his office—a flash of dark jacket, the purposeful stride of someone in a hurry. My stomach drops to somewhere around my ankles.

"They're coming inside," Zara confirms, voice tight with urgency. "This was a setup, Em. I think—I think your presence may have activated something."

I rise smoothly from my chair, ignoring the slight trembling in my legs. "Mr. Delgado, I've just realized I have another appointment. We'll have to continue this conversation later."

Confusion crosses his face. "But we haven't—"

"Check your email later today," I interrupt, already moving toward the door. "My contact information will be there."

Before he can respond, I'm out the door, walking briskly down the hallway toward the emergency stairwell I noted on the way in. Not running—running attracts attention—but moving with intention. My heart is pounding so hard I'm surprised it's not setting off seismic sensors.

"There's a team entering the building," Zara reports. "Four agents in the lobby, two more covering the parking garage. They're coordinating a sweep."

I push through the stairwell door, letting it close silently behind me. "Route?"

"Service exit on the ground floor. East side of the building. I'll meet you three blocks north. And if you get caught, I'm going to kill you before they even have a chance."

I descend the stairs quickly but quietly, listening for footsteps above or below. My mind churns through the implications. If this was a Bureau operation, if they spotted me on the surveillance feed, then I'm now officially compromised. No longer just AWOL but actively working against Bureau interests in their eyes. *Fantastic job, Slate. Really, top-notch work.*

Reaching the ground floor, I pause, listening. Nothing. I ease the door open a crack, peering into the corridor beyond. The service area is empty, but I can hear voices from the direction of the lobby. The sweep is underway.

I slip through the door, staying close to the wall as I make my way toward the service exit. My sweaty palms make it hard to grip the door handle. The voices grow louder—they're methodically checking each room, working their way toward me.

The service exit is just ahead, a plain metal door with a push bar. As I reach for it, I hear a shout from behind me.

"FBI! Stop right there!"

I don't look back, just slam into the push bar, bursting through the door into the alley beyond. Alarm sounds immediately fill the air—they've rigged the exit. I sprint down the alley, discarding my designer sunglasses, yanking off my suit jacket as I run. Transformation on the move—a skill every field agent masters and the reason I always wear layers.

"Two agents in pursuit," Zara updates. "Coming out the same exit. I'm repositioning to intercept you at Cedar and 7th."

I take a sharp right at the end of the alley, weaving through pedestrians on the sidewalk. Normal pace now, blending in. I pull a folded scarf from my pocket, draping it over my head like a casual accessory. Without the jacket and glasses, in motion among dozens of other pedestrians, I'm just another face in the crowd. At least that's what I tell myself so I don't lose it.

"I see you," Zara says. "I'm at the corner. The passenger door is unlocked."

I spot the car, walking toward it without an obvious hurry. Behind me, I hear the sounds of pursuit—agents communicating, trying to reestablish visual contact. But they're looking for Emily Agostini in a charcoal suit, not a woman in a white blouse with a scarf over her hair.

I slide into the passenger seat, and Zara pulls away from the curb before I even close the door.

"That was too close," she says, navigating through traffic with practiced ease. Her knuckles are white on the steering wheel. "What the hell happened in there?"

"I don't know," I say, struggling to catch my breath. My lungs feel like they're on fire. "One second I'm talking to him and the next we have agents infiltrating the building. I should have gotten out of there the second I spotted that surveillance device." I take a second to catch my breath.

"They have you on camera, meeting with him. They'll think you've flipped."

The reality of the situation crashes over me. "They'll think I'm working with whoever's behind the agents' disappearances."

Zara takes a sharp turn, putting more distance between us and Apex headquarters. "Did you at least get anything useful before everything went sideways? Please tell me almost getting arrested wasn't for nothing."

I shake my head. "Nothing concrete. But the fact that the Bureau is running surveillance on Apex actually makes me feel a little better. It means they're taking Fletch seriously. Unless for some reason it was totally unrelated, but I doubt it."

I stare out the window as the city blurs past, the weight of what just happened settling over me. I've gone from agent on leave to suspected traitor in the span of an hour. The path back to my old life just got exponentially more difficult.

And Liam is definitely going to kill me.

Chapter Fourteen

THE SAFEHOUSE DOOR clicks shut behind us, the sound of three deadbolts sliding into place offering little comfort. My body aches everywhere—muscles strained from tension, bruises forming from my encounter with Merritt, and a pounding headache from the adrenaline spikes over the past few hours. My body is a series of pot holes along a busy street.

"Finally," Nadia says, looking up from her laptop. The blue glow of multiple screens illuminates her face in the dimly lit room. "Where have you two been? I've been going out of my mind."

"Well," Zara drops her keys on the counter, "we thought someone might be tailing us, so it took about twice as long to get back. And we didn't want to use comms in case they were being monitored."

"Were you followed?"

"I don't even know anymore," I say flatly, collapsing onto the couch. "I don't *think* we were followed, but I can't say that for sure."

Nadia's eyes widen.

"Yep. That right there." I rub my temples, trying to ease the throbbing pain. "What's been happening here?"

Nadia's expression shifts from shock to something more serious. "Nothing good. Since you went dark, there's been an explosion of chatter across Bureau channels."

"About us?" Zara asks, heading straight for the coffee maker.

"About Emily, mostly." Nadia turns her screen toward us, showing what looks like an internal FBI bulletin. "They've connected you to Fletch's organization. They want you for questioning."

"Fantastic," I say.

"Elliott says it gets worse," Nadia continues. "New Mexico field office has been notified to be on the lookout for Claire Dunn and Fiona Laidlaw."

Our cover identities from our time out there. My stomach drops.

"If they're found, they're to be detained immediately," Nadia finishes. Which means we couldn't go back even if we wanted to. Caruthers must be involved now—he's the only one outside our group who knew our cover identities.

"Great," Zara mutters, dropping into the chair across from me. "Now I'm a fugitive, too."

"I'm sorry," I tell her, guilt washing over me in a wave. "You shouldn't be dragged into this. You haven't done anything."

"Guilt by association," she says with a shrug that's trying too hard to be casual. "Besides, where else would I be? Someone has to keep your ass alive."

Despite everything, I manage a small smile. "Still."

"Don't start with me, Em." She points her mug at me. "We're in this together. End of discussion."

Nadia clears her throat. "You know, maybe you should turn yourselves in. Try to explain. We have the information from Janice. It's far from a slam dunk, but maybe it could help them piece together what's been going on."

I shake my head. "If we hand over what we've got there's

no guarantee it doesn't just disappear down some bureaucratic hole. Someone in the FBI is making sure Janice's death isn't being investigated too closely. We can't trust the Bureau right now. Whoever this mole is, we don't know their motives or their endgame."

"And now they think it's you," Zara concludes.

A horrible thought occurs to me. "What if that's what Janice was investigating? What if she suspected me all along?"

"No way," Zara says immediately, her voice firm. "Janice believed in you. She would never think you were capable of something like this."

"How can you be sure?" The question comes out smaller than I intended, vulnerable in a way I rarely allow myself to be.

"Because I knew Janice," she says simply. "And I know you."

The certainty in her voice steadies me. We sit in silence for a moment, each lost in our own thoughts as the reality of our situation settles around us.

"Actually," Nadia says, breaking the quiet, "I might have some semi-good news. Depends on how you look at it. You know what? I'll let you decide."

We both look up.

"While you two were out getting shot at or finding bodies or whatever," she continues, typing rapidly, "I've been digging into the Bureau's servers."

"You what?" I nearly spill my coffee. "How? That's—"

"Highly illegal? Yeah, I'm aware." She doesn't look up from the screen. "But Zara asked me to look into some things, and desperate times, you know?"

I glance at Zara, who has the decency to look slightly sheepish. "Umm...*when?*"

"Before we left for Apex," she admits. "I figured we needed all hands on deck. She's a quick study."

"Wait a second," I say. "You said it would cost the equivalent of a *Lamborghini* to get that kind of access. Those were your words."

"That was before we had help," Zara replies, a satisfied smile on her lips.

I turn to Nadia. "How are you accessing classified FBI servers?"

She glances up for a brief second, then back to the computer. "Elliott installed a transmitter for me."

"Elliott?" I repeat, incredulous. "By-the-book, never-bend-a-rule Elliott?"

"He's more flexible than you'd think," Nadia replies, and something in her tone makes me raise an eyebrow.

Zara snorts. "She's got him wrapped around her finger."

"I wouldn't put it that way," Nadia protests, though her smirk suggests otherwise. "Let's just say I can be persuasive."

"Clearly," I mutter. "So what did you find?"

"It's more like what I *didn't* find." She turns her laptop toward us. "Records that should be in the system but have been recently deleted. And guess the common thread."

"Fletch," I answer, leaning forward to see the screen.

"Bingo. Reports, surveillance logs, meeting transcripts all erased within the past month. But the system keeps shadow copies for backup purposes, if you know where to look."

"And the content?"

"Still piecing it together. The recovery process is slow, and I'm being careful not to trip any alarms. But from what I've gathered so far, these files contain evidence of Fletch's meetings with our FBI agents, including detailed notes on what was discussed."

"Official meetings?" Zara asks.

"That's the thing—some yes, some no. Some of these agents were operating with authorization, like your operation. Others without. But they all had contact with Fletch, and they're all on Janice's board."

The implications hit me like a physical blow. "So the mole is covering their tracks, erasing evidence. All for Fletch."

I stand up and begin pacing, my mind racing through scenarios. Seven steps across, turn, seven steps back. When did I start doing that? And why is it soothing? "If someone inside the Bureau is actively working against us, it's going to be nearly impossible to clear our names. We're completely locked out of official channels now."

"Not completely," Nadia corrects. "We still have Elliott and Liam."

"For now," I counter. "But if they connect either of them to us, they'll be in the same boat. And I'm not willing to risk that."

Zara watches me pace, her expression thoughtful. "That leaves us with our original option. Our only option. We need to find Fletch."

"He's in the wind," I remind her. "And even if we could locate him, my cover is blown. He knows my real identity."

"*Maybe*." She leans forward, elbows on knees. "Maybe not. We don't know for sure. We're assuming the worst based on what happened in St. Solomon, but we never confirmed who leaked your identity."

"It's too big a risk."

"Everything we're doing is a risk," she counters. "But Fletch is the common denominator in all of this. He met with all the targeted agents. He's the answer to all of it."

I stop pacing. "Even if you're right, how do we find him?"

Zara exchanges a glance with Nadia, and I immediately know there's something they're not telling me.

"What?" I demand.

"There might be a way," Zara says carefully. "But you're not going to like it."

"Try me."

She takes a deep breath. "Theo."

The name hangs in the air between us. Theo Arquenest—

the man who brought us the Fletch case in the first place, the same man who disappeared after tipping me off about Janice's death. And the man who has been a thorn in Zara's side ever since we left for New Mexico.

"No," I say flatly. "Absolutely not."

"Hear me out," Zara pleads. "Theo has connections we don't. He brought us Fletch originally, which means he will know how to find him."

"You're the one who said you weren't sure we could trust him. What's changed?" I gesture wildly at the screens showing our faces plastered across Bureau bulletins. "For all we know, he could be the one who set us up!"

She doesn't reply, but holds my gaze. She *doesn't* know if we can trust him. I don't want this for her. I don't want to put her in a situation where she has to ask something of him. Where we have to rely on him.

"There has to be another way," I insist.

"If there is, I'm all ears." Zara's voice is steady, but I can see the tension in her shoulders, the way her knuckles have whitened around her coffee mug. "But we're running out of options, Em. And we're running out of time."

She's right, and I hate it. Every hour that passes is another hour the real mole could be destroying evidence, another hour of us being hunted. The weight of it all—Janice's death, the agents whose lives might still be in danger—presses down on me until I can barely breathe.

"You don't have to do this," I tell Zara, my voice gentler now. "Finding Theo, confronting him—that's asking a lot right now."

"I know." Something flickers across her face—determination, fear, resolve. "But I need answers too. I need to know if he played me, if he's been part of this all along."

The room falls silent again, the only sound the soft hum of computer fans and the distant noise of traffic outside. I study Zara's face, remembering our conversation the night before, her insistence that she needed to face Theo alone when the time came.

"Okay," I say finally. "If you think Theo is our best shot at finding Fletch, we'll try it. But we do it together. No solo heroics, remember?"

Relief softens her features. "Deal."

"So how do we find him?" I ask. "If he's avoiding Bureau surveillance, he won't be easy to track down."

A small smile tugs at the corner of Zara's mouth. "Actually, I think I know where he might be."

"You do?" This is news to me.

"There's a place he used to go when he needed to disappear for a while. A cabin outside Shenandoah. He took me there once. Said no one else knew about it." Her voice catches slightly on the memory.

"And you think he's there now?"

She nods. "It's remote, off-grid, defensible. Exactly where someone like Theo would go when things get messy."

"If we're doing this," I say, "we need to be prepared for anything. Theo may not be happy to see us, and we can't be sure what his agenda is."

"I know," Zara says. "But it's our best shot."

Nadia closes her laptop. "I'll keep working on the ghost files. Maybe by the time you get back, I'll have something concrete."

"Be careful," I tell her. "If someone catches you digging around in those files—"

"I know the risks," she says calmly. "Elliott and I have contingencies in place."

I want to ask what those are, but decide it's better not to know. Plausible deniability and all that.

Zara pulls me to the side as I head back for my bedroom, needing a shower and to gather my thoughts. "Hey," she says. "What about Liam? He wanted to be kept in the loop."

I hesitate. Old me would have said Liam didn't need to

know. But in the past twenty-four hours I've been beaten up, framed and almost arrested. I don't want to keep him in the dark. He needs to know we're going after Theo, no matter how much it pains me to tell him.

"Yeah, we need to contact him," I say. "Give him an update."

"He won't be happy," she says.

"Are any of us?" Nothing about any of this is ideal. But it's what's required.

Zara nods. "Okay. We'll head out first thing in the morning. The drive to Shenandoah will take a few hours and we'll be better off approaching in the daylight."

"Sounds good."

"You mind if I shower first?" she asks.

I motion toward the bathroom at the end of the hall. "Go ahead."

She gives my hand a quick squeeze before heading to the bedroom, leaving me alone with Nadia who is packing up to head back to her place.

"She's stronger than she looks," Nadia observes quietly.

"I know." I sink back onto the couch, exhaustion washing over me. "But this thing with Theo—it cuts deep. She blames herself for bringing him into our circle, for not seeing through him if he was playing us."

"And what do you think? Was he playing us?"

I consider the question, trying to separate fact from feeling. "I don't know. But I guess we're about to find out."

Chapter Fifteen

ZARA SITS in her car across the street from Theo's apartment building, her fingers drumming nervously against the wheel. The early morning light has yet to illuminate the front of the building, still just barely breaking through the clouds. She's been tracking Theo's location ever since they got back from New Mexico because she knew this day was coming one way or another. Em might have been able to stave her off for a while—and maybe she was even able to convince herself this could wait until later, but they need the information now and there's no avoiding it.

The guilt of going behind Em's back gnaws at her, but she pushes it back down. She never really went to sleep—she couldn't, knowing what she'd have to do. Instead, she waited until about four in the morning and quietly left the safehouse, keeping to the shadows and leaving without making a sound. If everything goes as she hopes, she should be back before Em even wakes up.

She would absolutely kill Zara if she knew what she was doing. She'd even made her promise. But Emily has already risked too much. She's been beaten, framed for murder and nearly arrested. And Zara isn't going to add to her pile of problems.

Plus…Theo is her mess to clean up.

Movement catches her eye at the building's entrance. Theo emerges, dressed in dark jeans and a leather jacket. That damn leather jacket she used to think was so sexy now just makes her want to puke. He scans the street with the practiced wariness of someone who knows what it's like to be hunted. And he looks thinner than the last time she saw him, shadows beneath his eyes that weren't there before.

There you are.

Zara slides lower in the seat. It's unlikely he'll be able to spot her from here but she isn't taking any chances. Her car won't draw his attention parked among the others along the road, but Theo has always been observant. It was one of the things that initially attracted her to him. He was clever and often noticed things others missed. And he used that skill to manipulate her.

Never again.

He pulls out his phone, tapping the screen and a few minutes later, a rideshare vehicle pulls up. Theo climbs in as the car pulls away and Zara takes a breath. Theo isn't the kind of person who keeps a regular schedule, but he *is* the kind of person who is addicted to his morning tea. And because he can be lazy, he prefers to go out and buy one rather than brew it on his own. He should be gone for at least fifteen minutes which Zara hopes will be long enough for her to get in and find what she needs before he returns.

Her heart races as she approaches the building, not from fear but from anger and anticipation. His apartment key feels heavy in her pocket and she can't stop fiddling with it as she paces through the lobby and heads for the stairs, keeping her head down. Thankfully no one else seems to be up at this hour. She takes the stairs up to the fourth floor, emerging into the hallway with a practiced confidence. At his door she takes a beat and listens for any sounds from within, but is only met with silence.

She slides the key into the lock and turns it smoothly. The door opens with a soft click, and she slips inside, disabling the security keypad with the code he thankfully hasn't yet changed.

The apartment looks different than the last time she was here a few months ago. Less lived-in, more spartan. It's clear he hasn't spent much time here either. In fact, the place looks more like a hideout than a home. Or maybe she's just seeing it in a new light. Regardless, she doesn't have time to waste. She moves methodically through the space, searching for anything he might have hidden. Theo's the kind of person who always likes to be prepared, which means he backs everything up and keeps copies of important documents in different places. There has to be *something* here that will lead them to Fletch.

The living room yields nothing of interest—no papers, computer or phone. The kitchen is equally barren, save Theo's favorite bottle of scotch, half empty above the refrigerator.

In the bedroom she finds more signs of temporary habitation: a suitcase partially unpacked, the clothes inside still creased. He's been in DC ever since they arrived, which means that like Merritt, Theo might be planning to get out of town for a while. Obviously, word is getting around about *something*.

The nightstand contains a burner phone, which Zara pockets without hesitation. The closet holds nothing other than a locked gun case and a couple of hangers with the clamps on them for pants. She's about to check under the mattress when she hears it—the distinctive sound of a key in a lock.

No. He's early.

She freezes, her mind racing with options. She could try to hide, but the apartment is too small for her to be concealed for long. She could confront him directly, but that might end poorly if he's armed. There is really only one option left.

The bedroom door is still partially closed. Zara quickly pulls off her jacket, messes up her hair and positions herself on the bed in what she hopes passes for a seductive pose. For some reason it's so much easier to tell Emily how to do this than to actually do it herself.

The front door closes, the footsteps moving casually through the apartment. They pause in the kitchen and the refrigerator opens then closes again. Zara forces herself to calm down and adopt a more neutral expression than the rage she feels. Part of her is almost glad he came back early.

The door swings open and Theo stops cold in the doorway.

"Hey, stranger," she purrs, leaning back on her elbows.

Theo's expression cycles rapidly from shock to confusion to wariness. "Zara? What in the bloody hell?"

She tilts her head, mocking hurt. "Is that any way to greet me after all this time? You didn't really expect us not to respond after you sent me that text, did you?"

His eyes narrow, scanning her face for any signs of deception. But she's completely resolved—she has this now. Seeing him has cauterized the wound that was their relationship. Theo is a master at reading people, but he won't be doing that anymore. Not with her.

"Where's Emily?" he asks, not moving from the doorway.

"Hell if I know." She stands slowly and takes a few deliberate steps toward him. "She came back on her own, I've been trying to find her ever since. I thought maybe she'd come here, but…"

"You lost track of her?" he asks. "The FBI is looking for her, Zara. They're saying she defected."

She smiles at him. "I think we both know that's not true." Theo needs to be focused on one thing and one thing only right now. She doesn't want him getting bogged down with talk. Not yet. Zara takes one of his hands and moves it to her waist, even though the move wants to make her shudder. Her face is inches from his, close enough to smell his cologne—the same one he's always worn when they were together.

As soon as his hand touches her waist it's like something comes over him. He pulls her into him, breathing in her scent. "I forgot how intoxicating you are," he murmurs as he bends to kiss her neck. Once upon a time that would have made her melt. "I've missed you."

Zara leans into his touch, forcing herself not to react negatively. She guides him to the bed, letting him think he has the advantage. He's distracted, focused on unbuttoning her blouse.

Perfect.

With practiced movements, Zara flips them so she's on top of him, pushing him into the mattress and straddling him. His eyes are wide with desire, so much the boy is practically drooling. She grins. "Remember that night in Boston?"

"You are a goddess," he says between heavy breaths. His growth is about to jump out of his pants. He grins at her, clearly anticipating what is coming. She reaches for his belt, undoes the strap, and deftly yanks it out of the loops and off his pants. With a grin a mile wide on her face, she takes both his hands and clasps them together, securing them with the belt which she then fixes to the top of the bedframe with as strong a knot as it will allow. It's not perfect, but it will do for the moment.

She then scoots down and undoes his pants, slowly easing them down with his help as he wriggles out of them. If he only knew what he's helping her do.

"Eager, aren't we?"

"You have no idea," she replies, her voice low and seductive.

She quickly hops off the bed and retrieves one of the coat hangers from the closet, breaking off the plastic clamp that would normally keep pressed pants from getting wrinkled. And before Theo can protest, she attaches it to his member just like a clip on a thick bag of chips.

"Ahh," he says, wincing. "That's a little tight, love."

"Shut up," she hisses, all pretenses gone. "One wrong move and this gets very painful for you, understand?"

Confusion crosses Theo's face, but he swallows and nods.

She settles back on his chest, one hand on the clamp as the force of her body keeps him in place. "Who told you to contact us about Janice?"

"I don't know what you're talking about," he protests.

Zara squeezes the clamp slightly. Theo yelps, a sound of agony echoing through the apartment.

"Oh *yes!*" She moans theatrically. "Right there!" Zara leans close to his ear. "Next time you scream, it better sound like you're having the best sex of your life. I can do this for hours."

Theo stares up at her, fear in his eyes and gasping for breath. "Zara, please. I don't know what you're on about."

For a second she wants to believe him. Like she always has. To admit all of this has been nothing but a mistake. But then she thinks back to that night in New Mexico. When she finally decided to investigate his background.

And it was cleaner than a freshly-polished car.

"You get one more chance to tell me the truth, or I break it."

Surprise flickers across his face before he can mask it. "How did you—"

"Because I'm not *stupid*," she says and tightens the clamp again. "Who?"

Theo grunts again, the sound coming out guttural and deep as he tries to process the pain. "I was just following orders," he admits through gritted teeth.

"Whose orders?"

"I don't know. It came through channels."

Zara tightens her grip further, the teeth on the clip burying themselves in the skin. Theo cries out and Zara matches his cries of pain with those of mock pleasure. She must admit, she's enjoying this a little too much. "Give me a name, Theo," she sing-songs.

"Fletch," Theo finally gasped. "The order came from Joaquin Fletch."

Why is she not surprised? The man has been instrumental in everything. She releases the clamp. "Why would Fletch want Emily to know about Janice?"

"I don't know the details," he says, sweat beading on his forehead. "I just do what I'm paid to do."

Fury bubbles up in Zara and she squeezes again just out of spite, causing Theo to cry out again. Tears form in his eyes, intentional or not. He is in some serious pain. Good. She considers it payback for the betrayal. All the heartbreak.

"What was Fletch meeting with the other FBI Agents about?" she asks.

"He never told me."

She grasps the clamp again. "Are you sure about that?"

"I'm sure, I'm *sure*," he says in a panicked tone. "You know how he is. Compartmentalizes everything. Doesn't want people to know what he's up to."

She releases the grip on the clamp. It would make sense for Fletch not to tell anyone what the meetings were about.

"Did you know about the deaths?" His silence gives her the answer. "Was he responsible for them?"

"Probably," Theo admits. "But I don't know the details. Again, he—"

"Yeah, save the song and dance," she replies, thinking. There must be another way to get what they need. And if Theo only has part of the equation, that means they'll need to go deeper.

"Listen closely. You're going to set up a meeting," Zara

says, her voice cold. "Between Emily and Fletch. Face to face."

Theo shakes his head. "Impossible. His security is too tight. He'll never agree to it."

"Emily is disavowed now, thanks to you and your friends," Zara reminds him, applying just enough pressure to the clamp to keep his attention. "She wants answers… about the Bureau, about Janice… all of it. And Fletch has those answers. You're going to make it happen."

"He'll never trust me if I suggest it," Theo argues. "He'll know something's wrong. Zara, he'll kill me."

"Then you'd better be very convincing." Zara leans closer. "Because the alternative is me leaving you here like this for housekeeping to find. After I've called in an anonymous tip about terrorist activity at this address."

Fear flashes in his eyes. He knows she means business.

"Yes, all right," he relents. "I'll try to set up the meeting."

"You'll do more than try," Zara corrects. "You'll make it happen."

She wants to twist the clamp harder, until his dick breaks off, if only to make him feel a fraction of the pain she's felt at his betrayal. She'd let him in, allowed her guard down, all while he was working for the man they were actively investigating.

"Why?" she asks, her voice softer but no less intense. "After everything we'd been through?"

He meets her gaze, his expression resigned. "I never wanted to, but I don't know if you've noticed, the world is becoming an unpredictable place. Simon… he was just the tip of the iceberg. There are hundreds of Simons out there, all with their own insane plans. And we can't stop them all. I had to protect myself. The only way to do that is with money—as much of it as possible."

Disgust washes over her. "You're despicable."

"I'm a survivor," he counters. "Just like you."

Zara removes the clamp but keeps his wrists secured. "If you haven't already guessed, consider this me dumping you. You're lucky I don't kill you."

"I know," he says quietly. "I always knew you were too good for me."

She ignores the comment, retrieving his phone from his pocket. "Unlock it."

He hesitates just long enough for her to reach for the clamp again. "5-2-7-9," he says quickly.

Zara opens his contacts and finds what she's looking for—a number labeled only as "F." She adds it to her own phone, then places his back on the nightstand.

"Here's what's going to happen," she says, standing up and gathering her jacket. "You're going to set up that meeting within the next 48 hours using Emily's real name. We already know her cover is blown. When it's arranged, you'll text this number." She shows him the burner phone she'd taken from his drawer. "If you try to warn Fletch, if you try to set us up, if you do anything other than exactly what I've told you, I will find you. And this little session will seem like a pleasant memory compared to what I'll do next."

Theo nods, his expression solemn. "I understand."

"You better." Zara moves to the door, ready to leave.

"Hey," he calls out. "You can't just leave me like this."

"Yes I can," she says to him. "Figure it out."

She leaves him there, closing the bedroom door behind her. In the living room she pauses just long enough to gather herself. The muffled sounds of Theo's attempts to free himself coming from the other side of the door. She'd been right, after all. Everything they'd had was a lie. He'd never really cared about her, just used her and Emily to infiltrate the FBI for Fletch. And if she'd been more diligent, maybe she would have figured that out before Janice had died.

She doesn't allow herself to cry. Not now and not here.

And strangely, some deep part of her feels better. Like a weight has been lifted somewhere.

As Zara slips out of the apartment and makes her way down the stairs, the reality of what she's done settles over her. She's gone behind Emily's back, confronted Theo alone, and potentially made their situation even more dangerous by forcing a meeting with Fletch.

But she's also gotten what they needed: confirmation that Fletch was connected to the Bureau conspiracy, a meeting and a potential path to answers. Fletch wanted Emily to know Janice was dead... why? To draw her back here? She can't say for sure, but they need to be extremely cautious. She may even need to call in a few favors.

But first, she needs to face Emily and explain why she broke her promise.

As she starts her car, Zara takes a deep breath. Em will be furious, and rightfully so. But this was necessary. Some tasks require crossing lines, venturing into moral gray areas.

That was why Zara had done it. Because she could wade into that darkness and still find her way back. Because Emily has already sacrificed enough. And because... this was her mess. She needed to face Theo alone—to confirm her suspicions. And to close that chapter of her life, without getting Emily involved.

Because sometimes, protecting the people you care about means doing things they'll never forgive you for.

Chapter Sixteen

MY EYES SNAP open to silence. I turn over and look at my phone. One minute before my alarm is set to go off. I switch it off and take in how quiet the place feels. Something about this isn't right.

I head into the hallway, only to be greeted by more silence. No smell of coffee in the air, no shower running, no Zara humming whatever nineties song is stuck in her head this morning.

"Z?" I call out, my voice thick with sleep. No answer.

I head into her room to find her bed a mess, though that's nothing new. She's not the kind of person who makes her bed in the morning. Maybe she went out for coffee. But why would she do that when we have perfectly good brew here and leaving the safehouse just opens us up to more risk than we need?

I tap her image on my phone and hold it up, but the call goes straight to voicemail. Furrowing my brow, I make my way through the safehouse, checking all the windows to make sure none have been compromised. As I do, a nasty feeling begins to brew in my gut. It's not like Zara to just leave without a note or a text or *something*.

Getting an idea, I head over to her computer setup on the dining room table. It's still showing the feeds from the hallway and outside the building. I wind the footage back until I find what I'm looking for: Zara leaving the safehouse around four-thirty this morning. She moves with purpose and without looking back, but I recognize that platinum blonde hair of hers sticking out of the edges of her hoodie jacket.

So she left on her own accord…but why?

No. She wouldn't have.

She *promised*.

A knock at the door draws my attention. I look back at the surveillance camera to see Liam fumbling with his key for the safehouse. I cross the room in three steps and let him inside in less than ten seconds, the door closed and locked behind him. He's buzzing with a nervous energy, which is very unlike him.

"Are you…okay?" I ask.

"Three tails." He's breathing hard, his hair disheveled, tie askew. "Had to ditch my car, took the Metro, doubled back twice." He yanks off his suit jacket, tossing it over a chair. "Almost didn't make it."

"Jesus, Liam." I wrap my arms around him, hoping I can at least help calm him down a little. "Are you sure you weren't followed here?"

"Positive." But his eyes dart to the window, and he pulls away as he checks the street beyond the curtain. "I wouldn't have come if I wasn't certain."

The sight of him so rattled sends a chill through me. Liam is always the calm one, the steady presence in the storm. If he's rattled, it means this is serious. "Here," I say. "Come sit down. Let me make you some coffee."

He glances back and nods, taking a seat at the dining room table. "I wanted to come make you breakfast again. But they almost caught up with me on Hudson. Thankfully I was turned away from them and they didn't get a good look at my face. Still…"

I move into the kitchen to start the coffee. We knew Liam would be under surveillance. But this feels a lot more intense than even just a few days ago.

Once he's caught his breath, he glances around. "Where's the terror?"

"Gone," I say, flipping the switch on the coffee maker. "Left early this morning."

"Why?" he asks.

"Why do you think?"

He screws up his face. "But I thought the plan was—"

I don't let him finish. "So did I." I grab two mugs from the cabinet, practically slamming them on the counter.

"You know she's just trying to protect you."

"Doesn't mean I have to like it," I say, pressing down the grounds into the cup, using enough pressure to turn coal into diamonds.

"Try not to be too hard on her," he says. "How many times have you done the same for her?"

I pause, frustrated that he's right. There have been plenty of times in the past when I've gone behind her back because it would keep her safe or out of trouble. To the point where she began threatening me if I ever did it again. I guess I can't blame her for a little payback. "Theo's not an ordinary mark. What if she gets in over her head, or—"

He gets up and wraps his hands around mine as I fiddle with the machine. "Zara can handle herself. *Especially* where Theo is involved."

I sigh. "I guess you're right."

"Plus, we have a bigger problem. They've ramped up the surveillance on me, and they're not even really being subtle about it. I even got a call from my mom last night asking why a dark car with government plates was sitting at the end of her driveway."

"They're watching your *parents*?" I ask. "Jesus."

"I told her not to worry about it, that it's just FBI precautions, but my dad won't buy that. Not in a million years. And the longer this goes on—"

"I know," I say, slamming the cup full of grounds back on the counter. "It's my fault. I get it, okay?"

He pauses and wraps himself around me this time. "I'm sorry, I didn't mean to imply this was your fault. This isn't your fault. Whoever is behind all this, that's who we need to be angry at."

I nod and pull away from him as he takes over the coffee duties. "But, I have an appointment with IA on Monday."

My stomach drops. "An interrogation?"

"They're calling it an 'information gathering session.'" His attempt at air quotes falls flat. "But yeah, interrogation is more accurate. They're looking to pump me for any information about you." He finishes the routine and sets the machine to run. The coffee begins to drip, its familiar aroma at odds with the tension in the room. I lean against the counter, suddenly exhausted despite having just woken up.

"You can't keep doing this," I say quietly. "Coming here, helping me. You're putting yourself at risk."

"I'm not abandoning you." His voice is firm, but I can hear the undercurrent of uncertainty.

"It's not abandonment. It's strategic." I try to keep my tone light, but there's no hiding the gravity of the situation. "You're more valuable to me out there, with your badge, than in a cell next to mine. Which is exactly where you're going to end up."

"Emily—"

"No, listen to me." I move closer, placing my hands on his arms. "If they connect you to me, to any of this, your career is over. And that's the best-case scenario. Worst case, they charge you as an accessory."

"I don't care about my career," he says, but we both know that's not entirely true. He's worked too hard, overcome too much to throw it all away now.

"What about the dogs?" I ask, playing my trump card. "What happens to them if we're both in jail? They go to your parents? Your brother?"

A flash of pain crosses his face. Our dogs are his world, his anchor in the storms we navigate.

"Low blow, Slate."

"I fight dirty when I have to." I attempt a smile that doesn't quite reach my eyes. "And right now, I have to make sure you stay safe."

The coffee finishes brewing, and Liam mechanically pours it into the two mugs. We sit at the small table, the silence between us deafening.

"They're going to find this place eventually," he says after a while. "If it's in your history anywhere, they'll track it down."

"I know." I stare into my coffee.

"We need to move you somewhere else."

"There is no 'we' in this anymore, Liam." The words hurt to say, but they're necessary. "From here on out, you have to stay away. No contact, no visits, nothing that could connect you to me."

He sets his mug down with more force than necessary. "And what about you? What's your plan?"

"Zara and I will figure it out." I sound more confident than I feel. "We'll find Fletch, get answers about who's behind this, clear my name. And plug the leak at the Bureau."

"Just like that?" A hint of anger creeps into his voice. "The Bureau's best agents are looking for you, Em. They have resources, connections, technology—"

"I know what they have." I cut him off. "I was one of them, remember?"

The silence that follows feels like a chasm opening between us. I hate this—pushing him away when every part of me wants to hold onto him tighter.

"So that's it? I just walk away while you're fighting for your life?"

"Yes." I reach across the table, taking his hand. "That's exactly what you do. Because I need to know you're safe. I need to know that when this is all over, there's still something to come back to."

His fingers tighten around mine. "And if it's never over?"

The question hangs between us, heavy with possibility. I've been avoiding thinking too far ahead, focusing only on the next step, the next lead. But Liam's always been the one to see the bigger picture, to make me confront the parts I'd rather ignore.

"Then I'll figure that out too," I say, trying to sound confident. "But I'm not dragging you down with me."

He starts to protest, but I silence him with a gentle squeeze of his hand.

"I need you to do something for me," I continue. "Tell Nadia she can't come back either. She and Elliott need to maintain plausible deniability in all this. If anyone asks, none of you have seen or heard from me since New Mexico."

"They won't like that."

"I don't care." My voice hardens. "This isn't a democracy. It's me trying to keep the people I care about from ruining their lives."

Liam studies my face, probably looking for any sign of weakness, any crack in my resolve that he can exploit. He won't find one. Not on this.

"Okay," he says finally. "I'll tell her."

Relief mingles with sadness. "Thank you."

We sit in silence for a moment, both aware that this is it—the last time we'll see each other until this nightmare is over. If it ever is.

"I should go," he says eventually, though he makes no move to leave. "The longer I stay, the more dangerous it is for both of us."

I nod, not trusting myself to speak. This feels worse than our goodbye before New Mexico, heavier with the knowledge of what we're up against. Back then, it felt temporary. Now, the uncertainty stretches before us like an abyss.

He stands, and I follow him to the door. We both know we shouldn't extend this goodbye, but neither of us seems capable of ending it.

"I love you," I say, the words inadequate for everything I want to express.

"I love you back." His voice is rough with emotion. "Stay alive, Emily. That's all I ask."

I nod again, swallowing the lump in my throat. "I will."

He cups my face with his hands and his lips find mine and they don't let go. We stay like that, drinking each other in until I'm forced to pull back. It takes all the willpower I possess and when I do, I find I'm literally breathless. With visible effort, Liam turns and walks away. I close the door behind him, each turn of the locks feeling like another barrier between us.

Only when I hear his footsteps fade down the stairs do I allow myself to break. I slam my fist on the door, needing some sort of outlet for the pain. The tears begin to fall and I let them. Then I wipe my eyes, take a deep breath, and reset.

There will be time for grief later. Right now, I need to find Zara, figure out our next move, and somehow, against all odds, find a way through this mess.

I check my phone one more time—still nothing from Zara. Wherever she is, I hope she's being careful. Because right now, she's all I have left.

Chapter Seventeen

I DISTRACT myself by taking a quick shower, getting dressed and thinking about anything other than Liam. Mostly about how I really want to tear Zara a new one for going behind my back. If I have any chance of getting to Shenandoah in time, I'm going to have to either rent a car or take a rideshare and neither is ideal. My only other ID might not hold up under scrutiny and Claire Dunn is a wanted person at the moment so my options are limited.

Still. I need to go after her. Of course, I have no idea *where* in Shenandoah she is. In fact, she may have been lying about that too, especially if she'd been planning this for a while. Great. That means my only hope of *actually* finding her is calling her nonstop until she picks up and tells me where the hell she is. And given I'm likely to strangle her the second I see her, I don't really expect that to happen.

But just as I'm finishing pulling on my boots, unsure where I'm going, the door to the safehouse opens and Zara enters, closing and locking the door behind her. She stops dead in the middle of the entryway upon seeing me, like a deer caught in the bright headlights of a semi truck.

Panic washes over her face for a brief second before it's

gone and her whole body slumps. "Well, shit." She pads into the living room, standing before me. "C'mon, let's get it over with."

"Oh no," I say. "It's not going to be that easy. You don't just get to stand here and take your beating. What the hell, Z?"

She holds up her hands. "In my defense, he wasn't supposed to be there. And honestly, it's a good thing *you* weren't. Otherwise, I wouldn't have been able to hogtie him."

I skip over that little nugget as I recognize it as her attempt to distract me. Though part of me wonders what the hell happened over there. "So you saw him. In person. And he saw you."

"Yep."

"Is he... dead?"

A slow smile spreads across her face. "No. But he probably wishes he was."

"Is he still in one piece?"

She shrugs. "Was when I left him."

I huff, pacing the room again. She can be so damn frustrating sometimes. "Look, I know you had this...vendetta you needed—"

"It wasn't a vendetta," she interrupts. "We—I needed to know if he could be trusted. And it turns out he can't."

I furrow my brow. "What happened?"

"He's been working both teams this whole time, Em. He's been running errands for Fletch, while at the same time serving us and the Bureau whatever Fletch told him to. The operation? At the Constitution? It was a setup."

"But..." I begin. "If Fletch knew we were FBI..."

"He played along," she says. "All to get us to take that damn drive from him. I think that's what infected the Bureau's computers and provided them access."

"Then he wasn't really drunk that night?"

She blows out a breath and sits on the couch. "I don't know. I'm not sure what to trust anymore."

I try to replay the whole operation in my mind. Theo brought us the case on Fletch, and after a thorough review, Caruthers approved the operation. The intel—planted obviously—showed Fletch and his business posed some threat to the FBI, but we weren't sure what. The plan was to surveil him for a few weeks, then plant myself in his ecosphere as a colleague. And when the time was right, get access to his personal data and find out just what the hell he and his operation were up to.

Only, it didn't exactly happen that way. We managed to pull off the op—even though I had to take a few risks to do it. All to obtain an encrypted drive that must have been nothing more than a trojan horse. If what Zara is saying is true, *we* were the ones who allowed Fletch to threaten the FBI. Look where it's left us—fractured and divided with the left hand not knowing what the right hand is doing.

I *knew* something about that night felt off. Theo had been there the whole way, an integral part of the operation, making sure to "distract" Fletch at exactly the right time so I could drug his drink. But now that I think about it, Theo was the one who provided the "drugs."

"I can't believe this," I say, sitting on the couch beside her. "This entire time?"

"I've been going through it in my head since I left his place," she says. "I don't think it was the entire time. But it's been for a while, at least. Maybe since the Procyon operation, I dunno, maybe before. Shit, I could be way off and he could have been playing both of us since Simon Magus."

I shake my head. "I don't believe it. Neither of us are that bad of judges of character that we'd just let something like that slide. It had to have happened in between somewhere. On one of those operations where we just weren't paying as close of attention. Someone got to him." I turn to her. "This isn't your fault."

"Says the woman who wants to blame herself for our boss's death."

Okay, point made.

"It doesn't matter anyway," she says. "What's done is done."

"Putting aside the fact that I'm furious with you, it *does* matter, Z. It matters because you cared about him. You still do. And you deserve to have someone in your life you can trust. Not someone who will use you and go behind your back like this. Did he at least say why?"

"Why else?" she shrugs. "Money. He seems to think something is coming… something bad. And he's trying to insulate himself."

"Fucker," I mutter. She called it, too. She knew something wasn't right while we were still in New Mexico. "What happened? Did he try to hurt you?"

"He never got the chance," she replies. "The idiot allowed himself to be locked into a compromising position."

My eyes go wide which produces a grin on her face. "*How* compromising?"

The fact that she doesn't answer and instead draws little circles on the fabric of the couch tells me everything I need to know. "And you… hogtied him?"

"Only halfway," she says. "Just his arms."

"He'll go to Fletch now," I say. "Expose us. And if Fletch is the one hunting me down, he'll know I'm in town."

"I know," she replies. "It was a calculated risk. I thought I could get in and out of there before he got back. But I think he must have had some kind of silent alarm I missed because he wasn't gone ten minutes when he never takes less than twenty for his tea runs."

"So are you going to tell me what happened, or do I have to beat it out of you?"

A mischievous look comes over her face. "I mean, it wasn't without its entertainment value."

"Spill."

She goes through the whole thing, about how she got into his apartment, which wasn't a cabin in the Shenandoah Valley after all, but right here in DC, only for him to show up and surprise her. Then, going into probably more detail than I'm comfortable with, she tells me about how she got him tied up and essentially forced him into running an errand for *us*.

"And you think he'll keep his word? About going to Fletch?"

"He will if he wants to keep his manhood intact," she replies. "I swear to God, Em, I was so furious I could have twisted it off right then and there."

I nearly choke on my own spit but manage a quick recovery. "That sucks. I'm sorry you had to do it."

"Me too. It wasn't nearly as fun as it sounds." She turns to me. "And I'm sorry I didn't tell you. But you have enough going on without needing to deal with Theo too. I knew if something happened, I could handle him."

I nod. "You definitely did. I just wish you'd told me you needed to take care of it on your own."

"And if I had, would you have let me?"

My shoulders sink. "No."

"Didn't think so. You're too stubborn for your own good."

"*Me?*"

We glare at each other and after a second we're both barely holding back. "Okay, okay, we're *both* stubborn."

"Do you want some breakfast?" I ask.

"No five-star treatment this morning?" she replies, getting up and heading over to the computer.

I hesitate. She looks at the computer and no doubt sees from the logs that Liam was already here and left. "What happened?"

I force a smile. "It's fine. We just decided…" I find I have to swallow before I can continue. "He's being watched at work. It's too dangerous for him to keep coming here. For any of them. Getting spotted at Apex… it changed the game. And on that note, I think we probably need to leave soon. Eventually they're going to track this place back to me. They'll be digging into my history."

"I thought you said it wasn't on any official records or—"

"It's not," I say. "At least, none that I know of. But if Janice wrote an errant note about it somewhere or they question one of the other agents I used to work with back in the day, they might remember it's here. The point is, it's not safe anymore. We should go."

"Where? It's not like we have a lot of options. Any hotels are going to have security cameras and avoiding those will be a pain in the ass. Not to mention they're gonna notice if two women check into a room and never come back out. Home share sites will be trackable, we need to stick to cash transactions. And—"

"We'll use Janice's second place," I say.

Zara pauses, considering the possibility. "Interesting. But doing that is assuming no one else knew about it. What if Merritt shared the location?"

I get up. "Let's just hope he was the professional he claimed to be," I say. "When is this meeting with Fletch?"

She holds up a burner phone. "I'm supposed to be notified. But, seeing how I left him, it may be a while."

"Good," I say. "That will give us enough time to pack and move. You really think a direct confrontation with him is a good idea?"

She closes the laptop and begins disconnecting cords. "It's the only way we can get any answers. Theo—under duress—claimed not to know anything. And as much as I hate to admit it, I believe him. Janice is dead. Merritt is a ghost. And the other living agents on Janice's list are probably as clueless as we are. He's our *only* option."

"But he knows I'm an FBI agent," I say.

"He knows you're a *former* FBI agent," she corrects. "And you need to convince him you're ready to let all of it go. The lifestyle, the work, all of it."

These are dangerous waters. It's not that I can't convincingly pull something like that off, it's that Fletch has already played us once. He's played *me* and gotten away with it. *He's* the reason for our exile and might even be behind Janice's death. He could be the one who was looking for me out in New Mexico. And all I need to do is stand in front of him and tell him I'm willing to forgive all of that for a little information.

"He'll never buy it," I say. "Especially if he has a detailed history on me." There's no reason to assume he doesn't. Theo always told us the man was meticulous in his research. We had to build quite the comprehensive file and background on *Emily Agostini* just to pass his first few levels of security.

"Em, you're going to have to find a way to make it work," she says. "Otherwise, all this is for nothing. And we might as well pack up because we'll never be able to come back to this town again."

Somehow her words galvanize me. There is a way to convince Fletch. I just need to find it. I need to make him believe I've been so wronged and so betrayed that I'm willing to do the very same thing to the FBI. Fletch is a narcissist and one thing to know about narcissists is they tend to think everyone else is like them in some way. All I need to do is focus on making that a reality. But I can't roll over, either.

"I don't guess there's any chance we can hire some backup, can we?"

"Already ahead of you. I know a few guys," she says. "But it isn't going to be cheap. And it definitely won't be legal. These aren't the kinds of guys the government vets."

"All the better," I say, heading down the hallway to my bedroom. "We'll need this to look as authentic as possible."

I head into my bedroom and begin throwing everything back into the suitcase I brought with me on the bus. The good thing about packing light is it won't take us long to get out of here and wipe this place down. Maybe the FBI wouldn't find it after all, but I can't take the risk of them showing up out of the blue and taking us both into custody.

And yet, for what I'm about to do, that's exactly what should happen.

Chapter Eighteen

THE TEXT from Theo arrives less than an hour after we've moved our setup to Janice's second apartment... the one where Merritt was making the dead drops and hopefully the one that no one else knows about, other than Mattingly.

> Meeting confirmed. 8PM tonight. Fletch's residence. Address to follow.

I stare at the message, my thumb hovering over the screen. After Zara's little stunt this morning, I'd been prepared for Theo to run, to cut all contact. The fact that he followed through suggests either Zara scared him more than I thought, or there's a deeper game at play.

An hour later, the address pings on the burner phone. Not a warehouse or nondescript meeting point, but a residential house in Georgetown. "Wait a second," I say after looking up the location through Google maps. "Did he send us Fletch's actual home address?"

"That's... ballsy," Zara says, studying the location on her laptop. The blue glow from the screen highlights the worry lines around her eyes. "Guess if things get rough we can always just go for the kitchen knives."

"He's baiting us," I counter, pacing our cramped safe house kitchen. "His turf, his rules. Like he's daring us to make a move."

"Or setting up an ambush."

"Yeah. Don't like it. Not one bit." But this is what we signed up for. Or more accurately, this is what Zara signed us up for. I don't blame her for making this choice on the fly, I just wish we had better intel—more prep. This working off the grid crap is killing me.

We spend the rest of the afternoon preparing and getting set up in our new, temporary home. Janice's place is smaller than the safehouse, but it will work for just the two of us. And now that we're no longer in contact with Liam, Nadia or Elliott, they'll be able to tell the truth when they say they don't know where we are.

I can't help but wonder how Liam's interrogation went. I've been worried sick all day, wondering if they're going to just decide he's lying and throw the book at him. And the worst part is I have no way of knowing. Honestly, he probably doesn't even know what the report will say. He'll just be working at his desk one day and IA will come over and tell him to come with them. And then he'll never see daylight again.

I'm overreacting, I know it. But I can't help myself. New Mexico was one thing, but this is so much worse. It feels like things have been turned up to eleven and I don't know how to bring them back down. I've endangered everyone by coming back here.

Thankfully, Zara is there to help me put it out of my mind. And by six, we're parked three blocks from Fletch's expansive townhome—if you can even call it that—waiting to meet our backup.

"Okay, be cool," Zara says as a nondescript panel van pulls up behind us.

"*Be cool?*" I ask.

"Yeah, don't embarrass me," she says and I can't tell if she's joking or not. We step out of the rental car and are greeted with the smell of old coffee and cigarettes as the men get out of the van. Each of them is dressed in what I'd call "combat casual." Black pullovers that no doubt conceal body armor underneath, camo pants and heavy-duty boots. One of the men, sporting a long beard and sunglasses despite the fact the sun went down three hours ago, gives Zara a nod.

"Chloe," he says.

"Wolf," she replies then nods to the other two. "Who've we got today?"

"That there's Bishop, and over there is Hawk," the man called Wolf replies. Bishop is clean-shaven while Hawk sports a similar beard and moustache to Wolf, except his is carrot red. All three men are physically fit, and from their demeanor, hyperaware of their surroundings, holding a quiet fervor about them.

"You've been briefed," Zara says. "Let's make this as painless as possible."

Each of the men nod and fall in behind us as we make our way down the street. "Are you sure about these guys?" I whisper as we reach the corner. "Wolf? Bishop? They're not just playing army here, right?" I've had experience with guys in the past who seem like they can handle themselves, right up until the live rounds start firing. That tends to separate the boys from the men real quick.

"Yeah, they're former Delta," she whispers back. "But they uh… well, they didn't see eye to eye with the Army, let's put it that way." She leans closer. "Dishonorable discharges."

"Wonderful," I reply.

"Okay," Zara says so everyone can hear. "You know your assignments. Let's get this done cleanly."

"Three-man team is light for this kind of operation," Wolf notes. His voice carries a slight Southern drawl.

"We're not expecting a firefight," I explain, adjusting my

jacket to hide the outline of my weapon. "You're here for insurance, not an assault."

"Still," Bishop adds, scanning the street for the third time in as many minutes, "If what you told us about him is true, guys like Fletch will have serious security."

"That's why you're staying outside," Zara tells them. "I'll be on overwatch from the building across the street. Emily goes in alone."

The men exchange glances but don't argue. Personally, I don't care if they approve or not. The only reason they're here is so Fletch doesn't think he can walk all over me in there.

We wait until 7:45 before Zara heads off to get into position. I hold until we receive the signal from her before leading the three men the final two blocks to Fletch's home. The Georgetown address speaks to serious money—old money, the kind that buys discretion and privacy. No obvious security presence on the street, which means it's either very good or very subtle. Probably both.

I press the intercom button at the gate. A camera above swivels to focus on me with an audible whir.

"Identification," comes a mechanical voice.

"Emily Slate," I answer. No point using the cover name I know is blown.

The gate buzzes, then swings open. As we walk up the short path to the front door, I'm acutely aware of Zara's voice in my earpiece.

"From what I can see we got three people on the first floor. Two more on the second. Assume there are more."

"Yep," I murmur. The three men stay a comfortable distance behind me, giving me space but also keeping a close eye. They're set up on their own comm, which is patched directly to Zara, but not to me. Because I have no idea what Fletch will say in there, I'm not about to give a bunch of mercenaries possibly classified information. Hopefully Zara will be able to see me in the house, and if I get into trouble, send in the cavalry.

The door opens before I reach it. A man in a tailored suit gives me a professional once-over, his gaze lingering briefly on my jacket—checking for weapons. But he doesn't insist I remove it or hand it over. Interesting.

"I'm afraid your invitation was to come alone." His accent is Eastern European, his manner coldly efficient. He smells of expensive cologne and gun oil.

"They'll stay out here," I say, motioning to the mercenaries. "But inside the gate."

He hesitates a second, no doubt receiving his instructions from a similar piece in his own ear. "This way."

I follow him through a marble-floored entryway that costs more than my annual salary. The polished surface clicks beneath my boots as we pass paintings that belong in museums, not private homes. We enter a study that looks like it was transported directly from an English manor house—dark wood paneling, leather-bound books lining the walls, a massive desk positioned before floor-to-ceiling windows.

Joaquin Fletch stands behind that desk, silhouetted against the city lights beyond. He looks exactly as he did eight weeks ago—silver-haired, impeccably dressed, with the kind of face that belongs on currency. The same face I dragged onto a hotel bed after I spiked his drink.

"Agent Slate," he greets me, gesturing to a chair opposite his desk. "Or is it just Ms. Slate now? I hear your employment status is somewhat... ambiguous these days."

I take the offered seat, maintaining eye contact. The leather chair is butter soft beneath me. "Let's skip the pleasantries, Fletch. We both know why I'm here."

A smile touches his lips. "Direct as ever. I appreciate that about you. You know, you played the part of Ms. Agostini well. Almost entirely believable."

"What gave me away?"

"Nothing," he says matter-of-factly. "But I never deal with someone unless I already know everything I can about them. Don't think I wasn't at least hoping we could get to *pleasure* before business."

There it is. He's referring to when he practically assaulted me with his mouth in an attempt to get under my dress before the drugs took hold. But he'd known the entire time. "I'm surprised you agreed to be drugged. Quite the risk."

"A necessary one," he replies, though I catch him bristle. "Theo insisted. He said you'd be able to tell. Apparently, you have quite the body count. Still, I was hoping they wouldn't act as… quickly as they did. We missed all the fun."

His casual response throws me slightly. I'd expected anger, resentment—not this almost collegial attitude. My pulse ticks up a notch.

"Cut the shit. You used me," I say, keeping my hands relaxed on the armrests. "To plant a Trojan virus in FBI systems."

"Only as a means to keep an eye on things. I was just securing my interests," he corrects smoothly. "The Bureau was getting uncomfortably close to certain operations of mine. I needed leverage."

"Your leverage got people killed." My stomach clenches at the thought of Janice, of the other agents who died under strange circumstances. "I know about the agents you've been meeting with. Agents who have conveniently ended up dead."

Something darkens in his expression, a flash of what might actually be genuine emotion. "I haven't killed anyone, Ms. Slate."

Bullshit. I want to stand up and grab that smarmy face of his and smash it into the desk. But I stay planted in my chair, my face neutral. Just being in this room, knowing this man played all of us right into his hands the last time we met makes my blood boil. "Right."

"I can see we have something of a trust issue here." He

motions to the wet bar that's built into one of his cabinets. "Can I get you something?"

"And give you the chance for reciprocation?" There's no telling what mix of drugs and narcotics he may have in that cabinet. "No thank you, I'm fine." I narrow my gaze but it only seems to amuse him.

"Very well." He proceeds over to the wet bar anyway and pours himself a glass of expensive scotch before returning to his desk. "By the way, I like your bodyguards. Very intimidating. And your previous partner... Ms. Foley, is it? She must be somewhere close. Maybe even somewhere with a line of sight right into this very room." He takes a sip of the scotch while smiling.

Something tells me even if Zara had a sniper rifle pointed straight at his head the bullet would never get there. Fletch brought me here because he's completely insulated. It would probably take a tank to break down the full security measures he's implemented here, however invisible.

"I was amused to receive Theo's call," he says. "Maybe even a little annoyed at first. But then I realized we could help each other."

"How's that?" I ask, genuinely curious. I'm here for one reason—to find out what happened to Janice. The man before me knows, but he's not likely to give up that information willingly.

"Let's get to that later," he says. "I assume you're here because there is something you wished to ask me. So please. Ask away."

I take a measured breath. I'm not sure how I imagined this meeting going, but it wasn't like this. I expected at least one of us to at least have a weapon on the table by now. But Fletch seems perfectly comfortable—at ease, even. Like this is a normal business meeting.

"What did you do to the Bureau's systems?" I ask. "That virus, what's the point?"

He nods, swallowing. "Purely a monitoring device, that's all." He replies. "Designed to notify me if my name came up in any… interesting… conversations."

"So then it's just a coincidence the Bureau has completely compartmentalized since it was uploaded."

He shrugs. "That's up to the Bureau. But I'm sure you saw what was happening before then. Why do you think I needed to monitor them in the first place? Because erratic decisions were being made. Protocol was not being followed. Normally, I know precisely how one of the alphabets will respond to any given stimulus. And yet, the Bureau had begun working off-book."

"What do you mean?"

"I'm not going to spell it out for you, Ms. Slate," he says. "Surely you saw it yourself. If not, perhaps you were part of the problem. And it's a good thing you got out when you did."

I have no idea what he's talking about—unless he means the spate of cases we'd begun to work with Theo. Of course, my department isn't the only one in the Bureau. Something else could have been happening that I didn't even see.

Then again, it could all be a farce, a made up excuse to justify his behavior.

"So you just wanted to keep an eye on things," I say. "And you were willing to put yourself at risk to do it."

"No risk, no reward," Fletch replies with a smile. "I will point out it worked. And we haven't had an issue with the Bureau since."

"Why were you meeting with the other agents?" I ask. "And why are four of them now dead?"

He takes a sip of his scotch, keeping a sharp eye on me. "In my line of work, it's important to have friends, wouldn't you agree?" I don't reply. "And who better to be friends with, than people who are sick and tired of being trodden upon by their own government? People who haven't been given their proper share in life?"

"You're saying they turned."

"I'm saying they were compensated for providing information. But when that information became less and less reliable, I needed another option."

No wonder Caruthers and Janice were willing to investigate Fletch when Theo brought them the case. He'd already turned some of our agents. They wanted to find out who and under what circumstances. *That* was the information I was supposed to retrieve from the hotel that night.

Instead, he'd been ready for us.

"Doesn't look very good for you that some of them are dead," I say. "What happened? Did you find out they could compromise your position and begin targeting them? Is that why they were put into witness protection?"

"You know, that's an interesting theory," he replies. "Unfortunately, I don't have any information about that."

He did it, then. He killed them because they could have exposed him. He must have added me to that list for good measure.

"Why did you kill Janice?" I ask. She suspected he was involved and asked Merritt to do recon for her. But she never got to read Merritt's intel.

"*Em!*" Zara hisses in my ear, but I ignore it.

"I'm afraid we had nothing to do with Agent Simmons' death," he replies. "As far as I know, that was a complete accident."

More bullshit. But I can't reveal that she was investigating him without tipping my hand. And the fact he's replying so calmly and rationally to a direct accusation gives me pause. I had hoped to elicit a reaction from him.

"All this talk of death," he says. "Let's move on to another topic, shall we?" Fletch sets his glass down, locking gazes with me. "What do you want, Emily?"

"I just told you."

He waves me off. "No, no. I mean what do you want out

of life? What do you live for? Especially now that you're no longer *officially* with the FBI. I read your file. You were as dedicated as they come. Hardworking, put your work life above your personal life. Solved cases even if it meant risking your own life or the life of others. And now all that's just…" He mimes a cloud of smoke. "…gone."

"I want to know who killed my former boss," I say.

"Let's assume you're right, and you find out. Then what?" he asks. "Imagine you get the answer to your question. Does it really change anything? Do you think they'll reinstate you once you 'solve the case' for them? Or are they just as likely to arrest you and bring you up on collaboration charges? Maybe you'll do time, maybe you won't. But you sure as hell won't get your job back."

I can't deny he brings up a solid point. My odds of getting back into the Bureau are slim to none. I'm not even sure Fletch *is* Janice's killer and if he is, I'll be lucky to prove it. It's not like the man to leave loose ends.

"You seem to be at an uncharacteristic loss of words, Ms. Slate."

"It's called thinking," I snap.

"You can't see a way out, can you?" He takes his glass and swirls the contents around. "Your old life, however altruistic, is over."

"Is this where you try to turn me?" I ask. "Like you turned those other agents?"

He leans forward. "You walked in here, alone and determined to uncover the truth. You obviously possess a set of valuable skills. And you don't work for the Bureau anymore." He pauses, I expect for dramatic effect. When he speaks again, it's with confidence.

"There's nothing to turn, Ms. Slate. I want to *hire* you."

Chapter Nineteen

I CATCH the laugh in my throat before it bubbles out. "You can't be serious."

"People in your position are incredibly difficult to find," Fletch replies, relishing the moment with a grin. "And I can guarantee you'll make more money than you know what to do with."

I hesitate, watching him closely. As far as I can tell, this isn't a ruse. He's serious about bringing me into his organization. "You realize I no longer have access to FBI files. I can't steal anything for you."

"I don't care about that," he replies. "I have the FBI under control. I want you to think bigger. More… international."

"Look," I say, doing my best to remain focused. "This isn't the reason I came here."

"I know. You came here because you have some misplaced sense of justice. But I think maybe you're starting to realize that justice doesn't exist. Not in this world, anyway. You have to look out for yourself; it's the only way to survive."

Funny, according to Zara, Theo said something similar. As much as the idea of working for him makes me want to throw up, this is something of a unique opportunity. If I reject him outright, I can forget learning any more about what might have really happened to Janice—how deep he's in with the Bureau—all of it. But if I accept, that might give me the in I need to get some real answers.

"What's the offer?"

Fletch smiles that shark-like smile again. "Three million per year as a retainer. One million per job, a guaranteed job at least every six months. Basically, you're getting paid to sit around and wait for my call."

The amount of money is staggering—more than I ever thought I would earn in my lifetime. And for a brief second, I can't help but think about what kind of life that would give me and Liam. What we could do with that—the number of people we could help.

But it would all be at the beck and call of a criminal. Someone who is profiting off the backs of the poor and helpless. And I'd never be able to live with that, no matter how much he paid me.

"What are the jobs?"

Something in his demeanor changes—almost like that night in the hotel. I can see the hunger in his eyes, the desire to "acquire" me. He thinks he has me dangling on the hook and I'm not about to disappoint him.

"Usually, nothing more than information retrieval. Sometimes security. You could even use some of those men out there as backup. But that would be at your own cost," he says. "It's a flat fee."

"And how do I know you're telling the truth and won't stab me in the back the second you get the chance?" I ask. "I wouldn't want any hard feelings over the incident at the hotel."

"Trust will come in time," he says, sitting back.

I mirror the action. "I don't know. It's a lot to think about."

He nods. "What if I sweeten the pot?"

"It's not about the money," I say.

"I know." He opens a drawer and removes a folder, sliding it across the desk toward me. "Let's call this a trial run. Once you're done, you can decide if you want to continue or not. And what the hell, I'll pay you the operation fee regardless of whether you decide to join us here or not."

I make no move to touch it. "And what exactly does this assignment entail?"

"As I said. Information retrieval," he says smoothly. "Something well within your considerable skill set."

"What kind of information?"

"The kind that you will find useful." His expression turns serious. "You asked me what happened to your former boss. For that, you need the autopsy report. I know who has it."

Despite myself, I lean forward slightly, wanting to tear open the folder and read what's inside. "Why would you help me with that?"

"Because we will never be able to trust each other unless we begin by being honest." Fletch leans back in his chair. "I know it's not about the money for you, Emily. A normal person wouldn't do the work for what you earn. What you really want is closure."

I shift slightly in my chair, finding myself uncomfortable for the first time.

"The assignment is simple. You'll visit this address." He taps the folder. "It belongs to Bryce Johannsen, one of the Bureau's coroners."

"I'm familiar with him," I say.

"According to information I found in the FBI's systems, he was ordered to perform the autopsy, then refrain from entering the results into the system. Instead, he was to keep the information secure—off site. According to FBI records, he only has the one home. It will be there."

I finally reach for the folder, opening it to find an address in Alexandria, floor plans, security information, and a few photos of Johannsen and his family. "You want me to break into an FBI Agent's home and steal classified data? And then what?" This is insane. Does he really think I'll do this? Plus, he could be lying about the autopsy. Why would the FBI want it kept off-site? I don't understand the big secret around what happened.

"You'll want to copy the data, then you'll want to get it to the proper authorities," he says. "Someone in the FBI you trust."

"You want me to deliver it back to the FBI," I say, skeptical. "Why?"

"Because, if we're going to be working together, we need to be able to count on each other," he says. "That's why this is a trial. You'll have to trust what I'm telling you is the truth. And I will have to trust you won't expose me to the FBI. Only then can we begin working together."

"Let's say I deliver it to someone I trust," I say. "But how do we prevent it from just getting buried again? Or destroyed? If there was an official order to keep it off the records, they're not just going to let me walk in there and hand it over. Especially now that I'm wanted for questioning."

He nods. "Ah, yes. The incident at Apex. Had you come to me first, I could have warned you they were being monitored. I believe your presence there may have… complicated the situation."

"You knew they were being monitored?" Then it clicks. Of course he did. He had the bug telling him.

"It's why I haven't worked with Apex for weeks now. As soon as I realized the Bureau was looking into them, I sought out other avenues. One of the benefits of… listening."

He's been using his access to dodge every bullet that's come his way. No wonder Janice went off-book to investigate him. Had she done it through proper channels, he would have found out about it. He may have found out anyway. But I won't know for sure until I read the autopsy results. Then again, if the autopsy results could in any way implicate Fletch, why would he lead me to them?

"Okay," I finally say. "You have a deal. But only if the information hasn't been tampered with. If you planted something for me to find or if it's been altered in any way—"

He puts his hands up. "Honestly, I'm as anxious to learn the reason behind her death as you are."

As I take the folder, I notice Fletch studying me with unusual intensity, his eyes moving methodically from my face to my build, even down to the way I stand.

"Is there something else?" I ask, raising an eyebrow.

"Just considering how valuable an asset you'll be," he replies smoothly.

"Mmm-hmm. There's still the matter of how to make sure this information gets into the right hands."

"Tell you what," he says. "I'll set up a meeting. Deliver it to my man tomorrow night at 9:15. I have someone on the inside who can make sure it isn't accidentally lost."

I narrow my gaze. He wants me to trust him to deliver the information about her death back to the people who ordered it not be entered in the first place?

The man finishes his drink, setting it down. "I can see we're going to need a little more trust. What if I were to tell you this Agent had no idea about my involvement, and for them, it will look like a simple handover? What if it were someone you knew? Agent Sutton, for instance."

"You don't have that kind of authority," I say. There's no way Fletch has infiltrated so deep he can craft an order for Sutton out of thin air. If he has, then the Bureau is in deeper trouble than I thought.

"Don't underestimate me," he says, his voice deepening. "I've been at this for a long time." I hesitate, unsure what to do. He's giving me exactly what I want. So why does it feel so wrong? And why is he so insistent?

Every part of me is screaming that something is off about

this. That Fletch is playing a deeper game here and I'm walking right into it. But without more information, how am I supposed to know what that is? And if he actually is telling the truth, and Johannsen has Janice's autopsy results, then I need to see them. I need to know what happened to her.

"Okay," I finally say. "You have a deal. I'll deliver it tomorrow night."

"Excellent," he says. "The address is 1001 Pennsylvania Ave. I believe you still have the phone from Mr. Arquenest's apartment. Please let me know as soon as you're done and I'll transfer your payment to a secure offshore account, along with all the access information. You'll be a millionaire by tomorrow night and you barely have to lift a finger."

"And then?"

"And then I'll be in touch," he says. "About your next assignment."

I stand, signaling the end of our meeting. Fletch rises as well, raising his glass to me once more. "Best of luck Ms. Slate. I look forward to working with you." The thought turns my stomach, but I give him a terse smile regardless.

The security man escorts me to the front door. Being in Fletch's presence feels like swimming with sharks—one wrong move and you're done.

Once I'm a safe distance from the house, I murmur into my concealed mic, "What the hell was that?"

"No idea," Zara replies. The mercs follow me out, watching my back and making sure we're not being followed. They're on edge, but not so much that they'll jump at the snap of a twig. I lead them back to the rental car, three blocks away where Zara is already waiting.

"Em, this smells like a setup," she says as the mercs head back to their van.

"And what if it's not? It might be our only opportunity to find out what happened to Janice. Even the FBI doesn't know at this point. Johannsen—he could be our only lead."

"Do you really think Fletch will find a way to get you a meeting with Sutton?" she asks.

"I don't know anything anymore," I say. "Except that my head hurts. How do spies keep all this crap straight? All these lies and subterfuge."

"Risks of the job," she says, getting in behind the steering wheel. "One thing's for sure. If you're going to break into an FBI agent's home, we need a full surveillance package. Which means I need to go shopping again."

"Agreed," I say. We don't want to leave any of this to chance.

So why does it feel like I'm taking my life into my hands?

Chapter Twenty

THE FOLLOWING morning I'm sitting in the car beside Zara, staring at the house at the end of the block that matches the location Fletch gave us. Bryce Johannsen's house, approximately fourteen-hundred square feet, two-car garage with three bedrooms and two bathrooms.

It's a modest home with clean flower beds out front that look like they've been prepped for spring. Either Johannsen or his wife must have a green thumb. I'm cataloging everything I can in an attempt to distract myself from what I'm about to do. Breaking into an agent's personal home is no small matter. What's worse is I may be doing it for nothing if Fletch was lying.

"Here we go," Zara says. A couple emerges from the front door, the woman locking it behind them. He heads for the car parked in the small driveway while she opens the garage door from the outside and gets in the Range Rover parked inside.

"He drives a Toyota and she drives a Range Rover?" Zara asks. "Hardly seems fair."

"Maybe he doesn't care about what kind of car he drives and she does," I suggest as he offers a quick wave to his wife before pulling away. Zara and I scoot down in our seats so he won't see us as he drives by. A few moments later, the Range Rover passes us.

"Okay, that should be it," she says. "Kid got on the bus half an hour ago, both adults are gone. You should have a couple of hours."

"Me?" I ask. "You mean you're not coming along on this one? I thought you were the master lock picker."

"Eh, to be honest it's getting old, breaking into all these places," she replies. "I'm not a burglar. Besides, *you* were the one who accepted the job, not me."

I purse my lips at her as she wiggles her eyebrows back. "Fine. At least make yourself useful and keep a lookout."

"Why do you think I'm here when I could be back at Janice's in a warm, comfy bed?"

I place the earpiece in my ear and give her *the* look before getting out and casually making my way to the house.

"You're doing great, you look like any other housewife in the neighborhood," Zara says in my ear.

"Shut. Up," I murmur as I check my surroundings to make sure no nosy neighbors are looking out their windows. I'd much rather do this under the cover of darkness but I'm not breaking into someone's house when they're all home. That's just asking for trouble. The best chance of finding what I'm looking for is when the family is out and I have a few hours to myself.

"Clear, go now," Zara says.

In one quick move I hop the fence into the backyard, landing without a sound.

"Looks clean, keep going."

I stay low and make my way around to the back of the house, looking for any cameras they might have back here. Fortunately, I don't see anything that looks like surveillance. The back of the property features a small deck area where a grill sits along with a table and umbrella that hasn't been used since last summer from the looks of it. The back door is a simple setup, with nothing more than a handle and a deadlock.

"At the back door," I say. "Working on the lock now."

Unlike the high-tech methods we used to get into Janice's apartment and Merritt's building, Johannsen's place just requires some good old-fashioned lock picking. Pulling out Zara's pick set, I go to work on the door and five minutes later I have the deadbolt done along with the handle.

"Look at that," I say. "Got them both without breaking either."

"Took you long enough," she replies. "Keep a watch out for the alarm system. You won't have long."

I nod and open the door, noticing a food and water dish right at the back door. There wasn't anything in the dossier about a pet. I close the door quickly to make sure nothing escapes and make my way to the front door where a keypad is flashing.

"Okay," I whisper. "It's a Securitech Panel, Model 905."

"One second," Zara says.

I watch the numbers on the small LED screen. "It's counting down. Twenty seconds."

"I'm getting it, hang on."

Fifteen seconds. Ten. Eight.

"Z!"

"The code is four-four-nine-six-one-six."

I punch it in quickly and the system confirms disarm.

"Em? Did it work? Did you get it?"

"Yeah," I say. It's only then I hear a noise behind me. I turn slowly, looking over my shoulder into the shadowed hall and only see a pair of reflective eyes staring back at me. "Oh."

"What?" she asks, anxious. "What is it?"

I take a few cautious steps forward, allowing my eyes to adjust. "It's a cat. A black one."

"Awww," she replies. "Is it friendly?"

I'm sort of afraid to find out. This cat could be the

sweetest animal on earth or it could lunge and tear my face off. I have no idea. "Um..." I reach out with one hand. "Pspspsps."

The cat turns and runs down the hallway, disappearing into the darkness.

"Guess it's not going to claw me," I say.

"It knows you're a dog person," she replies. "It can smell it on you. The filth of canine."

"I'm telling Timber you said that," as I survey the room.

"Noooo, I take it back," she says. "You can't cut me off from my boyfriend. I'm going to need him now that my real one has turned out to be such a shit."

I smile as I survey the house. It's clean, well-kept and organized. There's no reason for me to start looking in the main living areas—I doubt Johannsen would keep sensitive FBI information anywhere out here. But I do catch a few family photographs on the wall. They seem like a happy family as far as I can tell.

Following the cat's path down the hallway, I stop at the first door which happens to be a home office. "Bingo. Home office."

"Great, let me know if you run into anything."

The room is spartan, and well-organized like the rest of the house. A computer sits on a desk in front of the window, powered off. But when I touch the mouse it springs to life. "What are the odds the results are on the home computer?"

"Unlikely," she says. "If they exist, they'll probably be in physical form somewhere," she replies. "Anything on the home computer would be susceptible to hacking."

At least I don't have to worry about getting into that. But there are a lot of file cabinets and drawers to go through, including some stored in the closet. I take a deep breath and start pouring through it all.

TWO HOURS LATER I'VE GONE THROUGH JUST ABOUT EVERY file I can find in the room and there's nothing about Janice or anything FBI-related at all. It's all personal files, bank statements, taxes, purchase documents, insurance forms and so on and so on.

I take a seat in the chair that goes with the desk. "I think Fletch might be screwing with us," I say. "There's nothing in here."

"To what end?" she asks. "If he wanted to frame you, the police would be here by now and it's as quiet as a graveyard. Otherwise, it's just a waste of time."

I sigh. Maybe she's right and I'm just not looking hard enough. If I were instructed to keep something secure I doubt I'd keep it with my personal documents as well. "I'll keep looking."

Further down the hallway is the kid's room, which I don't bother with. I'll search it last if I have to. Instead, I head into the main bedroom. The cat from before is perched on the bed and sits up, alert as soon as it sees me.

"Hey there," I coo. "Pspspsps." The cat jumps from the bed and scampers around the closet door, which is only open by a hair.

"You are *terrible* with cats," Zara says.

"What do you mean? He's in my arms right now, purring."

"Uh huh. Let me hear him then."

"Fine. What else am I supposed to do? He's understandably skittish."

"Anything in the bedroom?"

I survey the area. Bed, dressers, small makeup table, and a few other pieces of furniture. "They make their bed," I observe. "Who does that?"

"I know, right? What a waste of time."

Making my way into the attached bathroom, I check for any hiding areas, looking under the cabinets and in the small attached closet. But it's nothing but bathroom products and towels.

I head back out to the bedroom and check under the bed, but it's clean. Nothing but a few pillows. Finally, I'm forced to head to the closet. I open the door all the way to find everything arranged carefully. A light inside illuminates the area, revealing the cat, sitting in the far back corner.

"Hey there," I say. "Just looking around." And that's when I spot it. A cutout in the wood floor where there shouldn't be one. And the cat is sitting right on top of it. "I think I have something. Looks like there might be a floor safe."

"Great, can you access it?" she asks.

"One second, there's a guardian," I reply.

"What?"

I bend down and put out a cautious hand. "Hi. Can you move real quick? I need to get where you are."

The cat watches me carefully; its eyes wide and reflective. But it doesn't move. Clearly this is going to be an ordeal. I reach out to move the cat but as I close in it hisses, showing me its sharp teeth.

"Did it bite you yet?"

"No," I say through gritted teeth. "I am a trained FBI officer who has faced down killers. I am not about to be stopped by a *cat*. I grab for the animal only for it to dodge me and swipe at my hand, catching the back of my skin.

"Sonofa!" I yell, pulling my hand back.

"Em! What happened?"

I look at the back of my hand where blood wells along the three claw marks along the back. "I was attacked."

Backing away from the cat slowly, I head back to the bathroom and grab some first aid supplies, washing my hand in the sink before applying a bandage and wrap to it.

"Do I need to come in there?" Zara asks.

"I got it, hang on," I say, frustrated. As soon as I'm in the kitchen I start going through the pantry until I find what I'm looking for. "Bingo." I give the bag a full shake and the cat comes tearing into the room, plants its butt right in front of me and stares up at me, licking it lips. "Yeah, I thought so." I pull a treat from the bag and toss it into the living room. The cat runs after it and I take the opportunity to head back to the bedroom closet and remove the false floor.

"Okay, got a Grant model ten-sixty," I say looking at the safe door. "Electronic lock. Looks like it might be keyed to their fingerprints."

"Thank goodness," Zara replies. "I thought this might be difficult."

"Give me a few." I pull out my small UV light and begin searching the polished surfaces for a clean fingerprint. It only takes a few minutes to find one on one of the door handles. I return to the office and grab some scotch tape and some glue. Five minutes later I have a perfect impression of the fingerprint on a hardened piece of glue, which I press to the reader. A second later it clicks open. "Ha! Got it on one."

Inside are a number of documents, as well as some jewelry. And on the very top is a five-page printout with the FBI logo on it. At the top is listed *Simmons, J.* "Z…" I say. "It's here. I've got it."

"What does it say?"

My eyes scan the page. But as they do, I find it more and more difficult to continue.

"Em? What's going on?" she asks.

I can't reply. It takes all my strength not to throw up.

Unbelievable.

Chapter Twenty-One

A HAND GRIPS MY SHOULDER. I look up through teary eyes and see Zara standing over me. She bends down beside me, taking the pieces of paper from my shaking hand.

"What is it?" she asks gently.

I can barely even register the sound of her voice.

"Here," she says, guiding me to the ground before I fall over or collapse. I'm vaguely aware of another presence in the room with us. I glance over and see the cat, watching from the doorway, its eyes boring into my soul.

Zara reads through the pages, scanning it with her usual level of scrutiny. "Oh, Em." She pulls me into a hug and holds on to me. "I'm so sorry."

It takes a moment for the absurdity of the moment to strike me. Here we are, two grown women, hugging on the floor of some stranger's home we've broken into while their cat looks on. If the homeowners were to come home now, they'd probably send us to the loony bin.

Finally she releases me and I take three deep breaths before I pick up the pages again and read them. But even as I do, the words don't seem to make sense.

From the coroner:

The cause of death appears on the surface to be an acute myocardial infarction. Despite managed risk factors, a deeper examination seems to indicate the infarction may have been brought on artificially. In fact, traces of triptohydrolazine were found in the victim's bloodstream, causing rapid coagulation of the arteries around the organ. While not conclusive, these factors may indicate foul play and should be investigated further.

"She was killed," I say. "Someone got to her and killed her. Just like we thought."

Zara nods. "Looks that way."

"Why would they want to bury this?" I ask. "What's the reason?"

"I don't know," she says. "Maybe they were trying to limit exposure. Like they've been doing ever since Fletch infiltrated the system. Maybe someone thought it might expose the Bureau—that the real results could make things worse."

"I suppose," I say, wiping my eyes. Given the fractured nature of the Bureau, it makes sense. "But who ordered it? Who would have known to?"

The look on her face tells me she's at a loss. And so am I. But this is information the FBI needs to know. "We need to get this out into the open."

"What about Fletch?" she asks. "Do you think he knew she was investigating him?" If he did, then he has the most motive for her death.

But then why would he lead us here, to this information if he was the one behind it? And help us to get it to the proper authorities? Something here isn't right—we're missing a bigger piece of the puzzle. "I'm not sure. Let's just get out of here. We don't need one of the Johannsens coming home early."

"Right, there's a copier in the office, isn't there?"

I nod. She heads off while I start wiping down any surfaces I've touched, along with making sure all the first aid materials have been replaced back where they were. Zara returns a few moments later with a copy of the autopsy. I replace the original back in the safe and lock it, covering it back up just like it was when we arrived.

"There you go," I say to the cat. "Now you have your spot back." He mews at me.

"Aww, what a sweetie," Zara coos.

"Yeah," I rub my hand. "Very sweet." We head back into the kitchen where I pull out one more cat snack before replacing the bag in the pantry. I toss it in the living room as Zara resets the alarm and we head back out the back door, using the lock pick set to lock it behind us. Less than three minutes later we're back in the car.

"That was pretty clean," she says as she pulls away from the curb. There's still no activity on the street. Either all these people are at work, or no one around here really cares about their neighbors. "And surprise, surprise, Fletch was actually telling the truth."

"Yeah, he was," I say, thinking.

"Now what?"

We have the official report, but it does us no good if someone is just going to bury it again. We need to get it into the right hands. But what does that even mean? Whose hands can we trust? "I want to see if Sutton really shows up."

"You think he was telling the truth about that?" she asks.

"I think someone is going to be there," I reply. "I'm just not sure who. We'll create two sets of documents. If the person who shows up is someone who we believe is trustworthy, I'll deliver the real report. Otherwise, they'll get a fake." I turn to her. "Is there any way you can track the location of say a padded envelope?"

"Sure," she replies. "I just need about an hour to set it up."

"Set up two," I say. "I want to be able to track them both. Just in case."

~

ZARA SITS IN THE CAR AS I STEP OUT INTO THE COOL AIR. Even here in this parking garage, I can feel the chill. We're parked about five blocks from the address where I need to deliver the package—which will be close to the J. Edgar Hoover building. In fact, this will be the closest I've been to the building since we left for New Mexico. Her face is a mix of concern and resignation. "Try not to get yourself arrested."

"No promises." I shut the door and pull my hood up over my head and shove my hands in my pockets. Walking these streets again feels both familiar and foreign at the same time. I keep my head down, my steps retracing a familiar path I've walked a hundred times before. It's funny, I know exactly which building I'm supposed to meet Fletch's contact in, though I've never paid it much attention. Other than the fact it has an ATM on the front, I don't even know what goes on in there. And I'm pretty sure it's no satellite office.

Presumably I'll see Sutton before I make it to the building. What can he be thinking, even if it is him? Does he know who he's meeting with? Or is this a kind of black-op situation we've got going on here?

Regardless, as I walk I find myself heading down a street parallel to the J. Edgar Hoover building. There is surveillance all over this area. I need to keep my head down and not provoke anyone's attention. But I can't help but sneak a look up at the building I used to work in. The building I may never set foot in again. And right there, in the window into the department where I've spent countless hours working late into the night, is Liam. His head is down over his desk as he concentrates hard on whatever it is he's working on. Why is he in the office so late tonight? Is it because IA gave him a hard time and as a result saddled him with a ton of grunt work? Or is he working on something for me, trying to find a way out of this mess? Given what I know about him, I wouldn't be surprised if either is the case.

As I sneak another glance at him, I can't help but resolve

this pit in my stomach that tells me everything about this is wrong. Even if Sutton does show up, how do I know he isn't another agent Fletch has already gotten to? How can I trust *anyone* in the Bureau right now, except the three people who have always had my back? One thing is for sure, Fletch has been pulling the strings since day one. Why should now be any different?

No, Sutton is not who I need to give this package to. It needs to get to Caruthers—despite the fact he's the one who wants me in for questioning. And just like that: it hits me. This whole time I've been doing everything I could to keep from being caught—from being found out. But that's not how I operate. The FBI wants to talk to me? Fine, then they can do it when I bring in this information myself. Combined with what we found at Janice's, we should have enough to at least launch an investigation into Fletch. I don't need him or his money. What I need is to trust the people I have worked with all my professional life. Not the criminal who is trying to tear it all down.

I pull out the burner phone, part of me wanting to call Fletch and tell him that it's off; that I'm not his errand girl. But instead, I dial Liam's number. He's here now. He can be the one to escort me in, take me into custody. That would be best for his career.

The only wild card is Zara. I don't want to make this decision for her. But she can take care of herself. If she doesn't want to turn herself in, I won't make her. In fact, I'll claim that I did all this on my own. They don't even need to know she was involved.

Fletch said I can't trust anyone at the FBI. But that's not true. There are still good people there. And I'd rather my life be in their hands than his.

I dial Liam's number, my fingers hovering slightly over the "send" button.

The second I press the button, I think the world has ended.

There is an earth-shattering *boom* that resonates through the air, shattering windows all around me and knocking me off my feet. I hit the concrete, covering my head and ears. It sounds like a jet crashing right beside me and for a few seconds I think I've gone completely deaf. Sound eludes me until I begin to hear it: a high-pitched wail or something like it. I chance a look up and gasp, my mouth filling with ash that's surrounded me, causing me to cough and hack, but I can't tear my gaze away.

There is a giant hole in the FBI building where only a few seconds ago there stood windows and walls, smoke pouring out of it like a pissed-off dragon breathing fire into the sky.

I look at the phone in my hand and realize what's just happened.

Someone planted a bomb.

And I was the trigger.

Chapter Twenty-Two

ALARMS FILL THE AIR. People scream. Glass and blood stains the concrete under my feet. Smoke nearly smothers my lungs. I cover my mouth with my sleeve just to breathe. But other than that, all I can do is stare up at the massive gash that now occupies a significant portion of the place where I used to work—the place that was my home away from home for most of my life.

Liam.

I look at the phone in my hand again. There's no way I can use it again to try and call him. It's obviously been rigged as a triggering device. This must have been Fletch's plan all along. He never wanted to work together. That explosion happened the second I pressed the send button. If I try to call another number, I could end up setting off another bomb somewhere else in the building. I need to get in there, to try and find him. I need to make sure he's okay.

The explosion is on the south side of the building, close to Pennsylvania Avenue. He wasn't in that section moments ago, but something could have happened. Or he could be trying to help. Or what if the internal damage is much more extensive than the external damage? I can't just assume everything is fine. I need to find him.

Sirens sound all around me, seemingly coming from all directions. It takes me a hot second to realize what this means. This is a terrorist attack on a federal building—one of the most important structures in the nation's capitol. They're not just sending police and fire rescue. They're going to send in the *fucking Army*. There's no way I'm getting out of this, and right now, I don't care. I just need to make sure Liam wasn't caught in that blast. Nothing else matters.

I waste no time sprinting toward the source of the explosion, closer to where the building runs parallel to 9th street, running as hard as I possibly can. It doesn't miss my attention that the building I was supposed to go into—the one Fletch gave me the address for with the ATM out front, has borne the brunt of the explosion. All its windows are missing and the frame of the building looks shaky at best. If I'd been in there, I could have easily been killed. Was Sutton in there already? Or was it all just a setup? Get me in there, and get me to call when Sutton didn't show up. The rage I feel at Fletch is only momentarily tempered by the worry I feel for Liam. The man set me up—just another one of his twisted games. And he may have killed the man I love in the process. He better pray nothing has happened to Liam, because he won't survive my wrath if it did.

Glass crunches under my feet as I sprint toward the building while everyone else runs away. I spot a couple of what look like tourists huddled behind a nearby pillar of the building beside the Bureau. One is cradling a man who looks to be unconscious.

Wincing, I can't help but stop and check to see if they're okay. The unconscious one is bleeding from a gash on the head.

"What happened?" I ask one of the women with the man.

She holds him like she's afraid if she lets go he'll die right here on the street. All three of them are covered in soot; I probably look similar.

"I... I don't know..." the woman mutters. "We were walking... and I just... I..."

"Here," I say, checking the man's head. I try to move where I can get some more light. "Let's lay him on the ground. If he's got an injury we don't—"

"Clear out of here!" I turn to see two men in suits running in our direction. They look like agents. From the other direction a DC police vehicle is coming screaming down the street. It slows when it sees the commotion.

I wave the agents over. "We have an injured civilian," I say. "We need an ambulance unit."

As they move into the light, I recognize one of them. Agent Marcus Lee. Damn.

"Slate?" he asks.

"Yeah," I admit.

Lee turns to his partner. "Here, take care of this. Get this man an ambulance." He turns back to me. "What the hell is going on?"

I shake my head. "No time. Get him some help. I'll check the building for any more injured." I turn and begin to run back in the direction of the building.

"Slate, hold up," Lee says, jogging after me. Wailing sirens fill the air around us. "You're... there's an order to bring you in."

"Really?" I ask him. "Now?"

He glances up at the building, the fire still pouring from the broken windows. For a split second I consider making a run for it. Lee is young and fit and could probably keep up. But the odds of me getting away from him and to Liam without getting shot are pretty low. Already I can hear the telltale *thump thump thump* of helicopters coming in. A pair of F-35 Raptors scream by overhead.

"Listen," I say. "Coll was working late tonight. I gotta make sure he's okay."

He hesitates before finally making a decision. "Okay," he says. "Lead the way."

We jog to the front of the building where a pair of men hold the doors open for the people streaming out, covering their mouths with their sleeves much in the same way I did. "You can't go in there!" one of the agents yells over the cacophony of sounds that have made it all but impossible to hear anything clearly.

"We need to search for injured agents," I yell back.

Beside me Lee holds up his badge. "She's with me. She has clearance." Damn. Maybe I'm not as much of a pariah as I thought. Lee is generally a by-the-book kind of guy. I wouldn't expect him to have my back on something like this. Then again, people do strange things in a crisis.

"Fire and rescue units are on the way, everyone stays out," the man at the door yells, his hand keeping me from entering. I don't have a choice; Liam could be trapped in there and I'm not stopping until I find him.

I grab the man's arm and twist him out of the way as I run past.

"Hey!" he calls back.

"Sorry, sorry, but we gotta get in there," Lee calls after us. He may have just saved me from having the back of my head blown off. We make our way through the smoke-filled hallways, passing people running in the opposite directions. The elevators won't work and when we reach the security gates to get to the interior of the building, everything is on lockdown. Officers with machine guns stand ready, helping to shuffle people out of the building.

"This way," I yell to Lee as I make an immediate right, heading around the security checkpoint. I don't know why he's following me other than the fact that he's a little younger than me. Maybe he still sees me as a senior agent instead of a fugitive. Whatever the reason, I'm not about to question it. I just need to get up to our floor. Check for myself.

Red lights fill the hallways, sirens going off everywhere as we run down an adjacent hallway that isn't in the secured portion of the building. It's the hallway that directs the tours to the memorabilia displays on the ground floor.

"What if he's already made his way out?" Lee calls from behind me. "Odds are he's evacuating with everyone else."

"I need to see it!" I yell behind me, not slowing down. As soon as we reach the area where the tour guide normally comes to meet the group of tourists, I wait for Lee to catch up, then snatch the badge from his neck and use it to open the access door. There's no security over here and just like that we're into the secured part of the building. I can hear the sirens outside and there's another earth-shaking rumble as more jets fly overhead.

Zara, please, if you have any sense, get the hell out of here. The second she heard that explosion she should have hightailed it out of there, though I doubt she did. She's probably still sitting in the garage, watching the chaos unfold. The city will be locked down in a matter of minutes and there will be nowhere else for her to go.

We find an empty stairwell and take the stairs two at a time until we're on the sixth floor where my old office is located.

Behind me, Lee stops to catch his breath. The hallway up here is empty, except for the sound of firefighters making their way through the building, heading for the damaged sections. "Why is Coll here at this time of night anyway?" Lee asks.

"I don't know," I admit. "He had a meeting with IA, because of—"

"Because they put out the call on you," he replies. "Right. Makes sense." He curses. "Branson is going to kill me for this." Branson is his CO, and from what I understand, a hard-ass. I realize Lee is putting himself in jeopardy for me and while I appreciate it, I can't worry about it right now. I need to find Liam.

We work through the maze of corridors, the only light coming from the emergency lighting system along the corridors and at every entrance and exit. When we finally reach our old offices, I burst through the doors to find the place completely empty. I run to Liam's desk, finding his computer still on—he didn't even log out. But he's not lying anywhere in a bleeding heap, which is a good sign.

I take a calming breath. He wasn't caught in the blast. He's probably okay.

But another thought immediately replaces it. What if he went to try to help? That's something I wouldn't put past him in an instant. Once he realized the building had been attacked, he no doubt headed in that direction.

"C'mon," I tell Lee, who has his hands on his hips, looking winded. Maybe I could have gotten past him after all.

"Where now?" he asks.

"Into the fire," I call over my shoulder.

"*What?*"

I snake my way through the corridors, encountering a group of firefighters who are making their way in our direction. Their masks and suits are covered in soot and dripping with water. No doubt from the emergency sprinkler systems that have gone off all over the building. But they don't pay us any attention. I thought for a second they might try to stop us, but I think they're more concerned with containing the fire.

I feel the heat before we reach it. It's like someone has opened a blast furnace inside the building and even though the emergency sprinklers are going off overhead, soaking me and Lee, the fire rages regardless. The heat is so intense I have to shield my face.

"Slate, c'mon, he's not here!" Lee calls over the roar of the blaze. People push past me and I realize it's another crew of firefighters, hauling a long hose. The one in front kicks it on and starts working to extinguish the fire. Another group approaches from the other side of the room, blasting the blaze with a compound that fills the air with an acrid smell.

"Emily, come *on*," Lee pulls at my coat, dragging me back. "Let them do their jobs!"

I scan the debris, looking for any sign of Liam—any indication he could have been in here. Of course, the blast covered at least three floors, he might have rushed to any of them. Still, I can't let go of the possibility—the chance that *I* might have caused something to happen to him. How many other people have I just hurt? How many have I killed?

Finally, I let Lee pull me away from the firefighters doing their jobs. "We need to evacuate," he calls, his face and suit drenched. I am in a similar situation, my body heavy with the weight of water. Lee helps me get back to the stairwell, leading me down and out back past the men with machine guns again. The same guy is still at the front door, yelling into a radio as emergency services have gathered outside, corralling people and setting up triage units.

A contingent of military personnel have set up around the perimeter of the building, keeping anyone from coming or going beyond the medical tents. There's no way I could get out of here even if I wanted to. That's when I see him. Liam, helping another agent to one of the makeshift tents that are still being set up.

"*Liam!*" I yell, hoping my voice will carry over the noise.

He pauses and turns, confusion forming over his face as he sees me and Lee exiting the building. He leaves the other agent with one of the nurses that are working the unit and breaks into a mad dash in my direction.

I smile, grateful that he's okay. That I didn't just kill the man I loved.

But before he can wrap me in his arms, I'm forced to the ground, ripped from Lee's arms as my face is pressed into the concrete and a knee digs itself into my back.

"Emily Slate," a gruff voice says. I recognize it as the man whose arm I twisted to get into the building. He must have finally recognized me. A pair of heavy zip ties binds my hands together and it takes all my strength not to pass out with the weight of this man on top of me.

"You're under arrest."

Chapter Twenty-Three

A COUPLE of hours later I'm shuffled into the entryway of Howard Hospital, an oxygen mask strapped over my mouth while my hands remain bound. At least now they're bound in front of me instead of behind, as I'm led into the hospital down one of the corridors by a nurse on one side and Agent Wilder on the other. Wilder, the man who tackled me to the ground in front of the building, is an older agent who works in the Cyber Division and apparently doesn't take very kindly to having his arm literally twisted. Liam tried to come with me, but SSA Rockford stepped in once he realized who they were dealing with. Rockford works for Internal Affairs and no doubt is anxious to have a discussion with me.

I doubt I'd even be here if I hadn't developed a nasty cough from all the ash and debris in the air. Despite Agent Lee's help, I never got the chance to speak to Liam or explain what I was doing there. And honestly, it doesn't matter anymore. All that really matters is he's okay.

"Agent, take a seat here," the nurse beside me says, leading me into a small room. She removes the mask and all of a sudden the scratchiness in my throat returns and I involuntarily cough. Instead, she fits me with a tube that sits over my ears and delivers oxygen directly into my nose.

"How long is this going to take?" Wilder asks.

"She needs to be assessed," the nurse replies. "We need to get her information and admit her first. I'd say she's going to be here at least a few hours."

Wilder blows out a frustrated breath. I'd ask him what his problem with me is, but I don't want to give the man any more ammunition than he already has. I need a lawyer, and fast. And I already know the first thing legal representation would tell me is to shut up and keep it that way, so that's what I'm doing.

"She's a flight risk," Wilder says. "We need to have her secured here."

"This isn't a jail," the nurse argues. "I have a hundred people in this hospital suffering injuries and we will get to them as soon as we can. For now, this is the best I can do."

"Then you won't mind if I handcuff her to this bed to keep her from running out of here," he says, pulling a pair of metal cuffs from the back of his belt.

The nurse huffs. "Do whatever you have to do." She turns to me. "Keep this on and ring that bell over there if you experience any other discomfort. We'll get to you as soon as we can."

I give her a thankful nod, being sure to stay silent. Wilder pulls out a knife and slices the zip ties off my wrists. He then pulls my right one to the side in a jerking motion, attaching me to the bar that runs along the side of the bed. "There we go. All secure," he says. I don't even bother looking at the man. Instead, I glance out the window to the flashing lights beyond. The hospital is a madhouse of activity; I can't even remember how many agents I saw. Some helping their fellow agents in, others demanding answers from people who had none.

And me, the lynch pin in the middle of everything.

Wilder searched me and took all my personal effects, including the envelope with Janice's autopsy results. The odds of that reaching the right people now are little to none, not that it matters. Hopefully Liam will find a way to let Zara know what's happened. Maybe there's still time for her to get away. I didn't see her either back at the Bureau or here, so I can only hope she found a way out.

"I don't get it, Slate," Wilder says, grabbing the remote for the small TV that's mounted near the ceiling. "What were you even doing there? You had to know you'd get caught."

I don't want to give him the satisfaction of an answer. And it's not really his business. He flips through the channels until he arrives at the news station he's looking for. The one that has a helicopter shot currently focused on the smoke pouring out of the FBI building in downtown Washington, DC.

I have to admit, Fletch played us well—played *me*. Though I have no idea how he managed to wire the FBI building to explode like that. From what I could tell, the damage was relatively limited. But the fact it happened at all speaks volumes.

Wilder turns up the sound so the news anchor's voice comes through clearly.

"—still looking at what remains of the explosion up here, Natalie. It seems crews have managed to extinguish all the flames, but it will take some time before the building can be declared safe again. Meanwhile, we've gotten word that search crews are already on site and are beginning to sift through the rubble."

"Is there any indication of how many people may be under there, Devin?" the anchor asks.

"Word from local sources tells us that area of the building was relatively deserted when the explosion took place, however two federal agents are currently unaccounted for by the FBI, along with one civilian contractor. We'll update you as soon as we learn more."

The image flips back to the news anchor, a pretty young

woman with blonde hair that's been pulled back and out of her face. She wears a serious expression, noting the grim task at hand. "Thanks, Devin. We've just learned there will be a press conference in less than thirty minutes where we hope to learn some more information about *how* such a tragedy could have occurred and who might be behind the attack. All other federal buildings have gone on full lockdown and the President has been moved to a secure location for his safety. Currently, there are no other indications of an impending attack, but word from the Secret Service and DC police is that they would rather err on the side of caution until we know more."

"Jesus," Wilder says, staring at the news program. "They're gonna crucify whoever is behind all this."

Sweat beads at my brow. Yeah, they're gonna crucify *me*. Even if I can somehow prove it was Fletch who set me up, I was still the one who pushed the button. I was the one who may have caused the deaths of two fellow agents. Not to mention I was already on the watchlist for being spotted at Apex. Without Janice here to explain all this, I'm the one left to take the fall.

Wilder *tsks* at the TV before turning to me again. For a split second I think he's going to see right through me and know I was the one who caused all this—that I betrayed and attacked the FBI. But he just sucks his lips between his teeth. "It's been a night. I'm heading to the vending machine. Want anything?"

What is this guy, my babysitter? "No."

"Suit yourself," he replies. "Don't go anywhere." He heads out of the small room leaving me alone for the first time. I can't help but think about where Liam could be right now. Is he still helping get everyone to safety? Wilder wouldn't let him come with us, though I'm sure he knows I'm here somewhere. But with everything going on, maybe he thinks it's better if he's not here to make it worse. *Hopefully* he's out there trying to find and warn Zara, or at least help get her to safety. I'm sure between him, Nadia and Elliott, they can handle it.

About ten minutes later Wilder reappears in the room, holding a half-eaten candy bar and a can of diet soda. He sets the soda to the side and fishes out an unopened one, putting it on the bed beside me.

"In case you get thirsty."

I give him a nod of thanks. I don't really know what to make of Wilder. He seems intense, but at the same time he's not such a bad guy. Maybe he was rough getting me in custody because he wasn't sure if I would put up a fight or not. I used to have something of a reputation in the gym. Maybe he figured a surprise takedown was the only way to get me into cuffs.

"Hey, you work up in VCU, right?" he finally asks, taking the last bite of the candy before crumpling the wrapper and tossing into the nearby wastebasket. I give him a glance without answering the question but it doesn't seem to matter. "That's Caruthers' unit, right?"

Why is he talking to me about Caruthers? Is he that desperate for small talk? Or is this some method of distraction?

He swallows. "Thought you should know, I saw them taking him upstairs to surgery."

My eyes go wide. "What?"

"Yeah, just caught sight of him on a gurney. Nurse said he must have been pretty close to the blast when it went off. They just got him in here."

Oh my God. I didn't even think about Caruthers being in the building, but of course he was. He always works late and arrives early. "How bad?" I ask.

"Couldn't tell. He didn't look awake, though."

My mind begins racing with the possibilities. Caruthers is a good agent, a good leader and the best boss I've had since Janice left. Could his injury have been on purpose? Could

Fletch have even engineered such a thing? And if so, how? I still want to know how he managed to wire up one of the most secure buildings in all of DC.

As I'm wondering just what will happen if Caruthers doesn't make it through the night, two more agents appear at my door. Both of them armed.

Wilder shoots a skeptical glance at me, then back to the door. "Help you fellas?"

"We're taking over security for the prisoner."

Prisoner? Really? Wow.

"This is my collar," Wilder says. "I think I have it under control. I'm going to transport her to processing as soon as they clear her here."

"No, sir, you're not," one of the men says.

It's then when the news program flips back on in the middle of the commercial break.

"—okay, we're getting word the press conference is underway," Natalie the anchor says. "We go now to Deputy Director Weiss, who is speaking on behalf of the Bureau regarding tonight's attack."

The image switches to Agent Weiss, who is dressed in a pullover and jeans, standing in front of a dais that is littered with microphones as he makes his statement to the press.

"—believe that this was a coordinated attack limited to the FBI building and the FBI building only. Based on our intelligence, we don't believe any further attacks are forthcoming. We already have teams working to determine exactly what happened and why.

"Furthermore, I have been in contact with both the DC Mayor and the President, who have both given us their full support in this matter."

"Was this a known terrorist organization?" a reporter off screen calls out, but the mic manages to pick up his words anyway.

"At this time we believe this was the work of one individual, though we're still assessing the evidence," Weiss says. My heart thuds in my chest.

"Then no one is claiming responsibility," another reporter says.

"Not at this time, no. And I'm happy to report that due to the quick thinking of some of our agents here on the ground, our suspect is already in custody."

"Is there any truth to the rumor that this was an inside job, perpetrated by one of your own?" another reporter asks.

Weiss looks uncomfortable for a half second before he recovers. "We're not prepared at this time to release the details of our suspect," he says. "That information will be forthcoming in the next few days. And now, I'm going to turn it over to Chief Randall, of the DC Fire Department." He steps back, allowing a man in a black suit with a white hat to take the stand and begin answering questions.

Wilder turns to me, then looks at the new guards again. "You," he growls. "You did this?" He lunges at me and I try to duck out of the way, though I'm limited in how far I can go. One of the guards holds him back while the other gets between us.

"This isn't for you, Agent Wilder. You're relieved," he says.

Wilder glares at me, a fire present that wasn't there before. "Yeah, I *am*," he says and storms off.

There's no containing it now. Wilder will make sure everyone in the entire department knows about me. I might as well get used to the idea of living in a cage.

Because there is no way out anymore.

Chapter Twenty-Four

I sit in a nondescript concrete room with nothing more than a table that's bolted to the floor and the chair I'm currently occupying. There are no windows in here, no way to see exactly where I am. The floor is old linoleum that looks like something out of the '70s and each corner of the room has a camera, all of them on and all of them pointed at me. At least they've had the decency not to chain me to the chair. I could get up and walk around if I wished, but I figure, what's the point? I've been in here for over two hours at least, though I don't know that for sure because there is no clock and I don't have a watch or my phone on me.

In fact, I've been outfitted with a *very chic* tan jumpsuit and a pair of brown slip-on shoes while my clothes and what remained of my effects were taken and placed into evidence. Zara would probably call this a fashion nightmare.

It's been three days since my arrest at the Bureau. I ended up spending the night in the hospital while receiving oxygen, but they determined there was no scorching to my lungs or any other permanent damage. Once that determination was made, I was whisked here, to some no-name off site facility without an official designation where I've been detained since.

Despite my numerous requests, I've had no contact with Liam, Elliott or anyone else. And I still don't know the condition of Caruthers, despite my repeated requests.

Instead, I've been placed in a single-person cell and been forced to wait. Until this morning, when they moved me from the cell to this room, where maybe I'll finally get to find out just how bad this will be.

The door finally opens to reveal a man in a dark suit. He sports a bushy moustache that doesn't quite fit his face and is on the thinner side. I spot a pair of suspenders under his suit jacket. He carries a briefcase in one hand and holds the door open in the other.

He's followed by a woman about my age, with dark black hair and a serious scowl where her mouth should be. She wears a pair of black glasses and is dressed in a similar dark suit.

Following the two of them is another man who seems more on the casual side, sauntering in behind them and taking up residence in the back of the room, leaning into the corner. He's wearing a dark tan suit and his dirty blonde hair nearly brushes his eyes. He also sports a five-o'clock shadow and stifles a yawn as soon as the door closes behind them.

"Ms. Slate," the man in the suspenders says. "I'm Agent Pendergast, with Counterintelligence. This is Agent Vostov from the BAU." He indicates the woman next to him before holding out his hand. I furrow my brow but take it cautiously, giving it a hearty shake.

"Ms. Slate," Vostov says and holds out her hand as well.

"Nice… to meet you," I say. "Shouldn't I have a lawyer present?"

Pendergast looks over his shoulder. "This is Mr. Keller, with the Department of Justice. He's here mostly as an observer but will be preparing a report for your official counsel as soon as they're assigned. As I'm sure you are aware, a case like this has special… requirements."

The door opens again to reveal a man with a dark beard and moustache, both immaculately trimmed. He's in a well-pressed suit and takes up residence beside Keller.

"Oh, and this is Agent Osgood, with the CIA," Pendergast says. "They've asked to sit in on this."

"You guys really pulled out all the stops," I say.

Pendergast and Vostov take the other two chairs across the table from me. "First of all, Ms. Slate—"

"Just call me Emily," I say. There's no point in anyone being formal here. I already know how this is going to go. I should, I've been on the other side of that table often enough.

He gives me a terse smile. "Emily. I'd like to start with you giving us your version of events as they unfolded. The Bureau is still piecing a lot of this together and if I'm being honest, we could use your help."

Wow. What a load of shit. I hope this guy doesn't do interrogations as his day job because he's terrible at it. The fact is the Bureau already has all the evidence they need, they're just trying to see how cooperative I'll be so they can gauge how much this is going to hurt them.

"Okay," I say. "I'll play along. But I want something in return. Give me a status update on Caruthers."

"We're not at liberty to discuss that right now," Vostov says in a voice that's overly calming. She's here to assess my mental state, to determine if I believe what I'm saying or if I'm lying through my teeth. She'll also make a recommendation once this "interview" is over about how much of a risk I am to the Bureau and how hard they need to bring the hammer down to silence me.

Keller over there is no doubt watching this so he can prepare his own list of charges from the Justice Department once the internal FBI investigation is concluded. But what worries me is Osgood. If the CIA is involved that means pretty much every department in Washington knows about me.

I sit back, determined to make them hand hold me through this. I'm not giving up anything, not until I speak to legal representation.

"Can you tell us what you were doing at 935 Pennsylvania Avenue on the night of the explosion?" Pendergast asks.

"I was in the neighborhood," I say.

"I see. Even though you already knew you were on an FBI watch list."

"Was I?" I ask. "I didn't realize."

Pendergast shares an exasperated look with Vostov. "Ms. Slate—Emily, we know you were aware of the warrant for your arrest. You were spotted colluding with an organization known to deal exclusively with nefarious individuals."

"I'm sorry," I say. "I didn't realize that shopping for a new security company automatically put me on the most-wanted list."

"We know that's not what you were doing," Pendergast says. "We have audio from your meeting with Mr. Delgado where you used your alias associated with Joaquin Fletch and even claimed to be working for him."

"Jesus," I say, staring at the ceiling. "I was undercover. You know, that thing you do where you pretend like you're someone else to get a suspect to talk? Ever heard of it?"

Vostov speaks up. "You had no official mandate—no case that had been approved by your supervisor. In fact, according to FBI records, you had been removed from duty six weeks ago by Deputy Director Simmons."

While that's technically true, it was part of my *other* cover. So no one would suspect anything when Zara and I showed up in New Mexico under new names.

"Who were you working undercover for?" she asks.

"It doesn't matter," I reply.

"Emily," Pendergast says, his voice sterner now. "I'm sure you know that this will go much better for you if you cooperate. You have a stellar record as a field agent. We just want to understand what could have turned things around for you. Was it because you were put on leave? Or did you have some axe to grind with the Bureau?"

"I wasn't dissatisfied with my work and I don't have a problem with the Bureau," I say, exasperated. I can't tell them I suspect the Bureau has been compromised without risking Liam, Zara and everyone else. I'll just have to bear the brunt of this alone.

"Then why would you plan such a heinous attack?" he asks.

I notice Keller and Osgood's attention shift slightly.

"I didn't plan any attack," I say.

Pendergast presses his lips together and reaches down to his briefcase, removing a tablet. He taps it a few times, turning it around so I can see it. "Security cameras picked you up in the building setting the charges an hour before they went off," he says, showing me still images captured from the internal security grid.

When I look at the pictures, I have to practically pick my jaw up off the floor. A woman, with my same build, same hair color and style and wearing the clothes I was wearing the night of the explosion is in each of them, though her face isn't fully visible. In some she's bending down, setting some kind of devices in rooms that I know had to have been destroyed in the explosion.

"That's...not me." I say.

Pendergast takes the tablet back and taps it a few more times, turning it back to me again. This time it shows me, caught on an outside security feed, making the phone call to Liam before the blast takes out the feed. He taps the next video, which shows me running toward the building, wearing the same clothes as the person in the still images.

"Next you're going to tell me that isn't you either."

"No," I say. "That *was* me. But I was never inside the Bureau until after the explosion. I haven't been for six weeks."

"That's convenient," Vostov says. "Because someone used your credentials to access the building at approximately seven-thirty."

"Guys," I say, sitting back. "Do you think if I was going to break into the Bureau and set *explosive charges*, that I would be stupid enough to use my own access credentials to do it? Why were they active anyway? Shouldn't they have been disengaged when I was identified for questioning?"

"We're looking into that oversight," Pendergast says. "But the fact remains that you were seen in the building, setting the very explosives that you then detonated from outside, using the phone seen in this video."

That part I can't argue with. "Look. Let's say I did this on purpose. Don't you think if I was about to set off an explosive, I would have stood further away? That blast nearly blew my ears off."

"Maybe you didn't realize the size of explosives you were using," Osgood offers.

"I'm not an idiot," I say. "Look in my record. Do I make careless mistakes?"

Pendergast hands Vostov a file folder which she opens. "It seems you had some issues with the Sloane trafficking case," she says.

I freeze. Low blow, Vostov, even for the BAU. "I was cleared of that." By Janice, no less. It had been at a very tumultuous time in my life—my husband had just died and I was eight months into an undercover op I couldn't just walk away from.

"Well, you were the one who asked," she replies. "What happened to your hand?"

"Stray cat scratched me," I answer. The wound has already scabbed up, but at least they bandaged it again for me.

"I see. Is there anything else you would like to say on your behalf?"

I let out a long breath. As much as I would love to explain

this whole thing from start to finish, that won't get me anywhere. They wouldn't believe me anyway and I'd be revealing that I know something is wrong with the Bureau. Hell, for all I know the same people who squashed Janice's autopsy are sitting right in front of me. And without Caruthers to back me up, all I would have is the word of Elliott, Nadia or Liam and I sure as hell am not dragging them into this.

But what really bothers me are those images of the woman on the video feeds. No wonder Fletch was examining me like he was studying for a test. He had someone ready to go on the inside, ready to plant everything in order to frame me. But if that's true, then it means Fletch really does have unfettered access to the Bureau.

"I know it probably doesn't matter and you're not going to believe me anyway, but I'm saying this so I'm on the record." I glance up at the cameras. "The FBI has a breach. Because whoever that woman was in those images, she wasn't me. I was across town for most of the evening until I arrived downtown around nine P.M. Someone else snuck in, impersonated me, and got out. Clean. Which means you have a security problem."

Pendergast glances at Vostov who only shrugs.

"You say you were across town. Where?" he asks.

I can't very well tell him I was breaking into another FBI agent's home and stealing information can I? I'm sure the report has already been destroyed anyway.

"It doesn't matter," I say, slumping in my seat.

"Very well," he replies. "Let's turn to another topic. Your partner in crime, Zara Foley."

I glance up at him, adrenaline coursing through my system.

"Yes, we know former Agent Foley has been assisting you since you arrived back in D.C. In fact, she's been very open about that fact."

They have Zara. She must not have been able to get away in time.

Wait.

Zara? Open about helping me commit crimes?

"Oh?" I ask carefully. "What did she say?"

"She gave us detailed information about your meeting with Apex," Pendergast replies. "As well as providing us with a comprehensive plan of your attack strategy. Of course, we'll be charging her to the full extent of the law. I believe Mr. Keller has already drawn up the paperwork from the Justice Department."

Keller nods along.

"Wow," I say, barely holding back a smile. "You really are not good at this, are you, Pendergast? Maybe try to be a little less obvious next time."

A frown crosses his face. "I don't understand."

"First of all, there is no master plan. So trying to bait me by telling me she gave one up is complete nonsense. Second, even if it were true, you're telling me the person who I've worked with for two solid years, who is like a sister to me, who has saved my life more times than I can count and who *always* has my back just decided to give me up? Just like that?"

Pendergast fumbles with the tablet in front of him. "Well, I mean it wasn't easy. She didn't—"

"Cut the shit," I say. "You don't have her because she's not involved in this. She's not even in the city. She tried to warn me off and I left anyway on my own. Understand? On. My. Own."

He exchanges another look with Vostov. She clears her throat. "Do you know the location of former Agent Foley?"

"No," I say. "But honestly, I wouldn't tell you if I did. You've already decided I'm guilty. So why don't we just save everyone's time and call it a day?"

Pendergast leans over and whispers something in Vostov's ear while Keller and Osgood look on. Finally, the two of them stand. "You'll be given formal representation tomorrow," Pendergast says. "I'm sorry we couldn't have found an easier solution."

"So am I," I reply.

Keller leads the way, followed by Vostov and Pendergast. Only Osgood remains, staring at me for a few minutes longer before finally taking his leave as well. I slump back in the chair, waiting for the security officer to arrive and escort me back to my cell.

Whatever this is, whatever is going on, there's not much I can do about it from in here. And without the evidence from Johannsen's house, Zara can't exactly do anything to help. The fact of the matter is we're dead in the water. Her only chance is to get out of town before they catch her in their net. I'm just glad they haven't caught up to her yet.

What I can't figure out is why would Fletch go to all this trouble to frame me? Was it because I embarrassed him that night two months ago? Because he thought he would get lucky and he ended up on the bed with his pants open instead? The man has more pride than most, and I could see that being his motivation. But the level of resources he's spent to put me in this position must be astronomical. Is he really that petty? And now that he's gotten his revenge, will he continue to infiltrate the FBI or will he move on to something else?

These questions continue to swirl around my brain as the security officer returns and places my wrists back in cuffs for my walk back to my cell.

And while I'm completely stone-faced as we walk, inside I'm screaming the entire way.

Chapter Twenty-Five

IT'S EARLY in the morning when I hear the sound of metal doors opening and animated discussion. My bed is little more than a piece of fabric-covered foam on a concrete shelf, but I've been so tired that I slept hard, and thus when I wake it's from a deep sleep—something with troubled dreams. It's one of those dreams that I never want to experience again, even if I can't remember exactly what it was. All I know is that it was bad and left a dark pit in my stomach.

"That's *not* protocol," a sharp voice says as another metal door clangs open. It's Agent Vostov.

"Look, I'm just doing what I'm told," another, younger voice says. "Do you want me to go back to the Deputy Director and tell *him* it's not protocol?"

I don't move from my shelf, but can't help squeezing my brows together. Is that Agent *Lee*? What the hell is he doing here?

"I'm going to get to the bottom of this," Vostov replies, clearly agitated. "Don't move until I get back." I hear her stomp away, her heels clicking on the linoleum floors.

"Here," Lee says. "I'm not putting my career on the line for her. This is the order. Let's go."

"Yes, sir," another voice says and I hear two pair of footsteps headed my way.

I sit up, slipping my shoes on and pulling my messy hair out of my face. I tense, unsure what's about to happen.

Agent Lee and one of the prison's security guards appear at my door. "Slate," the security officer says. "Assume the position."

I narrow my gaze. "What is this?"

"You're being transferred," Agent Lee says. "I need you to come with me."

"Where?" I ask. As bad as this place is, I can't imagine somewhere else worse. What are they going to do, shove me in a dark hole and never let me back out again?

"C'mon Slate," the guard says. "Turn around or I'll turn you around."

My body instinctively tenses again. I don't like threats. And I don't know what the hell this is. Why is Lee on a transfer job? Isn't he in Public Affairs? Did they find out he helped me get back in the Bureau and this is some kind of twisted punishment?

The guard unlocks the door but keeps it closed until I turn around with my hands behind my back. I could take him down and he probably knows it, but how far would I get? When they brought me into this place I went through two different rounds of security, and considering the windows of the van were blacked out on our drive here, I'm not even sure where "here" is. The guard pulls one arm tight and zips it to the other one, making sure both are secure. He then bends down and places ties with more slack around my legs so I can at least still walk.

"We good?" Lee asks.

"Lead the way," the other man replies. He escorts me out of the cell with Agent Lee in the front, heading back through the prison, past the interview rooms where they grilled me yesterday. I'm taken through one security checkpoint and then another before we see Agent Vostov storming her way towards us, a piece of paper in her hand.

"Hold up," Lee says, stopping all three of us. He holds a hand out to stop Vostov from getting any closer. "You verified the order?"

"I don't know what this is," she says, her face nearly red with frustration. "But I will appeal this decision. This is a dangerous individual here with a high flight risk. Moving her is extremely risky. Not to mention nonsensical. The most secure location for her is here."

"Look, Agent—"

"Vostov," she says, getting redder in the face.

"Vostov. I didn't write the order. It's like I told you; I'm just doing what I'm told. You want to challenge it, be my guest. Take it up with the director if you want. But for now, I need to make this transfer otherwise they're gonna have my balls in a vice, okay?"

Vostov looks like she wants to argue, but I'm assuming whatever is on the transfer order in her hand came from someone higher up than the person who put me here. Why they want to move me, I have no idea. I just know I'll be glad to be out of this place.

She points at me. "Fine. But if you lose her, it's your career. She's already attacked one building, there's no telling what else she's capable of."

So much for innocent until proven guilty.

"Duly noted," Lee says. "Now will you please move out of our way? We have a van waiting for the transfer."

"Pendergast will hear about this," she calls after us, but I don't bother looking back at her. I just let the security guard guide me along past the two final agents armed with assault rifles. They eye us as Lee shows them his own copy of the transfer order and they allow us to pass. We head down a long corridor to a pair of double doors that open onto a loading dock. There sits a nondescript white van with no windows in the back. It's made up to look like a regular sprinter van, but I know better. The back has specific seats for prisoners and places where they can be chained in place.

Another figure sits in the driver's seat of the van, but due to the darkened windows, I can't see who it is.

Lee leads us to the back of the van, which he unlocks with a key and opens, revealing two benches, each up against one side of the van. The benches are punctuated by small hooks in the floor and on the van's walls, where my restraints can be attached. The guard leads me up to one of the benches, sitting me down one away from the door. He secures my feet before turning me around and removing the ties around my arms. He then secures my arms to my front and attaches that to the hook on the wall behind me, limiting my movement. They're treating me like I could go off at any second and scratch someone's eyes out, though I guess that's not exactly out of the question.

Still, it seems like a lot.

"Okay for you?" the guard asks Lee.

"We're good," he says. "Thanks for the help."

"Safe travels," the guard replies and heads back towards the security doors while Lee shuts the doors on the van, leaving me alone in the cargo area. Without any lights it's dark back here. A second later the engine starts up and I feel us pull away from the site.

I take a deep breath, unsure what's about to happen. If Lee really is just following orders, then I'm likely to be taken to an even *more* secure facility. Either that… or it's something worse. Something I don't want to think about. Regardless, there's little I can do about it.

Unless…

I start pulling on the ties around my wrists, feeling them loosen ever so slightly. The guard didn't reattach them as tightly as they should have been and I can almost wrench my hand through the loop. It takes a few times and once I think I might have dislocated something, but finally I slip my one hand out of the tie, allowing both my hands to move freely now that they're no longer attached to the wall of the van.

I then turn to my feet. Unfortunately, those ties are tight—he didn't leave any slack for me to work with. I look around for anything that might be able to cut through the ties, but there's nothing.

Still, there has to be a way. I need to be free of these restraints when they open the door so I can at least have a fighting chance. I spend a solid fifteen minutes on the restraints, but they're not budging. And I can feel the van slowing down. Finally, it stops and I'm still attached to the floor.

Fine. If I have to do this chained to the van, that's how it's going to be. I reposition my hands so they look like they're still in the restraints attached to the wall as I hear one of the occupants of the van get out and walk around to the back. His feet crunch under gravel, which means we're probably not anywhere paved, like another facility. I need to be ready for anything.

The door unlocks with a sharp thud and my whole body tenses, adrenaline flooding my veins. I hold my breath and focus my gaze on the middle of the door.

C'mon. I'm ready for you.

The door opens to a bright light, brighter than I expected. We're outside, and it takes me a hot second to adjust, my eyes getting used to the sun again. But when they clear I see Liam standing in front of me, a kind of crooked grin on his face.

"What..."

He nods to the restraints around my wrists. "You got out of those already, didn't you?"

I glance down at my wrists, confused by what's happening.

"I... don't understand," I say. Agent Lee appears behind Liam.

"It's a prison break," he says. "Honestly, don't you ever watch the movies?"

Liam bends down to remove the ties around my legs. They click open, allowing me to step out of them. Before I can stand I find his lips on mine and I take a second to revel in his touch again before he breaks the connection.

"Sorry," he says. "I've just been really worried. I'm glad you're okay."

I'm breathing hard from both the kiss and the adrenaline that has nowhere else to go now. "Can someone please explain what's going on?" I ask.

Liam turns to Agent Lee. "You got this?" he asks.

Lee nods. "Yeah, you guys get out of here. I'll take care of the van. They'll find it crashed about ten miles from here. I've already got my cover story ready."

"Great," Liam says, taking my hand and leading me out of the van to an SUV that's parked alongside the deserted road. I glance in each direction; there's nothing out here.

"Where the hell are we?" I ask.

"I'll explain everything on the way," Liam says as Lee shuts the back of the van again and heads back to the driver's side. "Just get in. There's a change of clothes inside. Courtesy of Zara."

"Then she's okay," I say. "She got out."

"Well..." he says. "She's pissed. We all are."

"All?"

"Quit asking questions and get in already," he orders as he gets behind the wheel. I have no choice but to obey, hopping in the back where I find a set of my regular clothes from my suitcase, including a pair of shoes.

"Put the other clothes in the plastic bag," Liam says, putting the car into drive and tearing away from the curb. "We need to dispose of them."

"I'm assuming none of this is on the up and up," I say, getting out of the tan jumpsuit. "They're going to come for me."

"I know," he replies. "That's why we don't have much time."

Chapter Twenty-Six

It only takes us about thirty minutes to get back to the city. I still don't know exactly where I was being held, but I believe it was some black-site location close to Bethesda... and I suspect it wasn't an FBI facility at all. I have a feeling it might have belonged to the CIA.

On the ride back, Liam explains that just after my arrest, Elliott began snooping around in the internal FBI system, using what he'd picked up from Nadia to look for anything regarding what was going to happen to me. And the problem was, there was no actual record of my arrest. In fact, the system had been wiped of anything with my name on it, which threw up some red flags.

"When Elliott contacted me," Liam says, "he sounded concerned."

I tilt my head at the man. "Elliott?" The man is like a piece of stone. He doesn't generally show emotion.

"Exactly," Liam says. "Now you understand why we had to move so quickly. We figured if there was no record of your arrest, someone was planning on eliminating you. And they had you in the perfect place to make it happen."

"Pendergast?" I ask. "He seemed more interested in what I had to say than *eliminating* me."

"I doubt it was anyone you spoke with; that's just normal procedure in a case like yours."

"Yeah," I say. "Normal except for the CIA goon there listening to every word."

"Regardless, we figured you'd been targeted, like those other agents. They'd blame the explosion on you and then quietly make you disappear."

"Who is behind all this?" I ask. "Who wanted Janice out of the way? Was it Fletch?"

"We still don't know," Liam admits. "But we managed to create falsified orders signed by Weiss himself—you can thank Nadia for that—to get you transferred to another facility. Zara is monitoring all the comms and intercepting any calls Vostov or anyone else may be making about the transfer. It won't hold forever, but hopefully long enough that we can get you and Zara out of the city."

"And Lee?" I ask.

"He seemed really upset after they took you away the other night," Liam says. "He and I took a moment to talk and he admitted that he didn't believe you were guilty of what they were accusing you of. Especially after you ran back into that building." He gives me a playful shove as I finish getting dressed. "Which, by the way was the stupidest thing you could have done."

"I had to make sure you weren't in there," I say. "I wouldn't have been able to live with myself—"

"I know," he says, cutting me off. "But we don't need to go down that road. I was at my desk, I heard the explosion and I ran to help anyone I could. I got a few other people out and I stayed out. You were probably in there longer than I was."

"Do you have any word on the two missing agents? Or Caruthers?" I ask. They've been on my mind ever since seeing the news program.

"The missing agents, no. They were still sifting through the damage last I checked. But we did get a status update on Caruthers. He made it through surgery and is awake in recovery."

"Do you know why he was up there?" I ask.

"No idea. I didn't even realize he was still in the building. He wasn't over in our section the whole time I was there. I didn't even realize it was him until I saw him outside, on the stretcher."

I climb into the passenger seat and put my seatbelt on. "Liam, Fletch set me up. That phone—I don't know how but he programmed it to be the trigger."

"Zara's looking into that," he says. "What we can't figure out is *why* he set you up. What does he gain?"

"Trust me," I say. "I've been wondering the exact same thing."

∾

WE REACH JANICE'S SAFEHOUSE JUST BEFORE TEN IN THE morning. Part of me can't believe I'm back here. But I know this is only temporary. Soon the entire FBI will be on a nationwide manhunt for me, splashing my picture across every news station and cell phone they can push it to.

Before I can barely set foot in the door, someone slams into me, wrapping me in a hug that threatens to cut off my air.

"Z," I mutter. "You're gonna suffocate me."

"I should," she says before letting go. "For a while there I thought you were dead."

"We all did." Nadia stands from where Zara now has *four* laptops all hooked into each other and various other devices on the table, itself overflowing with a bevy of wires and power strips. She comes over and wraps me in a hug as well. "I'm just glad you're safe."

Elliott, who I haven't even seen since the night at the bar stands behind Nadia. "I'm glad to see the plan worked." Elliott isn't much on hugs.

"All thanks to you, I hear."

"I only did what I thought was prudent, given the circumstances," he replies. "None of us want to lose you."

"How did you even manage to find me?" I ask. "Where was I?"

"CIA black site," Zara replies. "It's not on any map. Trust me, I looked. When Liam finally got in touch with me he told me they'd taken you to Howard. From there it was a matter of breaking into the city's camera grid and looking for vehicles that left around the time you were discharged—which, of course, there is no official record of. According to the hospital, you were never even there."

"Someone went to a lot of trouble to erase me from the system," I say. "Fletch?"

"He has the access," Zara replies. "But I don't know. It seems to me if his goal was to frame you, he'd want your face on as many screens and your name in as many places as possible."

"He framed me all right," I say. "When they came in to interview me, they showed me still images of a woman who looked just like me setting the charges in the building, who apparently gained access with my credentials."

"Wait, why were your credentials active?" Zara asks. "Both of ours should have been deactivated when we went to New Mexico."

"The only thing I can think of is he—or the mole in the FBI—turned them back on for that very purpose. Counterintelligence was convinced it was me." I sigh. "And they have the phone—and Janice's autopsy report."

"We'll deal with that later," Liam says. "Right now, we need to get the two of you out of here. Nadia, don't you have a friend in Canada? We could—"

"Wait a second," I say. "I'm not going to Canada."

"Em, you can't stay here," Liam says. "They're going to use every resource they can to find you as soon as they realize those transfer papers were faked."

"I know. Which leaves us little time to get to the bottom of this. We need to find Fletch and get him into custody. He's the only one who can clear all this up."

"And you think he's just going to do that out of the goodness of his heart?" Liam asks. "Not to mention the man is under guard twenty-four-seven. How are we supposed to get to him now, especially after everything he's done? He could even be expecting some kind of retaliation."

I turn to Zara. "It's a good thing you didn't kill Theo. Not yet, anyway."

"You want to go after Theo?" she asks.

"I want to use Theo to get to Fletch. And pit them against each other."

"How?" Nadia asks.

"I'm still working that out," I say. "But Theo can lead us back to Fletch. I doubt he's still in the city."

"He's not," Elliott says. "We've been keeping surveillance on the area." He turns to Zara. "Using certain... assets."

"The mercs?" I ask. She nods. "Nice." Maybe those guys aren't so useless after all.

"There's also the matter of this mystery woman. There has to be a way to track her down. I can tell you exactly what she looks like." I hold my arms out in kind of a "like this" gesture.

"You said they only showed you still images, not video," Elliott says.

"Yeah, why?" I ask.

He turns to Nadia, speaking softly in her ear. She nods a few times. "Hang on," Nadia says. "Let me check something."

"I'm wondering if the images weren't planted for Counterintelligence to find," Elliott says. "Did any of them show your face?"

"No, just my clothes, hair, you know. She was turned away from the camera each time. But she was wearing the exact clothes I had on that day. And Fletch knew that I couldn't establish an alibi since I was breaking and entering into another FBI agent's home at the time. He set up everything perfectly."

"He did seem to put a lot of time and thought into this," Elliott says.

"And resources," I say. "I just can't believe he was willing to waste that much energy on me. And for what? If he wanted me dead, he had more than enough opportunities."

"He didn't want you dead," Zara says. "He wanted you disgraced and humiliated first."

"Yeah," I say and take a seat on the couch. Liam sits beside me. "Remind me never to go undercover with a rich asshole again. They've got too much money and time on their hands."

"Listen," Liam says quietly. "I know you don't want to hear this, but I really think you should consider getting out of the country for a while. At least until we can figure all this out."

I shake my head. "No way. I already tried that once. Not only did I almost end up quitting but it got us nowhere. Leaving isn't the answer. Even if I'm a fugitive."

"I know," he says. "But I just had to say it. Just so you know it's an option. I know you want to be strong and fight back. But there are some fights you can't win, no matter how hard you try."

"I appreciate that," I say. "I do. But I'm not letting them win. And if it means I end up back in another blackbox prison, then that's what has to happen. I can't live my life on the run, and I'm not going to let Fletch get away with this."

He places a supportive hand on mine. "Okay. How do we get him?"

I turn to Zara. "Do you know where Theo is right now?"

She shrugs. "More or less. He keeps trying to avoid my surveillance, but I always find him again. The idiot apparently doesn't realize he inadvertently told me everything about how he operates. And unless he changes things up in a major way, I should have no trouble tracking him down again."

"Except this time, you're not going alone. *Right?*" I put special emphasis on that last word.

"I mean, I could. You are kind of a heavy sleeper, Em. I wasn't exactly quiet."

"She's right," Liam says. "When you get into a deep sleep, it takes a second to pull you back out."

"Great, let's keep talking about my sleeping habits," I say, popping off the couch. "How soon can you find him?"

"Gimmie fifteen minutes," she says, winking at me before going to one of the other laptops.

"Hey, Em," Nadia says. "We might have something on these pictures."

"What do you mean?" I ask.

"Well, even with your clearance, it's not like you could have just walked into one of the most secure building in the world with a duffel bag full of explosives," she says. "And neither could a doppelganger."

"But... the building exploded," I say. "We all saw it. It's on the news."

"I'm not disputing that," Nadia replies. "But looking at the surveillance photos of the before and after on the building, I'm not sure this building did explode. At least, not from the inside like they're claiming."

"You're saying it was an external attack?" Liam asks.

"Here, look." She turns the laptop towards us. The images on the screen show stills from the J. Edgar Hoover building from local news programs, most of them in high def. "If we zoom in to the area where the explosion happened, you'll notice that the surrounding walls are blackened on the *outside*."

"Couldn't that have been from the fire?" Liam asks.

"Maybe some, but more likely it's residue from the initial explosion. Look how it's limited to only three floors and only about fifteen offices. Something like that could have been either installed on the outside of the building, or even launched from a nearby site, causing this level of destruction."

I glance at Liam and Elliott, all of us unsure.

"Look, what happens when a firecracker explodes in the palm of your hand?" Nadia asks. "You burn your hand, right? But if you have your hand closed around the firecracker, then you're looking for some new fingers. With the size of that explosion, we should be seeing structural damage here, and we're not. It's superficial."

"So you're saying no one actually got into the building to plant the explosives," I say.

"The only person who got into the building was to log your credentials. They probably left right after. Those pictures, they've probably been doctored. I'm betting the angles they show don't exist in the building. But Counterintelligence may not have accounted for that. In the confusion, they may have just assumed they were genuine because they came from *inside* the system. A system we know Fletch can access."

"It's a fair bet they're clueless," Zara mutters. "There's a lot they're missing these days."

I shoot Liam a quick glance. *Someone* clearly doesn't have a good opinion of their former department.

"Of course," Nadia says. "We'll need copies of the images to verify. I could compare them against every known internal camera location in the building before the explosion. I guarantee they don't line up."

"If they're still in the system I may be able to find them," Elliott says.

"Good," I say. "We have a plan then. Nadia and Elliott

will work on poking holes in the images while Zara and I track down Theo."

"What should I do?" Liam asks.

"Are the dogs fed?"

"Those dogs get better food than I do," he replies. Just the thought of them makes my heart ache. It's literally been months since I've seen them. I just hope they haven't forgotten me.

"Then I need you to set up the net. Assuming we track down Fletch, we're going to need some help bringing him to justice. It isn't like Zara and I can just waltz right up with him. You'll need to find Caruthers."

"He's still in the hospital," Liam says.

"I know. But he's the only one left who can corroborate Zara and my absence. We'll need his help to pull this off. You said Agent Lee was trustworthy. Rope him in if you need backup." He stares at me like he's looking for something. "What?"

"Has anyone told you you're hot as hell when you take charge?"

"Yeah?" I ask, staring up into those beautiful hazel eyes of his.

"*Oooookay*," Zara says. "There are other people here; rearrange each other's guts on your own time. We've got a schedule."

"Soon," I say, my hand on his chest. "Once all this is over." He nods. Honestly, I don't know what will happen when this is all said and done. What I do know is I'm not sitting back and letting other people make my decisions any longer.

It's time to go on the offensive.

Chapter Twenty-Seven

"THIS IS COZY," Zara says as the two of us remain huddled together on a rooftop overlooking a small park in Georgetown. We're probably only about four or five blocks from Fletch's house, an unintended coincidence, but I think it can work to our advantage.

"Better than a jail cell," I say, thinking about that tiny hole they had me in. "You wouldn't have liked it."

"You never know," she replies. "When I'm at home I like to get under the covers and pretend I'm in a cave."

"Trust me," I say. "It was not built for any kind of comfort. I'm just glad you ran when you did, I was so afraid they'd pick you up. They had freaking *tanks* out on the streets."

"I saw," Zara says. "I had to ditch the rental car cause I knew there would be no way I could get out once that explosion went off. But thankfully I managed to weave my way out of the area before the iron curtain came down."

"Smart," I say. "Leaving me behind."

She turns to me, shock on her face. "I *did not* leave you behind."

I crack a smile. "I know. Just messin' with ya."

"You're in an awfully good mood for someone who's an

international fugitive," she replies, looking back through her binoculars at the park.

"You're right there with me," I say. "There are two names on that list, remember?"

"Uh-huh," she replies, going quiet for a brief moment.

"Pendergast," I say. "He actually tried to convince me you'd flipped on me. That they'd taken you and in exchange for leniency, you'd given me up."

"Oh, he's right about that," she replies. "If I ever get caught, the first thing I'm doing is cutting a deal. Do you know how much dirt I have on you, Ms. Slate?"

"Wow, first thing, huh?"

"They're not even going to have the cuffs on before I start telling them everything from day one was your idea."

"You're incorrigible," I say.

"You love me," she shoots back. "Now shut up, here he comes." She hands me the binoculars and I catch sight of Theo making his way into the park, his hands stuffed in the pockets of his jacket. He glances around before taking a seat on one of the benches.

Zara pulls out a new burner phone and dials. Theo cocks his head, then reaches under the bench and pulls out an identical looking phone before answering.

"Glad you showed up alone," Zara says. I can't hear what he's saying on the other end, but I keep a sharp eye as Theo glances around, though he doesn't make a show of it. "Yeah, well *I* do," she says, more forcefully. "You can believe me or not, but this is your only chance. Otherwise, I go straight to my old bosses." She pauses. "Because he set us both up, that's why." She turns to me, giving me a little raise of her eyebrows at her acting chops.

"Okay, good. Meet me in fifteen minutes. I'll text the address. And don't deviate. I'll know if you do. I can see that fugly jacket a mile away." She hangs up. "Got 'em. He's mad."

"Good," I say. "I want to use that." I pause. "You sure

you're okay doing this? I know you didn't want to have to deal with him anymore."

"We need him to get the job done," she says. "That's the beginning and the end of it. If he can help undo some of this mess he's caused, it doesn't matter what I feel."

I drop my gaze. "I'm really sorry. About everything."

"Thanks," she replies. "But you're not the asshole. He is."

"Then let's go make him pay for it," I say.

∼

"THERE YOU ARE," THEO SAYS AS HE ENTERS THE SMALL CAFÉ. It's barely big enough to hold fifteen people and thankfully for us, is deserted at this time of day except for one other patron at the far end of the room with a pair of headphones on as she types at her computer.

I'm hidden behind a couple of curtains next to the entryway to the single restroom while Zara is positioned at a small table closest to me. I have a good vantage point of the table itself and Theo comes into view, sitting down across from her. "After our last encounter I wasn't about to let you back into my flat."

"That's good because I never want to step foot in that place again," Zara says. "Let's skip the formalities and get down to business. You saw the evidence. Fletch is pinning you as the fall guy for the FBI leaks... this *Solitaire* person. Emily is taking the blame for the explosion. And we both know Fletch is behind all of it."

"Look, the only reason I came here was to tell you you're way off base," Theo argues. "*I'm* not Solitaire. And Fletch would never pin this on me."

"Yeah?" she asks. "You sure about that? Because he's such an upstanding guy."

Theo leans a little closer. "We had a deal. One that I came

through on. I've been paid, all is done. Why would he go back on the deal now?"

"Let me think," Zara says in a mocking voice. "Maybe because he can't be trusted? And maybe because before now, the FBI didn't know about Solitaire. But Emily and I found references to them when we were searching through Janice's stuff."

Theo's relaxed features begin to tighten. "You did?"

"And guess what she spilled her guts to them about?" Zara replies. "They know Solitaire exists. And they're going to think it's you."

The man visibly swallows.

"What was Fletch's plan? To kill her in the explosion? Is that why he pointed us to that evidence? Because he thought it would be destroyed in the explosion?"

"I..." he hesitates and trails off.

"Thought so. But because she got arrested instead, *and* the fact we'd already done an investigation, that threw a wrench into things. Let me guess, he's already out of the country."

Theo doesn't reply.

"But if he can set you up as the fall guy, the one who orchestrated it all, they won't extradite him," Zara says. "Still think you can trust your *deal*?"

Theo huffs. "Okay, so what do you want me to do? It isn't like he gave me anything to use against him. He's not stupid."

"I want to know where he is and where else he might go when he's on the run," Zara says. "Because I'm going after him."

He leans forward again. "You can't do that." He reaches one hand across the table in a feeble attempt to connect with her, but Zara is having none of it. "He's dangerous."

"Don't you think I know that," she growls. "But no one tries to kill my best friend and gets away with it. We're going to clear Emily's name and get to the bottom of all this if it kills me."

My heart swells. It isn't often you hear someone speak so passionately about you. I also think some of her anger at him is driving this discussion, that all the hurt and pain he's caused her is coming back out as rage. And if Theo isn't careful, he's going to get fried to a crisp.

He shakes his head. "No, I'm out. Maybe I can't protect you, but I'm not going to stay around here and be someone's fall guy." He stands to leave. And while Zara could probably tackle him, I'm afraid she might rip his face off in the process and we still need him alive. Time to go to plan B.

I pull back the curtain just as he's about to leave. "How about you stay, Theo? Let's have a cup of tea." I pull another chair from the table next to them and take a seat in it as Theo slowly lowers himself to the seat. I signal to the barista who comes over to take our orders.

"Three earl grey teas, one with sugar," I say.

"Anything to eat?" she asks.

"A scone," Zara adds, though she doesn't take her gaze off Theo. He is unintentionally pulling back into his seat in order to avoid that gaze.

As soon as the barista is gone he turns to me, cautious. "You… got out?"

"Yep," I reply. "I cut a deal. Just like you're going to do. And maybe, just *maybe*, you won't spend the rest of your natural life in jail."

"You don't have anything on me," he says, though he's not as convincing as he probably hopes.

"We have aiding and abetting a known criminal," Zara says. "Not to mention conspiracy. You were the one who set up our meeting with him, you were the one who convinced us Fletch was a threat to the FBI and that the operation needed to go forward. And you were the one who made sure we got the flash drive in our possession."

"The FBI approved that operation," he says. "If they

arrest me for that they'll have to admit culpability. I doubt given the current political climate—"

"Shut. Up." Zara points at him, deadly serious. He does as she says.

"Here's the deal, Theo," I say as the barista brings over our teas, one with a cube of sugar on the rim of the plate. "We already have all the evidence we need. And you're not walking back out of this café a free man. There are eight agents already stationed around the building, which leaves you with two options. Go out that door, guns blazing. Or allow us to escort you out in handcuffs. It's your choice."

He shifts his eyes to the woman on the laptop who looks up at exactly the right moment. I couldn't have planned that better as it causes a visible change in him. He slides his eye over to the barista, who is in the middle of preparing Zara's scone.

"No way out," I say. "What's it going to be?"

"If I tell you his location… I want immunity," he says. "And a full pardon."

"And I want a purple unicorn that poops rainbows," Zara says. "You tell us where to find Fletch, and maybe we'll talk to the Attorney General."

Theo generally isn't the kind of person to wear his emotions on his sleeve. I've seen him in more tense situations than I can count and he's always managed to retain his cool. But not here. Sweat beads have formed on his considerable brow and he looks like the slightest sound might make him jump. I'm not sure if it's Zara or the situation, but he is *nervous*.

"What will Fletch do if he finds out you've betrayed him?" I ask.

"Let's just say it's a good thing I don't have any living family," the man replies.

"Theo," Zara says, leaning across the table. "You owe me this. Do the right thing."

The fight seems to go out of him. Whatever his flaws, it's clear he still cares for Zara. Maybe he felt like he didn't have any other choice but to work with Fletch, or maybe he thought he could play both sides and get away with it. But what he didn't realize is Zara isn't the kind of person who's ever going to tolerate that. As soon as he made that decision, he cut her out of his life forever.

"Okay," he says. "But you need to explain that I am *not* the mole. Whoever Fletch is working with, they have access way beyond what I could ever get. I was only ever a contractor, I had the lowest level of clearance. I had to get a special pass to use the facilities, remember? There is no way I could have broken into the system."

"Then who is it?" I ask.

"If I knew, I'd tell you. All I know is it's someone who has a high clearance. You already know the name."

"A current agent?" I ask.

"I don't know."

"Fletch knows who Solitaire is," I say.

He holds out his hands. "If anyone does."

"Okay. Where do we find him?" Zara asks.

Theo bends over the table, not looking at either of us. "Most of the time he operates out of his villa in Italy. He's probably there."

"Do you have an address?" I ask. Italy. That's not going to be easy.

He slides a napkin over and scribbles the address on the back. "If he's not there, he'll be at a chalet in Switzerland that he rents out. But he's probably at the villa. It has more security—especially if he knows you survived, which is why I assume he left in the first place." He hands the napkin to Zara. She pulls out her phone and immediately begins punching in the address.

"What should we expect when we arrive?" I ask.

"An army," Theo replies. "But he won't be expecting you to show up at his front door. You might be able to pull it off."

The barista brings over Zara's scone. It sits untouched on the table.

"You're coming with us," Zara says, still looking at her phone.

"What? Why?" he asks.

"This place is a compound," she replies. "I assume you've been there. Which means you're going to get us in and help us find him."

"Wait, hang on a second," he says. "I didn't sign up for that. You can't *make* me go anywhere."

"Wanna bet?" I ask. "Otherwise we hand you over to the FBI right now and you can argue your case *without* our help." I don't like the idea of taking him with us, but if Zara thinks we need him, then we may not have a choice. We'll be heading into a completely unknown area—we'll need all the intel we can get. We had planned on just taking him back to the safehouse and keeping him there until we had Fletch in custody and then delivering them both at the same time, but that may not be an option. We'll need to keep a sharp eye on him to make sure he doesn't try to warn Fletch we're coming.

"Okay, love. You win," he finally says and sits back. "What's one more death-defying adventure?"

"That's the spirit," I say. Zara pulls out her phone and makes a fake phone call, warning off the agents we had "surrounding" the place. She's pretty convincing at it as well. She motions to the barista for a baggie as I throw a twenty on the table.

"But once all this is done, you'll fulfill the bargain," he says. "I want a letter in writing before we leave."

"Sure," I say. "We'll get right on that." I don't care what this man says, he's going to help us whether he wants to or not.

He seems to consider arguing for a second before his shoulders slump under Zara's hard stare. She's beaten him down so bad he doesn't even want to fight anymore.

And honestly, that's the best revenge of all.

Chapter Twenty-Eight

IT'S BEEN a while since I've been on a plane. And never across the ocean before. Growing up in a little town in Virginia, we didn't take very many vacations. And the few we did were within a couple hours' drive of our house. And while I've been all over the country in the course of my job, I've never actually been *out* of it before. I don't really count St. Solomon, because it's still a territory. But this is an entirely different country, with an entirely different language. And all we have to do is find our man, subdue him, and bring him back in a place where we know no one, have no contacts or help and can't go around asking too many questions. Otherwise, we'll attract the wrong kind of attention and the last thing I want is to be flagged by the *Carabinieri*.

It took another day, but Zara managed to get us fake passports that matched our current fake IDs, though they were expensive. Between that and three tickets to Italy, she's just about used up all her foot money.

Elliott believes he is close in finding the evidence we need to help prove my innocence in the planting of the bombs, but he keeps running into roadblocks, despite Nadia's help. I informed them of the plan and that we would hopefully be back in two days with Fletch in tow, but if we weren't to release all of Janice's information to the one person we could trust: Caruthers. Liam managed to get in to see him at the hospital and he is awake and responding, but he won't be back to work for a while. He caught the edge of the blast and suffered a collapsed lung, which thankfully, they managed to re-inflate.

Still, he's our best chance for repairing the damage done to the FBI. He doesn't know anything yet, of course because I want to present all of Janice's evidence with both Fletch *and* Theo at the same time. Deliver the whole package all at once. That's the only thing that might begin to undo some of this damage. I don't expect to get my job back, or to ever work in the intelligence community again, but at least that way I might avoid jail time. I want to clear Zara's name too—she was only doing what she'd been assigned to do: protect me. She just took it farther than most would.

Needless to say Liam wasn't happy about the three of us jetting off together to Italy, but he didn't have much choice. It isn't like he could have come with us because we need him there, making sure everything goes smoothly for our return. He's the one who is going to get us a face to face with Caruthers, despite the massive security around the man.

It also feels weird to be flying as a civilian. The last time I was in an airplane I had to check my weapon, but at least I still had it. Now, I have nothing. But Theo has a contact in Italy who can help us out so we don't go to Fletch's completely unprepared.

As the man sits between us, with Zara on the far side looking out the window, I can't help but feel nervous. I don't know if he still buys the whole routine or if he's just playing along at this point, but what I do know is we can *not* let Theo out of our sights from the moment we land until we arrive back in DC. He may be planning an escape or a trap of some kind and we need to be careful. I don't like relying on him for anything, much less a means to get into Fletch's compound. But we also don't really have a choice. Zara spent hours researching the place, only to find that all construction documents or any pictures of the interior of the home had been scrubbed from the web. Probably a pre-emptive move by Fletch to make sure no one could ever compromise his security.

Eventually, the long flight begins to wear on me and I begin to drift off. We took the only daytime flight, which means it's an early morning heading out, but by the time we land it will be nighttime, despite only being in the air nine hours. So not only am I fighting jet lag already, but I'm also exhausted. This past week has been one of the most stressful of my life—especially considering I was nearly killed and arrested. And now we're headed halfway around the world to try and capture and bring back an international criminal in the hopes we can somehow prevent the organization I've spent my adult life serving from completely collapsing. That, and find justice for the woman who was more than just a boss to me. The only mother figure I'd had in my life since losing my own as a young teen. I never even realized how much I'd relied on Janice until she was gone. She was the person who could fix it, whatever "it" was. And even though she wore a hard exterior, probably shaped from years and years of slamming up against closed doors and walls, she was one of the most supportive people I've ever had in my life.

I'm really going to miss her.

"Good evening from the flight deck," the pilot says over the plane's intercom. "Just to let you know we're about a hundred miles or a hundred and sixty kilometers outside *Aeroporto Internazionale di Valbruna Alta – Giovanni Tassi* and will be landing in approximately twenty-five minutes. The temperature in Valbruna Alta is a cool fifteen degrees Celsius and weather conditions are clear. We expect a smooth landing."

I blink a couple of times, coming fully back to consciousness and glance over to see Zara practically has her hand on Theo's arm. Not for any reason other than to keep him where he is. She gives me a wink. "Figured you could use some shut-eye. I've been keeping an eye on him."

"By not letting me go to the toilet, by God," Theo says. "You'd rather I just wet the seat right here?"

"You're not going anywhere I don't have eyes on you," Zara replies.

"And just what am I supposed to do? Parachute out of the bottom of the plane?" he asks, incredulous.

"I wouldn't put it past you," she replies with a grimace.

Forty minutes later we're on the ground and moving through customs, using our fake passports—though Theo's is real enough, at least *one* of his real ones—and making it through without any issue.

Thankfully we packed light and are keeping all our bags with us as we head toward the taxi station outside the airport. The sliding glass doors hiss open and the chill of the evening sweeps in under my coat. It's colder here than I expected. The air is damp with the residue of a recent rain, but it's cool and crisp, smelling faintly of diesel and distant woodsmoke. There's a trace of pine, maybe from the nearby hills and the tang of espresso drifts into my nose from a nearby café.

"The first place we'll want to hit is Giovanni's," Theo says. "He'll have the hardware you need for the job. But it won't be cheap."

"Good," Zara replies. "Because you're buying. You're the one with all the money, remember?"

Theo huffs but doesn't say anything else as we wait for a car. The sound of mopeds dominates the area, and the taxis waiting for passengers are small, looking like they'll barely fit the three of us.

"Should we spring for a rental?" I ask. "That compound of Fletch's isn't anywhere near the city."

"Not here," Zara says. "Too open. We'll see if Theo's

contacts can't get us some wheels. I want to put our names on as few things as possible."

"Good point."

I have to admit, this place isn't what I expected. I was thinking Valbruna Alta was a bustling metropolis, but this is almost quaint. Obviously, there are a lot of shops, hotels and businesses around the downtown area, but that doesn't comprise more than a few blocks. Soon we're among the old structures, endless buildings that turn and twist in crooked ways, bordering streets barely wide enough for two people to walk side by side. The taxi takes us through areas I'm sure will be too small to fit, but they manage it anyway. It's a clear night, and I can see more stars here than I expected. The rest of the place is wrapped in the warm glow of streetlights and windows, as if the whole city is a warm hearth. Finally, the cab pulls up to a nondescript alleyway.

"*Tu sei qui,*" the driver says.

"*Grazie,*" Theo says, handing him a tenner. We get out, each of us with barely more than a backpack but as we do, I'm assaulted with the smell of cheese and something spicy. My mouth can't help but to water.

"We *have* to get something to eat before we leave," Zara says. "Not those crappy energy bars we grabbed in the airport. Like *real* Italian cuisine."

"I know the most beautiful spot," Theo offers. "Overlooks Lake Como. Completely outdoors and all the food is made right here."

"Yeah, you're not going," Zara replies. "You'll be tied to a radiator somewhere."

"Now is that the way to treat an ally?" he asks. "I'm here as a favor."

"You're here because you want to save your skin," I say. "Let's just get this over with. I'm not going to be able to eat until we have Fletch in custody."

"About that…" Theo begins.

"What now?" Zara asks. It's not hard to tell she's exhausted; we both are. We've been running on fumes for days, and the trip hasn't done us any favors. At some point, our bodies are going to just give out. I just hope we have Fletch before that happens.

"How exactly are you planning on... escorting him out? They're not going to just let us waltz in there and take him."

"Ideally, we go in and get him without anyone figuring it out," I say. "But more than likely we'll need to... subdue a few people."

"You mean kill them," Theo says.

Zara and I exchange a glance.

Theo smiles. "Yes, welcome to the world of international espionage. Before you had your badges to protect you. Now, you kill someone... that's on you. And because you're both fugitives, you're not looking at a rosy future if they end up adding murder to your list of... discretions."

"Just show us to the shop," I say without acknowledging his comment. I've been trying to work out just how we can get to Fletch with the fewest amount of casualties possible, but no matter which way I work it, it always goes wrong. *Someone* is going to spot us coming or going or both and they're probably going to take a shot at us. Hell, knowing Fletch, they'll probably take a lot of shots.

Theo leads us down the alleyway. A few lights illuminate the space and when I look up, the buildings seem to crowd in above us, like they're crushing us into this little space. Few windows or doors are open on this side, though light leaks through those that exist. Beneath our feet, the cobblestone is worn and wet. It's hard to imagine how much has happened in this place and just how old it is. This place has probably existed for two thousand years or more.

"Here we go," Theo says as we arrive at a large wooden door inset into its frame. "Giovanni's."

From what I can see there is no signage, no indication this

is a business at all. But given this person deals in illegal weapons, I wouldn't think they'd want to go advertising their location. This is something that's only passed around to those in the know.

Either that, or it's a trap.

"What do you think?" I ask Zara.

She takes one look at Theo and lowers her gaze. "I can hold him in a headlock if that would help."

"No, just…" We don't have a choice. We'll have to trust Theo at some point. It's either that or do what Zara says and take him back to a hotel and chain him to the radiator.

I take a deep breath and knock on the wooden door.

Chapter Twenty-Nine

THE DOOR OPENS to reveal a large man with a bushy moustache as wide as his entire head, which itself is as bald as a bowling ball. He wears a heavy leather apron under which is concealed a handgun and not very well. He isn't moving for the weapon yet, but I have no doubt he could have it trained on us in a matter of seconds.

"*Che cosa?*"

Theo steps around me. "*Gio. Sono Theo, ricordi?*"

The large man narrows his gaze. "Theo." The word comes out thick and heavy, like a lead weight.

"I'm here to collect on that favor you owe me," Theo says. "I've got a job that needs doing."

Giovanni—or who I assume is Giovanni, looks past Theo to me and then Zara. "Friends of yours?" he says in English, though he has a heavy accent.

"Business partners," Theo says. "Just need a couple of things."

The man seems to consider it for a moment before finally stepping aside and allowing us in. Apparently this is his home, as it's decorated as such. A small couch and TV sit on one side of the room, while a kitchen takes up most of the back. A set of very narrow stairs leads up to the second level, though I can't imagine with his broad shoulders he can get up them without turning sideways.

Gio closes and bolts the door behind us, unties his apron, which reveals a Glock 9 in his belt. He walks through the living room and opens the door to what looks like a closet. Except, instead, it reveals a small stairway that leads down.

"Come," he says.

I catch Zara sniffing the air for whatever Giovanni was cooking before we interrupted him, but I grab her arm and follow Theo downstairs.

Unlike the rest of the house, the basement is completely modern. I'm honestly shocked when we walk downstairs. The ceilings down here are higher than they are on the main level, and all the walls and floor are finished in high-end materials. Bright, fluorescent lighting gives the place a clean, modern aesthetic and for a second I feel like I've walked into a sports car showroom.

"Over here," Gio says, leading us to the back of the room where a large counter sits. It looks to be made of a solid piece of black marble, though that can't be. There's no way anyone could have gotten it down here. Behind the counter are large cabinets with sleek, metal doors. "What do you need?" he asks.

"Just a couple of handguns," Theo says. "One for each of us. And some flashbangs if you have them."

"I got them." Gio presses a button somewhere on the underside of the counter and the two cabinets behind him click before turning completely around to reveal they're holding a bevy of weapons. A Sig Sauer P226 Legion, Staccato P and an Uzi 9mm are the first things I notice. But there are also a couple of revolvers. On the other side of the cabinet are six M75 Balkan "egg grenades," a pump-action shotgun, a pile of *granata stordente* and a taser.

"We'll take three Sig Sauers and two of the flashbangs," I say. "And the taser. What's the voltage?"

"It's adjustable up to fifty-thousand," he replies.

I don't think we need enough voltage to kill an elephant. Just to stop someone for a few minutes. "Great. And thirty extra rounds."

"Just thirty?" Theo asks.

"That's ten apiece," I say. "We're not going to fight a war. If any of us has to fire more than ten times, we're dead anyway."

"Fair enough," he says.

"Oooo," Zara says, staring at one of the cabinets. "Is this a fully-automated Glock 18? I thought they were outlawed."

"All of this is outlawed," Gio says.

"Fair point. How much you asking?"

"No, I think we have quite enough," Theo interrupts. "What do I owe you for this, Gio?"

"Prices have gone up," he replies. "It'll be ten."

I catch Theo wince. "Sure. Same account?"

"Always." Theo takes a second on his phone while Zara watches carefully to make sure he's not sending off any errant messages.

"Sent," he says. "Thanks, Gio. Nice doing business with you." He shakes the man's hand before Gio starts handing over the weapons.

"There is one other thing," I say. "We need a ride. Something… inconspicuous."

"Purpose?" Gio asks.

"Extraction. We're going in to get someone and we need to make sure we have room to pull him out and get back to the airport."

Gio hooks a thumb over his shoulder. "Aston Martin in the back. I could rent out to you for say… five."

"Done," I reply.

"But," the large man says. "Any damages will cost extra."

I nod to Theo. "Pay the man."

Theo sighs and goes through the process again. "There."

Gio reaches under the cabinet and comes back out with a key fob. "It's behind the alley, one block over. You'll see it parked with some other cars." Theo begins to take the keys, only for Gio's large hand to clamp over his, causing him to wince. "I know what it looks like. Don't try pulling one over my eyes."

"Wouldn't dream of it," Theo replies.

"Actually," I say, taking the keys. "I'll drive. You navigate." I take the weapon he's provided and check to make sure the chamber is empty and it doesn't have any rounds before putting it in my belt under my jacket. I'll load it once we're in the car. "Thanks."

"You need more, my door is open to repeat customers."

We head back out, through the man's living room and into the nondescript alleyway again. I finally feel more like myself now that I've got at least the bare amount of protection on. The taser is heavy in my pocket.

"You really expect to use that thing?" Zara asks.

"Figured it couldn't hurt," I say. "Especially since we're trying to limit our body count."

"It will never happen," Theo says, a smile on his face. "If you want to get to Fletch, you're going to have to go through a few people."

"And if we don't just remember who goes down with us," I say.

"Maybe," he replies. "But then again, maybe I just stay here. You did just get me out of the country, after all. It would be a shame to go back so soon."

No wonder he was so amenable to helping. With Fletch gone, Theo probably wanted nothing more than to get out of town—and we were that opportunity for him. But unless he's planning on running, I don't see him getting away from us. At least, not until we get Fletch into custody. While I would love to bring Theo in too, it's not a prerequisite. Though, surprisingly, he hasn't tried to stab us in the back yet. Maybe he's betting we won't make it out of Fletch's place alive. And honestly, that's probably a solid bet. Going in there is very risky, but I don't see another way. The man isn't coming to us, so we need to go to him.

It only takes us a few minutes to get around the corner and find the correct vehicle. Thankfully it has a large section in the back where we'll be able to keep Fletch. Honestly, I don't know exactly *how* all this will go—if he'll come quietly or we'll need some kind of sedative—but I do know that I'm not leaving this country without him. He played me, put a target on my back and tried to not only ruin my reputation, but destroy everything I hold dear.

And he's not getting away with it.

"You're navigating," I tell Theo as I climb into the driver's side. The vehicle is lower to the ground than I thought and a fair bit sportier. And when I turn over the engine, it practically roars to life.

"Is this… a sports car?"

"That's Italy, love," Theo says. "If it's not a Vespa it's a road rocket." I'm gentle pulling the car out of the space and make sure to watch the narrowness of the alleyway that somehow accommodates two-way traffic despite being only the width of one vehicle. Theo leads us out of town, with Zara double-checking that we're heading in the right direction from the back. As soon as the city is behind us and there's nothing but farmhouses and tall trees out here, I open the car a little more, feeling it hug the curves of the land. The landscape stretches out before us, and thanks to the full moon, I have a beautiful view of the countryside and the Alps beyond. It's almost impossible to believe an international criminal lives out here in all this beauty.

But then again, it's exactly the kind of place I would expect someone like Fletch to live. He loves flaunting his money—of making sure people know exactly who is in charge by how big his house is or how fast his cars are.

In fact… that was one of the first things he said to me that night in the hotel. He wanted to show me one of his rare vehicles, to show me just what it could do. But if he knew I was an FBI agent, was that just him acting then too?

In all of this, I've failed to consider one very important piece. The fact that Fletch may have been lying when he said he knew who I was. We spent *weeks* doing surveillance on that man, inserting me into his life in different areas, social events, clubs, etc. Zara and I were meticulous in crafting the persona of Emily Agostini—an alluring, single woman making it on her own in the import/export business. Someone who would appeal to Fletch. All in an attempt to get into his inner circle, to get him to let his guard down long enough for us to find out just how big of a threat he was to us.

And then…to find out that it was all a lie. That he played us, practically invited us in, set the whole thing up so we would bring a Trojan Horse into our organization and make it vulnerable.

And yet… something doesn't feel right. Fletch himself admitted that he actually was drugged that night. And knowing what I know about him, that doesn't seem like something he'd willingly do. He wouldn't let his guard down like that around anyone, especially not a woman he barely knows. I don't care if my alter-ego had the best reputation in bed of anyone in the world, Fletch isn't stupid.

Which means… he's been lying this whole time. But why? I shoot a careful glance at Theo, who is looking straight ahead, a relaxed smile on his face. Ever since we arrived he's been in a better mood than I would like and I'm not sure why. Something about all this doesn't sit right with me.

Regardless, Fletch is the man who provided the device that has nearly taken down the FBI. We need to bring him in.

Maybe I can find out what's really going on once we get him in an interrogation room.

My stomach sinks at the thought. *I* won't be the one interrogating him. That job will fall to someone else. Maybe I can get something else out of him before we turn him over. Just for my own personal sanity.

"Okay," Theo says. "There will be a turnoff up here in about a hundred meters. It's hard to see and there is a gate which will be locked."

"Then we'll drive right past it," I say.

"Right. But further down the road is another path that the service personnel use. It also has a gate; however, it's hidden in a grouping of trees. I suggest we park outside the gate there and make our way to the house. That part of the property isn't as heavily monitored as the main entrance."

"Z?" I ask.

"Yeah, looks like he's telling the truth," she says. "I see the service road on the satellite. Should be a couple hundred yards from the gate to the compound."

"There it is," Theo says.

Off to our right, a large building rises from the landscape with both flat and pitched roofs. As we get closer, I realize it's not just one house, but many, or at least one very large, connected house. Lights glow from every window and even at this distance I can see men standing guard on different levels.

Theo was right, Fletch isn't taking any chances.

We pass the main entrance like any other car on the road, but as we drive past I notice that it's lined on either side by large Mediterranean cypress trees. Those lead up to a grand courtyard where a fountain lit up by spotlight sits, the water spewing high into the air. A couple of cars sit parked in the driveway but I have no way of telling if they belong to Fletch, his employees, or guests.

"Is he supposed to have any company this evening?" I ask as I look for the service road ahead.

"I'm not his calendar, love," Theo says. "But one thing is for sure, the man is definitely home."

"Why do you say that?" I ask.

"He only runs the fountain when he is," Theo replies. "Kind of like when the Queen flies the flag at Buckingham."

I snort. Appropriate given what I know about Fletch.

The service road appears quickly and I slow, pulling in with the lights off and park next to a large grove of trees. The car isn't visible from the road, nor is it right beside the service gate. A camera sits beyond the gate, but it looks like it's designed to catch license plates. It should be easy enough to dodge.

The three of us exit quietly and Zara hands me the weapon she loaded along the way.

"Where's mine?" Theo asks.

"You don't get one," she replies. "If someone starts shooting at you, do everyone a favor and block the bullets with your body."

"I'm not going in there without some kind of protection," he replies.

"Here," I say, holding out the taser. "At least if you use it against one of us it won't kill us."

"That hurts, Emily, it really does."

"Shut up and take it or I'm cuffing you to the steering wheel," Zara hisses.

Theo reluctantly takes it.

"Okay," I whisper, even though there's no one around to hear us. "Theo gets us into the house without getting spotted… hopefully. Once we're inside, we locate Fletch, bind and hood him, and then we get the hell out of there. There's no way we don't run into resistance, so we're shooting to warn or disarm only."

"Got it," Zara says.

"If anything goes wrong, we use the flashbangs to cover our escape. We rendezvous back here as quickly as possible."

"And if we don't have Fletch?" Zara asks.

I don't have an answer for her. This all depends on us getting him. There is no failure option. If we don't get him in custody, we might as well never go back home.

She seems to understand without me saying a word. "I have an IR jammer that should take care of any local cameras for a few minutes," she says. "But anything else we'll have to deal with as we go."

"Works for me," I say, turning to Theo. "You cross us—"

"I know, I know," he says. "I'm starting to regret taking this deal."

"Good, I want you scared and alert," I say. "Ready?" Zara nods. Theo gives a reluctant nod as well.

"Then let's get it done."

Chapter Thirty

I TAKE the lead up to the house with Theo behind me and Zara bringing up the rear. Thankfully we're all dressed in dark clothes, while Zara has on a hat that obscures her bright hair. We move quickly and with purpose, crouching as we make our way up parallel to the service road. I'm on high alert for any additional cameras when I spot our first security officer walking the perimeter. He's dressed in black as well, except he's wearing a dark red tie. He's not carrying any obvious weapons, but from the way his suit coat bulges as he strides, I can tell he's packing.

He says something in Italian as he walks and I assume he's mic'd. He strides past us on the other side of a thick hedge.

Zara gives me a hand signal. *What do you want to do?*

I tap the side of my clavicle.

She nods. In one deft move she hops the hedge behind the guy and as soon as he turns she has him in a choke hold, putting pressure right on the vagus nerve and holding it there as the man struggles against her. He goes for his weapon but I'm on him and have him disarmed as his face begins to go purple.

"Don't suffocate him," I whisper.

"I'm not, but it takes a second," she hisses back. Finally, the man's eyes go glassy and he slips from her grasp, his body going slack.

I drop the magazine from the gun and unload the round in the chamber before tossing all the pieces into the nearby hedge as well. "Theo," I whisper. He appears over the hedge. "Help us move him over there."

The man sighs and grabs the man by his shoulders as Zara and I take his legs. We lift him up and over the hedge so he's hidden behind it. I grab the small wireless radio piece that's in his ear and place it in my own. I'm met with a smattering of Italian, none of which I can understand.

"Here," I say, handing it to Theo. "Keep a sharp ear. Let us know what we're running into." Zara fishes around the man's belt until she finds a small keycard, which she pockets.

He reluctantly takes the earpiece and places it in his own ear. "Normal patrols," he says after a few minutes. "Doesn't seem like they're on high alert for anything. This is just a normal night."

That's a welcome relief. Though I'd hate to see what this place is like when they're expecting trouble.

"Do you have an idea of how many we're dealing with?" I ask. This is the second time we've infiltrated one of Fletch's homes. And while the first one was relatively benign, I have a feeling this is going to be much more difficult.

"At least four different voices so far," he says. "But I'd expect a lot more. Maybe ten."

"*Ten* guys?" Zara says. "Who does he think he is, the pope?"

"The pope can't get laid," I say. "C'mon, we need to make this as quick as possible. Someone will notice this guy missing eventually. We're on the clock." I turn to Theo. "Which way?"

"Up here," he says and we follow him across the small courtyard to the side of the house where a large arched opening leads into the interior part of the compound. I flatten against one of the walls, doing my best to listen for any additional security. Zara is beside me and I notice she already has her weapon out and ready. I'm not quite there yet, I want to see if we can do this without firing a shot.

Theo motions us to follow him through the archway, which leads into a sort of vestibule before heading off into what looks like an interior garden and large swimming pool, both brightly lit and done up in a classic Roman style. The vestibule features doors on both sides and Theo chooses the one on the right, trying the handle only to find it locked. Zara rounds the wall and places the electronic keycard from the security officer to the handle, which then gives easily.

"You didn't really expect it to be open, did you?" she asks.

Theo doesn't respond, only carefully opens the door, checking inside, before heading in. Zara follows and I bring up the rear, watching behind us to make sure no one spotted us going into the house.

Inside, the tile floors do nothing to help muffle our footsteps, and the stucco walls are reminiscent of what I'd expect this place to look like. It's nice and warm in here, and it seems like almost every light in the house is on. That's going to make moving through here more difficult.

Theo stops at the edge of a wall with a life-size oil painting of some seventeenth-century dignitary. He points beyond the wall, where a staircase leads to the upper floor before the hallway heads into the massive kitchen. *Upstairs*, he mouths.

I nod before checking the blind corners and then crouch-running over to the stairs. These can't be the primary stairs for the home, they're too narrow. More than likely they're for the service personnel or for the kitchen staff to deliver food to the upper part of the home.

I carefully take the stairs, noting there is a window right at the first landing, which I duck below. I sneak a quick peek out there and see it faces on the back of the property, overlooking the pool. Out there I can see two more men walking around, patrolling the grounds. How long do we have? Ten minutes? Maybe less?

At the top of the stairs I pause, waiting for the others. So far, so good. If we can get Fletch back down this way, we'll be in good shape. But we still need to find him. And from here, the hallways split off in three different directions.

"Which way?" I ask Theo as he and Zara join us.

"I don't know where he'll be," Theo replies. "He has his own pool hall up here, and a bar, along with a theater. He could be in any of them."

Great. I would suggest we split up but I know the second Theo is alone or even with just one of us he may try to get the advantage. "We'll do it systematically," I say. "One after the other until we find him."

Theo nods, though not very enthusiastically. He heads down the left corridor and we follow until we hear the sound of footsteps at the other end. There's nowhere else to go other than a door to our right, which I immediately open and usher us through. We close the door behind us as the footsteps grow closer.

But when I turn to look where we are, I find that we're in the bedroom of a little girl. She's sitting up in bed, a book in her hands, though she's looking at the three of us. If she's surprised to see us, she doesn't show it.

"Um…" Zara says.

I smile at the girl, though my heart does that thing. A second ago I was fine—I was solid as a rock. And now my system has been flooded with so much adrenaline my hands are shaking. Theo never said anything about any *kids* being here.

Theo grins at the girl and gives her a quick wave. "*Ciao. Come ti chiami?*"

"Luisa," the girl replies.

"Luisa, *è molto bello. Cosa stai leggendo?*"

"What are you doing?" I hiss.

"Trying to keep her calm," he replies.

"She seems calm enough to me," Zara replies.

The girl holds up the book she's reading. "*Loca e la Volpe.*"

"Great, is she going to give us away or what?" I ask.

"Luisa," Theo says. "*Tuo padre è qui?*

She shrugs.

"*Dovrei verderlo,*" Theo ads.

"What are you telling her?" I ask.

"Just trying to figure out where Fletch is," I say.

"Wait, did you say *padre?*" Zara asks. "Is this his kid?"

"Fletch doesn't have any kids," I say. "At least not from the intel we sourced."

"You didn't have the whole picture," Theo says before turning back to Luisa. "*Andiamo subito a cercarlo. Buon libro.*"

"*Grazie,*" she says and turns back to the book. Theo makes a motion with his finger that we should get moving. I peek out into the hallway to find whoever the footsteps belonged to has passed. Fletch has a daughter? How can that be? Does that mean he has a wife and other kids too? None of that was in his dossier or in any of the intelligence we sourced when doing our recon on him.

"What else aren't you telling us?" I whisper to Theo as we make our way down the hallway again.

"Nothing important, love," he replies, though I don't like the way in which he says it. He's too confident, and he spoke to Luisa like it was nothing. What if he told her to go warn her father we're coming?

I grab Theo by the collar and hold him against the wall. "What did you tell her?"

"Nothing," he insists. "Just that we were here to meet her dad and to enjoy her book. That was it."

"You're sure," I say. "We're not walking into—" But before I can finish, I hear shuffling at the other end of the hallway.

"*Fermati qui!* Stop!" A flashlight hits me in the face, temporarily blinding me as Theo squirms out of my grasp.

"Em!" Zara yells and I pull out my weapon, but as soon as my vision clears I see four men surrounding us on all sides, their weapons pointed directly at our heads.

"I wouldn't do that if I were you, Ms. Slate," Fletch says, pushing between two of his men. "After all, you wouldn't want to start a firefight in my hallway and scare my daughter, would you?" His face breaks into the widest grin I've ever seen on a man.

I could fire, maybe take out one of the guards. And maybe Zara could get a second one. But that'd be it. We'd both be dead before we could hit the floor. I glare at Theo who only offers a weak smile as if to say *I told you so*.

"Hand them over and this will all go much better," Fletch says.

I glance at Zara. We're outnumbered and outgunned.

And now… we're at this man's mercy.

Chapter Thirty-One

"I HAVE TO ADMIT, I wasn't expecting to see you here," Fletch says as we're led into an expansive room on the second floor of his villa. There's a pool table on one end and a full bar on the other, complete with a mirror back, making the room look even larger. The windows of this room face out on the front of the property and from here I can see the large fountain, lit up in blue and white lights, as well as the bevy of expensive cars that are parked around it.

The room also holds two couches. After a quick search which relieves us of our weapons, Fletch's men sit both Zara and me on one couch while the man himself goes to pour himself a drink at the bar. "Can I get you anything?"

"I wouldn't mind a Vodka Collins," Zara says. Theo stands by the doorway, his arms crossed and his head down. "Or a merlot."

"I was just asking to be polite," Fletch says. "I don't think giving you a glass right now would be very conducive." He shoots a knowing glance at me.

"How long have you known we were here?" I ask.

"Well, when Fermi stopped responding, we figured something was wrong. And then Marco found your car down by the service gate." He goes to the bar and pulls a short glass and a bottle of expensive-looking scotch. "But it was probably the nanny cam that was the nail in your coffin."

"In your daughter's room," I say. "Great."

He turns to us, a smile on his face. "Or maybe it was Theo there, when he sent me a coded signal to let me know something was wrong."

Zara and I turn to Theo at the same time, but the man continues to hide his face. "How?" Zara demands. "I've been watching you like a *hawk*."

"Subdermal device," Fletch says, pointing to the back of his shoulder. "All my men carry one. All they need to do is tap it twice to let me know to be ready. And Theo's warning came about eighteen hours ago."

"You spineless little—" Zara begins as Theo wilts under her gaze.

"Now, now. Try not to be too hard on him," Fletch says, taking a seat across from us in the other plush couch. "He was just doing what I paid him to do. Like all my men. We're all just cogs in the machine."

"Like you paid him to get us to look into you," I say. "So you could get the device into the FBI system."

"That's right," Fletch says, raising his drink.

"Except," I say. "There's something about that which isn't quite right, is there?"

He begins to take a drink but arches his eyebrow at me.

"You weren't aware of the plan as it was conceived, were you?"

"Of course I was," he replies. "It was my plan." He hesitates from taking a drink.

I shake my head slowly. "No, you never would have *willingly* allowed yourself to be drugged. You didn't know *what* was going on. Someone else planned the whole operation. You're just a cog yourself."

"Ms. Slate, it was *my* plan."

"No, it wasn't," I say. "It was Solitare's plan."

His eyes flare and he glances sharply at Theo, who only keeps his head down. "Solitaire used you, didn't they? They used you to get into the FBI's system and you had no idea about it. But *he* did." I point to Theo. "I think you're both protecting this person. I want to know why. What do they have on you? *Both* of you?"

Fletch smiles, this time taking the drink and polishing it off. "You know, you really are a talented investigator. It's a shame your career has come to such an abrupt end."

"No thanks to you," I say. "You wanted me killed in that blast, didn't you?" Fletch glances at me, then at Theo again. "No, *you* didn't. You were just following orders again." I sit forward, but am immediately pulled back into the couch by one of his goons. "Who is doing this?" I demand. "Who is targeting me?"

"You know, as much as I would *love* to sit here and answer all your questions, I'm not going to. You've come all this way, taken all this time and we haven't yet shown you the proper Italian hospitality. You need to get out and see some of the countryside." He motions for the men behind us to move us.

"We already saw the countryside on the way here, asshole," Zara says.

"Then you get to see it again," he replies. "Think of it as a parting gift from me to you."

"Wait," I say as the men stand us up, preparing to escort us out. "I found Janice's autopsy. The heart attack under suspicious circumstances. You know what happened, don't you? I deserve answers." That's how all this started. If I'm going to be taken out into the middle of nowhere and shot, I want to at least know why.

"Do you?" Fletch asks.

"Yeah," I reply, staring him down. "Did you kill her?"

"Me?" Fletch asks as if he's offended by the words. "No, of course not."

"Then who did?"

He eyes me for a moment. "Some no-name grunt who we contracted to do the job," he says. "No one important."

Even though I spent all this time trying to prepare for it—even knew it in my bones—I can't stop the revelation from hitting me like a ton of bricks. "Why?" I manage to whisper.

"Because we needed to find you," Fletch says. "She suspected Theo over there and was closing in on me and you hadn't shown back up yet. See, when the breach began, we figured you would be activated, put in charge of the investigation. Instead, the Bureau took you and hid you somewhere. And we needed a way to get you back."

"This was all... for me?" I ask. "Why?"

"Because like you, I am sometimes just a cog in the machine," Fletch says. "You've proved a very difficult person to kill, despite our best efforts."

Solitaire, I think. Whoever they are, they want me dead. "If I'm going to die anyway, then why not just tell me who it is?" I demand.

"Because those are my orders," Fletch says. "Perhaps it's one final indignity. The fact that you don't *get* to know. Frankly, I'll be happy once this is all over and you're out of my hair." He motions for the men to take us. "I'll be there to oversee everything in a few minutes. Get them ready."

This *bastard*. I don't have time to consider the implications of his words, or to even divine if he's telling the truth. I need to find a way out of this.

No. *We* need to find a way out of this.

I turn to Zara, and slide my gaze to her left. Right where Theo stands, his head still lowered. She narrows her gaze for a second before it dawns on her. She nods.

"Wait," she says as the men parade us past Theo out the doors. She stops right in front of him.

He doesn't glance up.

"Theo, look at me," she says.

He finally raises his gaze to meet hers. The man looks miserable—which he should. He betrayed us over and over again. And now he's sending us to our deaths.

"I just want you to know, I forgive you," Zara says. I swear the man looks like he's on the verge of tears. She leans in, pressing her lips against his and he practically crumples under her. The men holding her relax their grip for a split second, long enough for Zara to slip her hand into Theo's pocket and pull out the taser, which she then turns and uses on the closest man to her. He hits the floor just as I drive my knee into my escort's groin. He yells in pain as Zara decks Theo across the jaw and we run, bullets clipping the door frame behind us.

"Where do we go?" she yells.

"I have no idea," I yell back. "Just keep moving." If I were a lesser person, I'd head back for Luisa's room and use her as a hostage. But I'm not putting her in danger. That's something her father would do, not me. Instead we fly down the stairs and back out the way we came. Our only chance is to try and get back out, but I'm not even sure our car will still be there.

At the bottom of the stairs we practically run into another guard who is coming our way, probably attracted by the gunshots. Zara shoves the taser into his neck, sending him into immediate shock as he collapses, convulsing on the ground. I grab the handgun out of his belt before we hop over him and head for the same door we came in, only to see more guards running past.

I pull Zara to the side wall as we hear multiple footsteps descending the stairs behind us. We run in the other direction into the house's main living room, only for another bullet to go whizzing by us. I hop over the first piece of furniture I see, which happens to be an old wooden cabinet that sits in front of a couch. Landing on the couch, I roll to the floor as Zara ducks behind another wall partition. Pulling the weapon, I fire three warning shots back, just enough to give us some breathing room. The footsteps stop, but then more bullets come crashing through the room, taking out lamps, glass windows and ceramic vases probably worth tens of thousands of dollars.

I spot Zara from my position behind the couch. She's pinned. And so am I. I'm not sure we could get out of here without taking a bullet. It's only then when I hear shouting from what sounds like outside. The gunshots abate for a second, though I don't know why. I glance at Zara and we nod together. This may be our only chance. Or they might be trying to bait us into showing ourselves. Whatever the reason, we can't waste this opportunity.

I vault myself over another piece of furniture, heading for the far end of the room with Zara running parallel to me through the hallway just on the other side of the arches that lead out to the pool area on this side of the house. Lights flash through the windows like searchlights as Zara and I turn the corner, looking for any door to get out of this Tuscan maze.

Finally, I find the main doors and throw them open, only to be greeted by half a dozen searchlights pointed directly at our faces.

"*Metti giù l'arma!*" Someone yells. "Put down the weapon!"

I hold both hands up, and slowly lower myself to the ground, laying the handgun on the marble.

"Get on the ground and place your hands behind your head." I glance at Zara. There's no telling what is going on or who this is. It could be more of Fletch's private security. All I can see are lights and the muzzles of guns pointed at us.

As soon as I'm on the ground I feel hands grab my arms and pin them behind me, placing them in cuffs. From her grunts, I assume the same is happening to Zara.

"Well, well, Agent Slate. Funny to meet you here," a familiar voice says. A voice I've only heard once before, but is *very* clear in my memory.

I glance up and see the man light a cigarette, which illuminates the face of CIA Agent Osgood.

It's only then that I realize just how truly screwed we are.

Chapter Thirty-Two

"So," Osgood says, taking the seat across from me. I've been sequestered in what I can only assume is an Italian jail somewhere close to Fletch's compound because it only took us about fifteen minutes to get here. I haven't seen Zara since they loaded us into separate cars, but I did get a good enough look to see that they had subdued most of Fletch's men and were in the middle of what looked to be a full-on raid.

It's funny. Over and over, Fletch either tried to get me pinched or killed and yet it was the CIA that finally succeeded. He failed to get me at Apex and had I not run directly into the FBI building when it exploded there's a good chance I would have gotten away there too.

"I have to admit, I didn't think I'd see you again so soon," Osgood adds. "And in another country, no less."

"Lawyer," I say.

He puts both his hands up in a defensive gesture. "Let's just take a beat here," he says. "You don't even know why you're here."

"I can take a good guess," I say. I'm here because I'm a fugitive from the United States on a terrorism charge and Italy can choose to extradite me for a political favor. I'm here because not only was I found in the home of a known criminal, there is evidence tying me to his operation in not one but *two* other instances. I'm here because I screwed up and instead of going to the authorities I just kept digging myself deeper and deeper.

And now, I'm about as deep as I can get. "Where is Zara?"

"Agent Foley is fine," Osgood says. "She's two rooms over. Speaking with my colleague."

At least I know the CIA isn't in Fletch's pocket. He may have a lot of influence, but even *he* doesn't have that much power.

"Just get me my lawyer," I say. "I'm not going to talk to you or anyone else." I escaped a federal prison. Even if I weren't on the hook for anything else, there is that to consider.

"If you want to speak with a lawyer, that's your right, of course," Osgood says. "But it might be premature. Instead, why don't we talk about the past forty-eight hours."

I motion for him to go ahead.

He doesn't bother pulling out any files or taking out his phone. Instead, he just crosses his legs, folds his hands together on the table and stares at me. "Using falsified documents, you managed to procure transport out of a FBI detention block which then conveniently disappeared, leaving no trail behind. You then obtained false passports under an assumed name and used them to transport yourself, Agent Foley and Mr. Arquenest to a foreign country, where you purchased illegal weapons and then attempted to storm the property of an international citizen. How am I doing so far?"

I shrug, not wanting to give him the satisfaction. But everything he said is true.

"This individual, Mr. Joaquin Fletch, is a known information broker for several unscrupulous clients. In fact, we've had our eyes on him for a couple of years, but the bastard is slippery. He doesn't make mistakes, nor does he do anything without reason."

I pause, waiting for the other shoe to drop.

"For instance, he employed you to help him instigate an attack on the J. Edgar Hoover building in Washington D.C. which resulted in two deaths and nearly forty injuries."

Jesus. I didn't realize the number had been that high. But honestly, we're lucky it wasn't higher.

Wait a second. "You know that Fletch was behind the attack?" I ask.

He gives me a very subtle nod. "It was brought to our attention that the person who set the charges along the building was deliberately chosen because they look like you. The FBI has her in custody now, a Melody Tanner, from Philadelphia, I believe."

"They have her in custody? How?"

"Your fellow agents are responsible for that. And she has made a full confession about her part in the destruction of the building and implicated the man who hired her, the aforementioned Joaquin Fletch." Osgood pulls out a pack of cigarettes from inside his jacket pocket, along with a lighter. He offers the pack to me but I just shake my head. He takes a cigarette and lights it, breathing deep, then turning his head and letting out the smoke so it doesn't blow in my face.

"I was also told that the FBI could find no triggering program on the phone you used that night to activate the bomb. They did, however, find a transmission station on the roof of a building a block away. They believe it was triggered from there."

"But..." My mind tries to grasp this. "It exploded as soon as I hit the button, it had to be me."

"We believe they were monitoring the cell signal of the phone, waiting for you to dial any number. And once you did, they then set off the bomb. You probably already know this, but neither you nor the phone were supposed to survive the explosion. And there would have been a street camera pointed right at the building where you were supposed to make your… drop, I believe?"

"Everyone would have assumed…" I begin.

He nods. "It turns out those deaths are not on your head, Agent Slate."

"I still don't understand," I say. "What's the situation with the FBI then?"

He pulls out his phone as it vibrates in his pocket and puts it away, the cigarette hanging from his lips. "It turns out the data your previous boss collected has been received. An Agent Caruthers was handling things when I last left the situation."

He narrows his eyes. "Which brings us to this evening. Let's skip over the fact that you illegally entered the country. What were you planning to do at Mr. Fletch's compound?"

I sigh. No sense in holding back now. "We had planned to take him into custody and return him to Washington with us," I say. "In hopes that we could make him answer for the damage he'd done to the Bureau."

He nods. "Ah. I see. Then you weren't there to kill him."

"Killing him wouldn't have helped us," I say. "We needed him to testify."

"Makes sense," he says. "You'll forgive me but I had to ask. You know, when I reviewed your record before the FBI interviewed you I had my suspicions something wasn't right. You're not the kind of agent who goes rogue."

I can't help but be a little stunned. "Why were you at his compound?" I ask. "We thought you might be part of his security force at first, but—"

"No, actually we were working off the FBI's recent intelligence. The data provided to us from an Agent Sandel was enough to give us the clout we needed with the Italian Government to finally go after Mr. Fletch. It just happened that you were there at the same time."

Elliott. "We didn't have a choice," I say. "Our clock was running out."

Osgood takes another long drag of his cigarette. "Of course, you couldn't have gone about it in a worse way."

"Arquenest," I say.

He nods. "Given the paper trail between him and Mr. Fletch, I don't think we'll have any trouble hanging this on him. He's obviously been involved for a while and we have a *lot* of questions for Mr. Arquenest. And when we're done, the FBI is sure to want to take their turn." He stubs the cigarette out on the metal table.

"What does that mean for me and Zara?" I ask.

"You are in the country illegally," Osgood says. "And you did break out of a federal prison. You'll have to face that music when you get back. As far as the CIA is concerned, you assisted in the apprehension of a dangerous criminal. Had you not been there, Mr. Fletch may have spotted us much sooner which would have resulted in a larger loss of life."

"We were a distraction," I say.

"And a good one at that," Osgood replies, smiling.

"Wait, did you know we were here before you arrived at Fletch's house?"

"Of course, we had people at the airport who spotted you getting off the plane," he replies. "The FBI expressed concern that you might try to apprehend Mr. Fletch yourselves. It just happens that our goals aligned." He stands and holds out his hand. "Well done, Agent Slate."

My jaw has to be hanging open by a good mile. I finally stand and take his hand, giving it a weak shake. "Um… no problem?"

"As soon as we finish with Agent Foley the two of you will be on a plane back to Washington, courtesy of the CIA. I wish you luck when you get back. With all the recent turmoil, I'm not sure what your future looks like." He turns to head back out.

"That's it?" I ask.

He stops, looking back over his shoulder at me. "Unless there's something else."

I nod. "The mole, inside the FBI. Fletch knows who it is. They call themselves *Solitaire*. I believe they were instrumental in the breach. *And* I believe they hired Fletch to help facilitate the lie."

A concerned look comes across Osgood's face. "Yes, we spoke to Mr. Fletch about that. He claims *he* is this… Solitaire."

"What?" I ask.

"He's taking full responsibility for the breach and for the attempts on your life," Osgood says. "Admits to orchestrating the whole thing."

"But… that's not right," I say. "We have evidence showing—"

"You mean the suppositions from your former boss?" Osgood asks before shoving his hands in his pockets and coming back over to me. "Look, Agent Slate. I don't know how the FBI works, but when an international criminal admits to a crime that it looks like they themselves perpetrated and are accused of, we don't tend to argue."

"No," I say. "Fletch was being played. Someone set him up as the fall guy."

"Do you have anything I can go on?" Osgood asks. "Anything other than what was in Simmons's notes?"

I pause, thinking. All we've ever had on this *Solitaire* person was questions. Even Theo doesn't know who they are. But Fletch did. And the fact that he's willing to take the fall for this person makes me nervous. Fletch isn't the kind of guy who seems like he'd bow to anyone.

And yet… someone got to him.

"Listen," Osgood says. "You're tired, probably hungry and still jet-lagged. We'll get you a good meal before we send you back to face the music, okay?"

"Yeah," I say, taking my seat again. Could Fletch be Solitaire all along and was just playing the part? I guess I could see how that would be a benefit, completely separated from the person who looks like they're pulling all the strings. And yet, at the same time, still be the puppet master.

I don't know anymore. All I know is my head hurts, I want a drink like no tomorrow, and a shower wouldn't hurt either. The fact that I'm not going to have to do any of that in a prison is the only thing keeping me going right now.

"I'll take that as a yes," Osgood says on his way out. "Hang tight. You'll be out of here in no time."

~

"OH MY GOD," ZARA SAYS AS SHE STUFFS HER MOUTH FULL OF pasta. "And I thought Liam's cooking was good." She points her fork dripping with sauce at me. "I was always jealous as hell because you got the boyfriend who knew how to cook, but this blows him completely out of the water."

"I'll be sure to let him know," I say, staring off into the distance. We're sitting at a small café in town, though we're the only two people in here. There are four CIA agents keeping watch. One at the door to the kitchen who keeps getting in the way of the server, one at the door to the café and two outside, watching the area closely. They're not even trying to fit in. Basically they're a set of warning signs, telling people not to come anywhere near us.

Zara managed to convince Osgood we needed a *proper* meal before leaving, so he allowed us this one pleasure before we hop on a plane back to Washington. But I can't help the pit deep in my stomach. Who knows what's waiting there for us when we get back? I wouldn't be surprised if there were a garrison of agents there to take us into custody as soon as we step off the plane.

This might very well be my last meal as a free woman.

"Would you at least blink, please?" Zara says, stuffing her mouth again. "You're going to pop a capillary."

"Sorry," I say. "I've got a lot on my mind."

"Want my advice?" she says. "Look around. You are in *Italy*. One of the most beautiful places in the world. You are eating the best goddamn food I've ever had in my life. And sure, maybe we'll be going to prison for the rest of our lives. But that's a future Emily problem. Right now, this is pretty sweet."

I sigh and pick up my fork. "I wish I had that ability," I say.

"What ability?"

"To put the future away for a few minutes," I reply. "To not worry about what's going to happen next. To relax."

She reaches over and gives my wrist a quick squeeze. "The way I see it, we could be lying in an Italian morgue right now. But we're not. We're here, enjoying this food. And you wanna know the best part?"

"What?"

"Theo is the one in prison." She grins. "He *hates* confined spaces. He will not do well."

"I guess that is a plus," I say.

"And did you see how I decked him?" she asks, almost giddy. "I was gonna use the taser on him but I didn't get the chance. Still. Your ol' buddy Z did pretty good." She swirls another lump of pasta on her fork and shoves it in her mouth, practically groaning at the taste. I catch the raised eyebrow of one of the CIA agents.

"Aren't you worried about what happens when we get back?" I ask. "About what Weiss will do?"

She shrugs. "I guess. But there isn't anything else we can do about that, is there?"

I check the exits again and she immediately puts her fork down. "Emily Rachel Slate. We are *not* running."

"I didn't say we were!"

"You were thinking it."

"I didn't even say anything."

"I know you," she replies, picking up the fork again. "You're wired to look for a way out. A way to fix things. But you know as well as I do that evading the CIA would only make things worse. You'd never be able to go back home. You'd never see Liam again. Is it worth looking over your shoulder for the rest of your life for that?"

"No," I admit. She's right, of course. Running would be the coward's way out. And I need to face the music. We did what we came here to do—even if it wasn't in the way we planned. Both Fletch and Theo are in custody. And hopefully, with the information garnered from them, the Bureau can start repairing itself, both the physical building itself and the damage done to its organizational structure.

"C'mon," Zara says. "Try to at least enjoy the food a little. We gotta live in the moment while we can, right?"

I look at the plate of food before me, clearing my mind of everything ahead of us. It *does* look mouthwatering.

Finally, I pick up my fork and dig in.

Chapter Thirty-Three

I SEE the flashing lights before the plane even touches down. A set of five vehicles out on the tarmac of Dulles International Airport, all SUVs. The plane makes its landing and pulls over to one of the private hangars, where the vehicles all sit waiting.

Thankfully it was an easy flight. One where Zara couldn't quit fawning over the fact we got to take a private CIA airplane back. And given it was just us and two other CIA agents in the entire plane, we had it mostly to ourselves. She kept asking me to compare it to my last private plane experience and I couldn't help but rib her a little about it, telling her the other plane was plusher, and I was offered champagne. Despite her repeated requests, our *escorts* weren't about to serve us alcohol.

As soon as the pilot kills the engines, the agents get up and open the door. I find I can't help my heart from beating as hard as it possibly can. Zara turns to me, and gives my hand a squeeze. I hate that I've dragged her into this—it never should have been her fight. And now she's going to face the same fate as me.

Finally, I stand and head past the CIA agents, thanking

them for the escort before stepping out into the cool early spring air. The sun has almost set, leaving the sky a beautiful tapestry of blues, pinks and oranges and I can't help but admire it for a moment as I descend the stairs of the plane.

It's then I see him. Liam standing out in front of one of the SUVs, with Nadia and Elliott close by. Suddenly I'm running and I find myself in his arms without even knowing how I got there.

"You're here," I say.

"I'm here," he replies.

"What's going on?"

"We're taking you back to the Bureau," he replies. "For debrief." I pull away from him and see Zara and Nadia embracing while Elliott looks on.

"Reinstated?" I ask Nadia.

She nods. "After what we went through to track down your doppelganger, the Bureau thought it was only appropriate."

"It was quite the challenge," Elliott replies, his hands clasped behind his back as always. "And took a considerable amount of time and resources."

I pull away from Liam and grab both of them at the same time, pulling them into an unexpected hug. Elliott resists at first, before finally relaxing into it. "Thank you. Both of you. We would be in an Italian prison if it weren't for you."

"We couldn't leave you hanging," Nadia says. "Not after everything."

"I'm getting in on this," Zara says, grabbing on to all of us.

Liam clears his throat. "Uh, guys?" He motions to the other agents who are looking at us with puzzled expressions.

Zara and I let go of the others as we all straighten out our clothes. "Caruthers?" I ask.

Liam nods. "We're going to meet with him right now."

"He's out of the hospital?"

"He's on… extended leave, but wanted to be there when

you returned. We have a meeting with Deputy Director Weiss."

I expected as much. But just the fact that Liam, Nadia and Elliott are here—that they allowed them to meet us instead of someone like Wilder—speaks volumes.

"Okay," I say, exchanging a glance with Zara. "We're ready." Zara and I get into one of the SUVs with Liam while Nadia and Elliott get in another.

"Hey, Agent Slate."

I look at the driver's seat. "Lee?"

"I promise I'll take us right to the Bureau this time," he says. "No losing the vehicle under mysterious circumstances."

"How did they not reprimand you for that?" I ask.

"Oh, they tried. But Agent Kane helped me out a little. You'll have to ask her about it."

What the hell has been going on in the three days we've been gone? I'm not sure what to think anymore.

"It'll take us about an hour," Lee adds. "Traffic is a bitch at this time of day." He pulls away behind one of the other SUVs while the rest follow us.

"How was Italy?" Liam asks once we're on the highway.

"I wish we could have stayed longer," I admit.

"Maybe one day," he says, which causes me to furrow my brow. Is he saying there's a possibility I won't be in jail for the next fifteen years? Or does he just mean after?

"I'll tell you one thing, buddy-boy," Zara says, turning around in her seat. "You finally have some competition in the kitchen. You're going to have to up your game. And I expect weekly deliveries to our cells."

He chuckles. "I'll see what I can do."

∽

WE ARRIVE AT THE BUREAU THROUGH THE BACK, SO I DON'T get a good look at the damage on the front, but they still have the roads blocked off and there is scrim covering part of the building from where I can see. We head into the underground parking garage, through two security checkpoints before getting out and heading to the elevators that will take us back upstairs.

Even though the rest of my team is here with me, the ride in the elevator feels like the longest of my life. Normally I would be more confident, considering we could technically call this a win. But without Janice here to protect me any longer, I'm not sure what Weiss will do. I think the best possible outcome is a quiet resignation, no fuss. I think back to when I was prepared to resign in New Mexico. I've already mentally gathered myself for this, it was just a little delayed.

The real question is how many charges they'll be throwing at us. Because I don't care what they found or who confessed to what, someone needs to take responsibility for this. And the fact of the matter is, the attack never would have happened if I hadn't been involved.

We take the elevator up to the top floor, bypassing our department entirely. As we step out, I notice one end of the hallway is already blocked off for construction repairs. Men in hard hats are moving through the hallway with flashlights and tablets, working on assessing the damage.

"They're pretty confident there's no structural damage," Liam says. "Nadia was right. It was mostly superficial."

"That's good," I say, though I don't really feel it in my heart. I'm more worried about what we're about to face at the other end of the hallway.

As we reach the doors to one of the conference rooms, it's opened by an agent I don't know before we arrive. He holds one arm out to Liam. "Slate. You and Foley only. The rest will have to stay out here."

Liam gives me a reassuring nod as I lead the way in, followed by Zara. The agent closes the door behind us, leaving Liam, Nadia and Elliott outside. The blinds to the conference room are drawn, so I can't see them. But the windows that look out on the rest of the city are wide open.

But when I see who is sitting at the conference table, I freeze. Agents Vostov and Pendergast sit on one side, while my boss, SSA Caruthers sits on the other. He wears a sling around one arm and his face is bruised, dark circles under his eyes. A crutch is propped up against the table beside him. When I see the state he's in, my heart sinks.

"Sir," I say, shakily. "Are you—"

"Slate, take a seat," the man at the head of the table says. Deputy Director Weiss—the same man who was on the TV telling the reporters they had the suspect responsible for the blast in custody. I guess that's still true.

Caruthers gives me a reassuring nod and I take one of the seats a few down from him while Zara pulls up a chair beside me.

Weiss stares me down but doesn't say anything while Pendergast and Vostov both open file folders in front of them. Caruthers sits back, eyeing Weiss carefully. It's like we're all sitting in some kind of stalemate, waiting for the other person to make the first move.

"Are they waiting on us?" Zara whispers to me.

"Agents," Weiss says, his voice booming through the room. "Seems like you've had quite the trip."

I know better than to say anything. If there's one thing I've learned being in the FBI, it's when to keep my mouth shut. Sometimes, when I'm up against an ego that needs to be checked or someone who has accused me of something I didn't do, I don't have a problem saying so. But in this case, I take full responsibility for my actions. Whatever is coming is warranted.

"You know," Weiss continues. "We wanted you in here much sooner. To clear up a few… irregularities."

He's referring to when I was caught dealing with Apex. "Yes, sir. That was a mistake on my part. Not Agent Foley's. I was prepared to come in, but I needed a certain piece of intel first."

He glares at us before turning to Caruthers. "I understand it was your idea to sequester these two in New Mexico under new identities?"

He clears his throat. "It was a joint venture between me and Agent Simmons," Caruthers says. "We thought it was the best possible option, given the circumstances at the time."

"To hide two of our agents within our own organization?" Weiss asks, incredulous.

"Agent Simmons—"

"Agent Simmons is dead," he says, cutting the man off. "I'm asking *you* for an explanation."

Caruthers seems to gather his strength. "Given that we were facing an unknown breach that seemed to target Agent Slate, *I* decided it would be best to move her for her own safety. However, if you know Agent Slate, you know she doesn't do well without a goal. We decided it would be best to keep her on the job while we tried to determine the seriousness of the threat against her."

"And Agent Foley?" Weiss asks.

"Was sent to assist Agent Slate. I felt that due to her lack of backup on her case in St. Solomon the circumstances warranted it."

"Not to mention I wouldn't have let her go alone," Zara adds.

I glare at her. *What are you doing?* I mouth.

She just winks at me.

Weiss hesitates a moment before turning back to Caruthers. "Were you aware she had returned to DC without authorization?"

"No," I say before Caruthers can answer. "No one was. I came of my own volition."

"Because of what happened to Agent Simmons," Weiss says. "I understand the two of you were… close."

I nod.

He sighs and glances at the information in front of him. I can only assume it is the autopsy report. "I understand we have you to thank for this." He holds up the papers we took from Johannsen.

"Yes, sir," I say.

"Another oversight on our part, apparently," Weiss continues. "I was unaware this autopsy had not been entered into the official record." He glances at Caruthers. "We've recalled and apprehended the four other agents who met with Mr. Fletch. It also appears Agent Johannsen was on his payroll, and was told to obscure this information from the Bureau."

"Why?" I ask.

"We believe it was to prevent any further investigation into Agent Simmons' death," Caruthers says. "I believed the autopsy was tied up in red tape. In reality, it had been removed entirely."

"Fletch gave us that information," I say. "But since he figured I'd perish in the explosion, maybe he didn't care."

"Or he knew by then it wouldn't matter," Weiss says. "It appears we have Agent Simmons to thank for not only exposing who was behind this attack on our institution, but helping lead you to him." He turns to Caruthers again.

Caruthers addresses all of us. "Thanks to the help of some of our more… enthusiastic agents… I was given the evidence showing that not only was Joaquin Fletch behind our internal breach here at the Bureau, but also the attack five days ago that resulted in the loss of two of our agents. We've also determined he was the person behind the deaths of the four other agents who had been targeted much in the same way as Agent Slate had." He takes a deep breath. "Unfortunately, this situation was due to the improper vetting of a trusted source that led to the breach."

Weiss looks at his notes. "This Theodore Arquenest," he says. I catch Zara flinch.

"To be fair, sir, Arquenest played the long game. His intel on every operation before his final one was solid, and led to arrests and an overall improved record. Agents Foley and Slate can speak to that."

"I'm concerned that Agents Foley and Slate may have been in league with him," Weiss says, looking at Zara. "Weren't the two of you in a relationship?"

"We were," Zara replies. "Until I began to grow suspicious of his actions while we were in New Mexico. From that point on, I suspected he might not be who he appeared to be."

"And you didn't think to inform the Bureau," Weiss says.

"Who would she have informed?" I ask. "Fletch had a direct line into our deepest communications. He would have just wiped anything that mentioned him or Theo. Just like he wiped any record of my arrest on the night of the explosion." I glance at the two agents across from me. "The Bureau was compromised. We had to perform our own investigation."

"Yes," Weiss says, looking at Pendergast and Vostov. "We've been discussing your actions. Agent?"

Pendergast clears his throat. "Emily, the Bureau is concerned with your behavior, and rightly so. You've demonstrated a disregard for authority, even going so far as to have members of your own team orchestrate your escape from prison so you could continue on this crusade of yours. Frankly, it makes us hesitant to trust you."

"Wait a second here," Zara says. "Em didn't orchestrate anything. What, do you think she called us from a butt phone and gave us a master plan? No, we did that on our own. There is no conspiracy. The fact of the matter is Fletch wanted Emily dead. When Agent Sandel looked into it, there was no arrest record, no assignment record. She could have been put in a black box or dropped off a bridge and no one would have known the difference. When he didn't kill her in that explosion, Fletch was going to use the *FBI* to take her out. And had we not interrupted that process, he might have succeeded."

"That's ridiculous," Vostov says. "We never would have let that happen."

"Really?" Zara asks. "Were you watching her twenty-four seven? Can you assure me a black order that looked like it was signed from Weiss over there giving explicit orders on what to do with her would have been ignored? By *everyone*? Because you sure complied with the one I came up with."

"Okay, okay," Weiss says, holding his hands up. "We're drifting off topic here. The real reason we're here is to determine what to do with Agent Slate, and by extension, Agent Foley and the rest of Slate's team. Given the recent breaches, we can't discount the possibility Agent Foley is right. It will take months if not years to find and repair all the damage Fletch managed to do to our organization. But I don't want to lose good agents because of it." He turns to Pendergast and Vostov. "Based on your professional opinions, what are the odds that Agent Slate has gone rogue?"

Pendergast turns his gaze towards me. "While there is evidence that she tends to buck authority and use irregular methods, I don't believe Agent Slate is a threat to this organization."

I'm spared a moment of relief before he speaks again.

"However, I'm not sure she is in the best place for her talents."

"What does that mean?" I ask.

"It means you have a specialized skill set," Vostov says. "Not to mention you're obviously a determined and dedicated agent. Both of you. We think the Bureau can put you to better use."

"Better use?" Zara asks.

"What's your recommendation?" Weiss asks.

"I want them working for us," Vostov says. "At the BAU. There are dozens of cases, if not more that could use their skills. And the job would offer slightly more autonomy."

"Wait a second," Zara says. "Are you *promoting* us? For breaking Em out of jail?"

"If anything it's a lateral move," Pendergast says. "But with better benefits."

I look at Caruthers, then Weiss. This can't be real. They're messing with us, right?

Weiss leans forward, folding his hands together. "Slate. This may come as a shock to you, but you and Agent Foley have some of the highest hour-to-case ratios in the entire Bureau. You work harder than most of our agents. The only problem is you pull shit like this, where you go off on your own without authorization. Now normally I'd say that's grounds for an early retirement. But in your case, I know that just means you'd go to another organization and we can't afford to lose you. Your stats for number of cases closed dwarfs most other departments."

"It's not like I'm alone," I say. "I mean, it's a joint effort."

He nods. "I know that. Which is why when you take this new job, and you *will* take it, you'll be taking your team with you. I realize you all work better as a unit. I want to keep it that way."

All of us? In our own unit?

"I'm still not sure I understand," I say. "What about the whole 'breaking out of prison' thing? Isn't that a felony?"

"Well, considering you weren't the one behind the attack for which you were being arrested, I don't think we need to go through the paperwork, do you?" Weiss says, turning to Caruthers, who shakes his head. "The Bureau has a lot of repair work to do, and we don't need to make the process any harder than it already is."

"I'm not sure what to say," I admit.

"Say *thank you*, shake our hands and get the hell out of here before someone changes their mind," Weiss says. "You'll be reporting to Agents Pendergast and Vostov. You start on Monday. Take the weekend to get your heads straight. And inform the rest of your team out there. I know they're probably doing everything they can to listen in."

It's like a giant weight has been lifted from my chest. I exchange a brief glance with Zara who shrugs, but with a smile on her face. Almost like she knew this might happen all along. Did she have some inside information? Is that why she was so calm in Italy?

I'll deal with that later. Instead, I stand and shake everyone's hand once. It's odd, considering two of these people were just presiding over my arrest interview a few days ago. Now they're going to be my bosses?

"Hate to lose you both. But I know Simmons would have been proud. You know how hard it was for her to speak highly of anyone and she did of both of you," Caruthers says.

"Thank you," I say and my eyes want to well up with tears, but I manage to hold back.

"No, thank you," he says, shaking Zara's hand as well. "It won't be the same around the office without you."

Zara gives the man a careful hug. They've known each other longer than I have, and I can see real emotion on her face. I think she's as conflicted about this as I am.

When we get to the door, I pause. I still can't believe this is real. Then again, I almost did die not once, but twice. Maybe this is that karma thing people are always talking about. "You want to tell them, or do you want me?" I ask.

"Oh no," she says. "That honor is all yours. I'm just happy to sit back and watch."

"Okay," I say. "Then let's get started."

Epilogue

As soon as I'm in the door, two dogs slam into me, knocking me completely to the ground. One second I'm standing, like a normal person, and the next I'm being smothered by dog kisses as they compete to see which one can make my face the wettest. Considering I haven't seen them in almost seven weeks, I'll take everything I can get.

"Guys," Liam chides. "Let your poor mother breathe a second."

I grab onto Timber with one arm and then Rocky with the other and just hold them while they both try to jump around, too excited to keep their energy in. But I need this. Timber is one of the last connections I have to my past, and Rocky has helped complete our family. The fact that I've been away from them for so long feels criminal.

"Okay, okay," I finally say and Timber takes off, running full bore down the hallway in search of a toy while Rocky sits obediently next to me, his tail swishing back and forth on the floor.

"I guess they're happy to see you," Liam says. "I showed them your picture every day to make sure they wouldn't forget."

"You did not," I say, pushing myself back up as Timber returns with a large octopus in his mouth, trying to push it in my hand.

"Somebody got a new toy," I say. I toss the octopus down the hall, causing Timber to run straight after it. I give Rocky a quick nod and he takes off as well, both of them vying for the large stuffed toy.

"God, I feel like I've abandoned them," I say as I set my backpack on one of the chairs. "First St. Solomon and now this."

"They're fine," Liam says. "Sure, they missed you. But that's all in the past now. You're home."

I take a seat in one of the chairs, finally feeling all the pent-up tension in my shoulders release. "I need a massage or something. I shouldn't even be here."

"Stop saying that," he says, taking the seat next to me. "You went through an ordeal and you survived. And now it's over."

"Yeah," I say, though it still doesn't feel real. After being on the run for so long and looking over my shoulder constantly, it's going to be weird getting back to normal life. At least, as normal as it gets around here.

After we explained to the rest of the group about the new assignment, Zara and I headed back to our old desks to collect what few things we had left behind. It's going to be weird no longer working out of that building—not seeing all the same familiar faces all the time. Instead, we're being moved to an off-site facility in Virginia, one with no signage, no indication of what is actually inside the building. It's just a normal office park, like any other. But we still aren't quite sure what awaits us in this new role. That will be determined on Monday, apparently.

Thankfully, everyone seemed receptive to the change. Even Elliott, who can be something of a wild card sometimes. But he expressed a strong desire to face the new challenge, and obviously Nadia and Liam were on board. It'll be strange, just the five of us. But we've been working together long enough now that I know I can trust each of them with my life. In fact, were it not for their help, I'd still be sitting in that black site, awaiting my fate.

Actually no, I'd probably be dead.

"C'mon," Liam says. "You're exhausted. Get into something comfy and I'll start working on dinner."

"You don't have to do that," I say. "Let's just order something. That way neither of us has to move." I seriously feel like I've been run over by a truck. Between the flights, the insanity at Fletch's and then the meeting this evening, I could probably sleep for a solid year.

"Sounds good to me. What do you feel like?"

"Whatever," I reply as Timber comes over and puts his head on my lap. I stroke his bony little head, feeling the soft fur under my fingers. "Did you give him a bath?"

"Both of them," Liam says. "Trust me, it had to be done. They were ripe."

"By yourself?" Timber and Rocky are not small dogs. And bathing them can be an adventure in itself.

"I managed to do one at a time. Took the better part of four hours, but we got it done, didn't we guys?"

Rocky follows him into the kitchen where he grabs a stack of paper menus we've been saving for just such an occasion. He sets the menus in front of me. It reminds me of our time in the safehouse. Which is now back to being a normal apartment. And Janice's second apartment is still being dissected for anything useful. "Dealer's choice," Liam says.

I wave my hand. "Really, anything is fine."

"Are you okay?" he asks.

"Should I be? I mean, I guess I should, but doesn't this all feel a little too convenient?" I ask. "Fletch is taking the dive for something he didn't do. Which means this Solitaire person is still out there. Theo is in an Italian prison waiting interrogation by the CIA, but given his penchant for escapes, I wouldn't be surprised to learn he gets out."

"He's not going to get out," Liam says. "The CIA won't allow it."

"I wish I had your confidence." There are still so many unanswered questions. "And we still don't know if someone may have a bug in the Bureau's systems."

"It will take some time to sort it all out," he says. "But I think we at least have a handle on it. Now that we know where the cracks are, we can fix them." He pauses. "I'm using the term 'we' metaphorically here. You and I won't be doing that. The information from Janice proved invaluable. I didn't tell you, but the Bureau came up with something from her apartment." He gets up and heads to the bedroom, returning with an envelope in his hand. "I was going to save this for later, but you look like you need it now."

"What is it?" I ask.

"Open it," he replies.

The envelope is marked with a red *E* scrawled across the front. "It's open," I say when I examine the back.

"The Bureau examined it already," he says. "They weren't going to leave anything to chance."

I pull my features together as I remove a letter from the envelope and unfold it. The second I see the scribbled letters, my eyes begin to well.

Emily,

I've never been good at this sort of thing, but I'll try anyway. I've never told you outright, because I don't believe in ego fluffing. But considering how this case is going and how many tails

I've been shaking lately, I figured I better get it out somewhere before it's too late.

But the point is, ever since the day you walked into my office as a fresh-faced graduate all the way through your career, I have always admired you. Your tenacity, your commitment and your moral compass are everything we look for in the Bureau. But more than that, you remind me of myself at your age. And yet, you've shown wisdom beyond your years. You have the makings of a great career and I believe you will go far. More importantly, you are a good person. The kind of person we should all strive to be. You have reminded me what it means to be someone who gives a damn, and for that, I can't thank you enough.

Know that whatever you do, no matter what path you take, I am proud of you.

Your friend,
J

I WIPE BACK THE TEARS, MY VISION SWIMMING AS I STRUGGLE to read the last few words without completely breaking down. Ever since we got the news, I haven't allowed myself time to grieve. To really live with the idea Janice won't be around anymore. And as soon as I open those gates I feel the emotions flood my system, overwhelming me. Liam takes me by the shoulders and I let it all out, the catharsis of weeks of bottling it all up finally coming out.

We stay like that for what seems like hours before I fall asleep from exhaustion, all thoughts of dinner forgotten.

And when I sleep, I dream of the woman who was like a mother to me. The woman who helped shape me into the person I am now.

I don't remember much about the dream. Except that she was smiling.

And that's enough.

The End

To be continued...

Want to read more about Emily?

SOME PLACES ARE BUILT TO HEAL. OTHERS ARE DESIGNED TO hurt.

Special Agent Emily Slate has just been appointed to lead a new team within the FBI. It's a fresh start. A new boss. A new mandate. But no time to breathe.

A series of disturbing reports from a remote psychiatric facility land on her desk—patients suddenly cut off from family, strange staff turnover, and whispers of something far more sinister beneath the surface.

The deeper she and her team dig, the clearer it becomes:

this isn't about mental health. It's about power, control, and silence. And someone inside will do whatever it takes to keep the truth buried—even if it means killing to protect it.

As the lines between sanity and conspiracy blur, Emily must navigate the shadows of an institution built on secrets… before she becomes its next patient.

The Killing Jar is a chilling new entry in the Emily Slate Mystery Thrillers by bestselling author Alex Sigmore. Perfect for returning fans and new readers alike, this standalone mystery delivers razor-sharp suspense, gripping twists, and a heroine who never backs down—even when the system is designed to break her.

To get your copy of *The Killing Jar*, CLICK HERE or scan the code below with your phone.

New Series Alert!
A twisted killer lies in wait…

I HOPE YOU ENJOYED *FIRE IN THE SKY*! WHILE YOU WAIT FOR the next installment in Emily's story, I'd like to introduce you to Charlotte and Mona, two amazing detectives who are after a very twisted killer.

WHEN A WOMAN'S BODY IS DISCOVERED IN OAK CREEK, LOCAL *police quickly dismiss it as an accidental drowning from years ago. Brought in from Chicago to help with the case, Detective Charlotte Dawes has worked on more murder investigations than she'd like to remember. An examination of the body tells her what local police refuse to see – somebody moved the victim to this remote location.*

After a local artist is found murdered, her body positioned to match one of her final paintings, the sinister truth can't be ignored. More disturbing still, the artist's other works seem to predict who in the small town will be next to die, in increasingly macabre ways.

As fear grips the town, Charlotte discovers a link between the first victim and a local cop, and it's clear the killer has planned their moves meticulously. In a community where everyone guards their secrets, Charlotte must determine who's truly playing on her side, before she becomes the next target…

WHAT READERS ARE SAYING ABOUT *THE DARKEST GAME*:

'This is the start of something special… prepare to fall in love with this new world and its darkly addictive pace.' Reader review,

'I was completely held hostage by my Kindle the whole way til the end.' Reader review,

'Okay, wow! This book was just… whoosh! Mind blown… a masterclass in suspense. Gripping, intelligent, and so compelling, I reread it the moment I finished. I haven't been able to stop thinking about it since.' Reader review,

'I'm kind of fangirling right now. Honestly, I was blown away by how much I enjoyed it.' Reader review,

Interested? CLICK HERE to snag your copy of THE DARKEST GAME!

Now Available

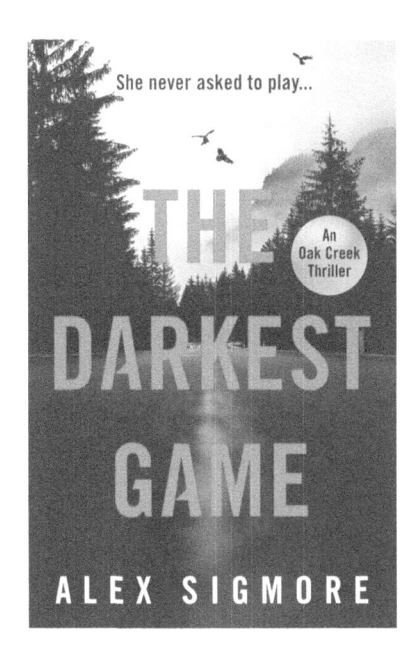

I can't wait for you to read it!

CLICK HERE or scan the code below to get yours now!

The Emily Slate FBI Mystery Series

Free Prequel - Her Last Shot (Emily Slate Bonus Story)
His Perfect Crime - (Emily Slate Series Book One)
The Collection Girls - (Emily Slate Series Book Two)
Smoke and Ashes - (Emily Slate Series Book Three)
Her Final Words - (Emily Slate Series Book Four)
Can't Miss Her - (Emily Slate Series Book Five)
The Lost Daughter - (Emily Slate Series Book Six)
The Secret Seven - (Emily Slate Series Book Seven)
A Liar's Grave - (Emily Slate Series Book Eight)
Oh What Fun - (Emily Slate Holiday Special)
The Girl in the Wall - (Emily Slate Series Book Nine)
His Final Act - (Emily Slate Series Book Ten)
The Vanishing Eyes - (Emily Slate Series Book Eleven)
Edge of the Woods - (Emily Slate Series Book Twelve)
Ties That Bind - (Emily Slate Series Book Thirteen)
The Missing Bones - (Emily Slate Series Book Fourteen)
Blood in the Sand - (Emily Slate Series Book Fifteen)
The Passage - (Emily Slate Series Book Sixteen)
Fire in the Sky - (Emily Slate Series Book Seventeen)
The Killing Jar - (Emily Slate Series Book Eighteen)
A Deadly Promise - (Emily Slate Series Book Nineteen)
Solitaire's Song - (Emily Slate Series Book Twenty)

The Ivy Bishop Mystery Thriller Series

Free Prequel - Bishop's Edge (Ivy Bishop Bonus Story)
Her Dark Secret - (Ivy Bishop Series Book One)

The Girl Without A Clue - (Ivy Bishop Series Book Two)
The Buried Faces - (Ivy Bishop Series Book Three)
Her Hidden Lies - (Ivy Bishop Series Book Four)
One Dark Night - (Ivy Bishop Series Book Five)

The Oak Creek Thriller Series

The Darkest Game - (Oak Creek Thriller Book One)
Never Strike Twice - (Oak Creek Thriller Book Two)

A Note from Alex

Hi there!

I don't know about you, but this one actually brought tears to my eyes. I always feel all of my books deeply, and when faced with great loss, I can't but help feel as my characters would. Even though I often consider them separate from me in many ways, they are also very much an integral part of me. So I wanted to you know how difficult this book was to write.

But even in difficulty and hard times we manage to find the good. Emily and Zara are back at work with a brand new mission, one that opens up a lot of new opportunities for them. And personally, I'm really excited about what's coming up.

Of course, there are still a few unresolved threads hanging in the background. And if you've been with me from the beginning, then you know we're not done with those yet.

All good things come in time, so for now, I just want to say thank you for continuing to support your small-time local author who is absolutely thrilled to be writing these books for you.

I can't wait to see what comes next.

Sincerely,

Alex

P.S. If you haven't already, please consider leaving a review or recommending this series to a fellow book lover. Your support is crucial for continuing Emily's adventures. Thank you, as always!

Made in United States
Cleveland, OH
16 September 2025